Human Rights

Philip Hoyle

I0545411

This Edition Published in 2016 by Stanhope Books, Essex, UK

www.stanhopebooks.com

Cover design by Barbara Owczarek © 2014

ISBN-13: 978-1-909893-22-1

Chapter 1

Tuesday 6th June 53

The sun streaming in through the window wakes me from a troubled sleep, glancing at the clock on the bedside table I see that it's still only five o'clock in the morning and as tired as I am there's not much hope of any more rest. Until springtime it was relatively easy not to think about the summer solstice but since the days started getting longer it's been preying on my mind more and more frequently. This is about the fifth year that I've been aware of the Human Rights although in previous years they've not really affected me, I'd not been fully aware of them. This year is very different, this year it will be my brother Jim's turn.

Jim is thirteen months older than me and turned sixteen just last Wednesday, he's one of the *lucky* ones who have to wait less than a month past their birthdays. Mum, dad and Jim are really excited about the whole thing but I'm not sure. No, I am sure. I'm sure I'm not excited, I don't want any Human Rights. I've never understood why they're so important, as far as I can see all they bring is pain and misery and now in only two weeks and a day I'll probably never see my brother again. Until a year or so ago we'd been very close however we drifted apart during his final preparation year. On the positive side my birthday isn't until June 26th (five days after the longest day), it won't be my turn until the year after next meaning I'll be nearly seventeen years old. A whole year's stay of execution.

Of course my parents were desperate for me to be born on the summer solstice, everyone wants to have a child born then. They planned everything just right and it had nearly worked. I'd been due on the correct day but had gone and spoilt everything by being a few days late. It wasn't my fault of course and I don't really think my parents blame me but it does sometimes feel they do. In a way I can understand their disappointment. It would have given us all many benefits. I think my mother would have had a caesarean section if the money had been available but of course it wasn't. Not that it would have been easy or safe, it's one of the serious crimes that would be referred to the High Court so they would have had to have hidden all signs of the operation very carefully. Besides which there was no certainty that the doctor wouldn't have turned them in anyway so maybe it was all for the best, what do I mean maybe? Of course it was for the best.

Normally I'd be looking forward to the four week summer holiday and a break from school round about now but not this year, what with Jim. I push back the covers of the bed and get up. I'd anticipated waking early and I've got yesterday's homework to do this morning. I cross the room to my desk and sit down, the computer detects my presence and activates the touch screen with the details of my history essay in the middle. I don't care much for history and have always been a little uneasy about the fact that we never look into anything prior to the Third World War. That only ended fifty odd years ago, I'm sure there must have been any number of interesting things before that. Possibly even two other World Wars although I wouldn't dare to say anything like that at school or I'd be in trouble. Officially it was the war that happened in the Third World but if it had only happened in the Third World why had it affected the whole world?

I think it's more likely that it was the third time that there had been a war involving the whole world. I'd love to be able to investigate, that would be a history essay worth writing. I don't even know where to begin, the information would definitely be online but classified and any attempts to find it would no doubt be recorded. There aren't many people old enough to remember the war personally, well not round here anyway, what I really need is a book. They're almost impossible to come by, when they do turn up they are prohibitively expensive and generally works of fiction rather than reference books. Possession of books whilst not actually illegal is frowned upon and tends to single the owner out as being a little bit odd. Even fictional titles can be quite enlightening about the past though, once I got my hands on one by George Orwell called simply *1984*. Obviously a year, although the current year being 53NE meant the title was not actually much help for dating it. It had been published in 1949 and my copy had been printed in 2015 so the events predicted in the book clearly hadn't happened in the suggested timeframe. Although thinking about it now, this old vision of a past future feels quite similar to the way in which we live today.

I have to write an essay about Europarl and its endeavours to protect our human rights as citizens of the United States of Europe. My mind wanders to thinking that Europarl is just Big Brother with a different name, I banish the thought quickly, rest my fingers on the keypad of the desk and start to write:

Europarl is the abbreviated name of the European Parliament. By the end of the war the population of Europe had been decimated, tiny communities of survivors were spread thinly across the continent. The landscape was badly affected too, not many of the buildings that were still standing would remain standing for long and there was a very real risk that there would be a complete collapse of the human civilisation, other continents were just as badly affected as Europe. However Europe had the advantage of Luxburg, previously a very small country towards the north of Europe which managed to survive the war completely unscathed thanks to an electromagnetic shield of some description. This made it the perfect place to set up the administrative centre in charge of rebuilding after the war.

Due to the hugely reduced population across Europe it was decided that the best course of action was to create a large country with a centralised government working for the good of the surviving population and to ensure the rapid repopulation of the region. To ensure that everyone was treated fairly under the new system a set of ten human rights was established as an integral part of the constitution of the country.

Every citizen has the right to life, this right is closely linked to three of the others namely the right to have a family, the right to work and the right to equality. At the festival of the summer solstice every year all the people who have had their sixteenth birthday in the last year are assigned a spouse, they are chosen carefully to ensure the best diversification of the gene pool as well as to ensure that there are sufficient shared interests for a successful and happy marriage. Each new couple is assigned a house, this could be in any of the settlements across the whole country where the population is currently below the standard population size of one thousand adult citizens. New settlements are built as and when they are needed and situated according to the natural resources that are available and are required. The location chosen for each couple is based upon their natural abilities and suitability to the work available in the area. In exchange for working all families are provided with their food, drink, housing, clothing, heating or cooling depending upon the area of the country and/or the time of year and basically all the necessities of life as well as a small wage to pay for luxury items. This means that all the people in all of the states are treated with absolute equality.

Everyone has the right to an education. Every settlement has two schools, one for girls and one for boys. The school year starts at the end of July, everyone starts school at the start of the school year following the year in which they turn six – this year running from the day after the summer solstice up to the following summer solstice. This means that someone whose birthday is on 21st June will start school approximately four weeks after their sixth birthday whereas someone born the following day will not start school until after their seventh birthday. Everyone has ten whole years at school regardless of what age they started, during this time students are assessed continuously to identify the best way they can serve the community. The main part of this assessment though is reserved for the final preparation year, the last year before they leave school, during this year the school hours are extended so that they are the same as a standard working day and a lot of practical training is undertaken.

All people have the right to healthcare. All the settlements have a hospital that provides for all the most common ailments in that particular settlement. What facilities are included are dependent upon the type of industry in the area, the natural risks of the area and the nature of the population. In the event of an individual patient's requirements being beyond the scope of their local hospital they will be transported to the nearest hospital offering the necessary treatment. In the event of incurable diseases the patients are transported to the capital city of Luxburg for onward passage to the next plane of existence.

All citizens have the right to privacy, this is protected by means of the curfew. Everyone has to be back in their house by 22:00 and in their bedrooms by 00:00, the doors are then locked to ensure each person's privacy and security.

The exceptions to this being those people that work outside normal working hours and of course parents are able to interrupt their children's privacy. The right to privacy also promotes the right to think freely as this is easily accommodated during the hours of privacy.

Every year at the Human Rights celebrations everyone who is of voting age, this being all the adults in the community, have the right to vote. Each voter chooses a representative for the settlement in which they live, the candidates are all members of the Europarl in Luxburg and don't actually visit their potential constituencies but in the weeks leading up to the celebrations they have broadcasts on line which everyone is encouraged to watch to enable them to make their decision.

Anyone who commits a crime within the community has the right to a fair trial. For minor crimes there is a courthouse within each settlement but any serious crimes are referred to the High Court in Luxburg where all defendants are assigned a legal representative.

It's now six o'clock, I hear the soft click of my bedroom door unlocking so I can go downstairs now if I want to although the front door of the house won't be unlocked for another hour. A quick glance in the corner of my homework shows I've written a little over nine hundred words, the essay was supposed to be about a thousand but since I've covered all ten Human Rights and it's near enough the required length I decide to call it finished. I touch the send icon and get up from the desk and head to the door, I open it as silently as I can and walk down the stairs staying close to the wall to avoid making the floorboards creak. Whilst all the houses in my settlement are relatively new, Chelmsford was built only seventeen years ago, they're built very quickly and therefore not particularly well and are prone to creaks and noises. I head into the lounge and sit down, I switch on the main screen and wait for the rest of my family to come down.

The morning news is showing, they are reporting that this year the birth rate across the whole population of Europe has exceeded twenty-five per thousand for the first time since records begun. This combined with an annual death rate of less than ten per thousand is really good news for the country. The birth rate has been rising steadily under the careful guidance of Europarl, this means that for this year's celebrations the population of The United States Of Europe stands at 145,340. Over 48,000 of these people are living in places other than Luxburg. The big excitement though is that there will be a new city needed this year. It seems likely that it could be near us in the south east of the state of South Britain as more people will be needed to service the power generation facilities in the North Sea.

All of the electricity for the whole country comes from a huge facility in the North Sea which uses power from both the waves and the tides to drive generators. Not only does this provide for all our energy requirements but it also has the useful side effect of a significant reduction in the height of the waves arriving on our shores. This is a real benefit for us being as we are so close to the coast in a relatively low-lying and flat landscape. Before this facility was built all of the electricity was produced in a large power station in Luxburg but as the population increased along with the associated energy demands it no longer met the requirements. It still exists and can be put back online if required but the wave and tidal power is constantly there and gets rid of the requirement to mine coal so the settlement of Chelmsford was born and my parents were in the first population intake.

Our settlement is currently the only one in South Britain, the majority of the states don't have anyone living in them at all. Most of the settlements are in the northern parts of mainland Europe.

Being a seaside town can be quite dangerous due to the toxic nature of the water but the sound of the waves is nevertheless very relaxing. The main cable comes straight into the power substation here in Chelmsford which is where the vast majority of the people here (including both my parents) work.

I hear a footfall on the stairs and my dad pokes his head round the door, "Ed, you're up early again, everything alright?"

"Yeah I'm fine, had to do my history homework anyway."

"Ah, I was the same as you, always leaving it to the last minute or even later! Still, not long till the holidays now eh? I'll go and get some breakfast going, I think we've still got some bacon if you fancy it."

"Thanks dad."

I turn off the viewing screen and follow my dad into the kitchen where he's already got a frying pan on the hotplate. I pick up a jug from the counter, put in a couple of teabags in and fill it from the boiling water tap. By the time I've made the tea dad's got the bacon sizzling and I can hear Jim and mum on the landing. A few minutes later we're all sitting round the table with a bacon roll each which is a little ostentatious for a Tuesday. In fact we don't normally have a cooked breakfast at all but when we do it would normally be on a Sunday when there's more time without the pressure of having to get to work or school. Unless mum or dad are on shift but that's not very often these days as they now both have fairly senior positions at work.

The front door unlocks whilst we're eating and by half past seven I have the house to myself, my parents having headed off to the substation and Jim to school. I don't need to be at school until nine but I decide to head out early for a wander, as the door shuts behind me it's a still, beautiful sunny day without a cloud in the sky. I head down the road towards the beach squinting in the glare of the sun, after half a kilometre I'm clear of the buildings of the town and I can hear the breaking waves. Another kilometre down the road and I'm level with the substation and almost at the high water mark. I can see the line of rubbish along the top of the beach and the muddy clay stretching down to the waterline. It's about half way between high and low tides although I've no idea whether it's going in or out. I reach the high tide line and walk along it away from the substation, I can see the generation machinery in the distance but I'm scanning the rubbish. Sometimes you can find interesting things here.

Almost straight away I find a long stick probably from a broom which I pick up to help me pick out anything interesting. Despite the ease with which I found the broomstick it looks as though today is not going to be my lucky day, I've now gone round the curve of the beach so that I'm no longer visible from the town but have seen nothing of any interest. I need to think about heading back now in order not to be late for school, just as I'm about to turn around I see a tumbledown structure on the backshore. It would be almost invisible if it weren't for a plume of smoke rising from a small fire just in front. I decide to take a risk and investigate, heading directly towards the shack I quicken my pace.

When I'm about ten metres away from the fire a man crawls out of the entrance of his shack and beckons towards me, "Morning…" he calls.

"Hello?"

"You're wondering why there's a man you don't recognise camped out on the beach, that's good. I'll tell you, I was waiting for you!"

My blank face encourages him to go on.

"I thought you'd show up sooner rather than later and I was right, I've only been here a couple of days. This is such a stroke of luck that you're like this too, someone who can think for yourself, someone who's inquisitive enough to be wandering along the beach by the *poisonous* sea when most people are at home waiting until it's time to head off to work or school. Do you want some breakfast?"

He lifts a small fish skewered on a short stick off the fire and waves it vaguely in my direction. I wave it away explaining that I've already had a bacon roll, he smiles and takes a bite out of the fish and continues his explanation whilst spitting out small bones.

"Bacon! Not had that for ages, but I live in hope. All I seem to catch is squirrels and they get a bit samey after a while, that's why I'm on the beach now to try my luck on fish and to wait for you of course! You're quiet aren't you?"

"Yes, I've never seen you before and you claim to be waiting for me, are you surprised that I'm a bit puzzled?"

He throws the remains of the first fish into his fire and picks up the second by spearing it with the same stick. Looking at him I'd say he's a little older than my parents, maybe in his mid-forties, but I get the impression that he's actually quite a bit older. It's hard to guess as his hair is long and matted and his face is obscured by several weeks of beard growth so I ask his age.

"You're wondering if I remember the war, aren't you? The answer is yes, I was ten years old when the war finished, lost all my family and had to fend for myself in a landscape totally destroyed. You know before the war this place was more than twenty kilometres from the sea, it was a fairly large city too. More people lived here than the whole of the country now, well the official recorded population. There's quite a few people like me around so it's hard to tell the actual head count. You'd better run if you're not going to be late for school, come and see me another time, I'll be here until after summer solstice, there are lots of things we need to talk about. But don't lead any rights enablers to me, eh!"

He turns his back on me and wanders off down to the incoming sea, I put my stick down and start a steady jog back along the beach. By the time I reach the school entrance I've got sweat dripping off my face and I'm slightly out of breath but I'm on time. I head quickly to the changing rooms by the gym and have a quick shower and get a change of clothes to freshen up before heading to registration. After all that I'm only just in time and everyone else is already sitting at their desks when I sit down at mine although luckily there is no sign of the teacher yet.

All through the day my mind keeps wandering back to the strange old man on the beach, I never even asked his name but he seemed to know me. I find his assertion that there are quite a few people like him intriguing, are these people that Europarl doesn't know about? I feel sure they must do, after all I didn't do anything particularly out of the ordinary to find him, or maybe I did, I don't often meet other people on the beach. If they do know about these people wandering around outside the system do they tolerate them or do they hunt them down? He knew that I'd go down to the beach at some point, how did he know? He didn't seem worried about trusting me. By the time the final bell goes at four o'clock I've decided to go back to the beach and find him again. I should be able to spend over an hour with him without being missed at home, that should be long enough to answer at least some of my questions.

Fifteen minutes after the bell has gone I'm back at the beach, this time the tide's right in and I walk through the occasional breaker which doesn't seem to do me any harm as I make my way along the coast. There's no fire this time but I see the old man sitting with his feet in the sea, he doesn't turn towards me or acknowledge me in any way until I sit down.

"I'm glad you've come back, what do you know about the war already?"

"Nothing at all" I tell him, "except that we're not told anything about it which I think is suspicious."

"It certainly is suspicious, you'd be mad if you didn't think it was. Have you never wondered how a small area of land in the middle of Europe managed to survive the war completely unscathed? A war that destroyed all the buildings everywhere else, that resulted in a rapid rise in the sea level, a war that left large areas of previously fertile land a virtual desert. This small area of land, a city that had been adopted as the home of the European Parliament only a few years before the start of the war, survived in its entirety. Now what does that tell you?"

"I thought Europarl was set up to rebuild the country after the war!"

"No, Europarl existed a long time before the war started, Europarl started the war…"

Chapter 2

Over the next couple of weeks the old man whose name I learn is Jack tells me his story as well as much of what he knows about the current system of government. I don't spend hours at a time with him, in fact he's insistent that I don't come down to the beach any more than I would normally do so or spend any longer there than I usually would either. The reason he provides for this gives me a slight shock, not the reason itself but more the fact that I'd not realised it by myself – everyone in the country is *tagged*. A device that Jack calls a chip is implanted into every new-born child using an ordinary hypodermic needle and syringe as it is so tiny. It is administered at the same time as the initial inoculations that we all have to prevent the major diseases and could be anywhere in the body. Each chip has a unique code which identifies the person making it possible to track anyone's location at any time. He admits that he has tracked me himself and that is how he knew that I was a regular visitor to the beach. He is not tagged himself, living as he does outside the system, to a Europarl observer watching me from Luxburg I would appear to be alone on the beach.

As I already knew, the date system was changed at the end of the war but since he was amongst the many people who have lived outside the control of the state he is able to tell me that this year is 2102 as far as he's concerned. In the second decade of the 21st century practically the whole world was deep in recession, nearly every country in the world had huge international debt. Years of excellent healthcare meant that many people lived well into old age and the failing or rather failed economy couldn't support the situation. More and more businesses were facing bankruptcy and many people lost their jobs meaning the dwindling working population were supporting an ever swelling number of dependants. The recession continued, over a decade passed with almost no economic recovery. Taxation spiralled and eventually the public got fed up with paying more and more for less and less return.

There were riots, it got very messy indeed, a large number of people died in the riots themselves but many more still died when the governments brought in their respective military forces to control the mobs. They couldn't control the mobs anywhere and the mobs knew this because in those days there was a worldwide communication network available to the general public that enabled anyone to be in touch with anyone else almost instantly. The troops were withdrawn and the mobs were left to their own devices. Weeks passed, shops and homes were looted, cities burned, more people died. Services began to fail, not many places had electricity and the broadcasting networks fell silent. Telephones and other communication systems failed, nobody knew what was happening. The rioting all but stopped and many of the survivors started leaving the cities, trying to escape to rural areas. As bad as things were this was the calm before the storm.

The first bombs hit major cities. Major cities all over the world were affected, many of the bombs were nuclear bombs. The majority of the people left in these cities died instantly from the blast and many of those who didn't died in the fires that raged afterwards. There were large numbers of unfortunate people who having managed to avoid these fates fell to acute radiation sickness. For the rest it was just the beginning of their problems. Nobody could understand what was happening. Many people expected there to be a nuclear winter, large quantities of soot had been released into the atmosphere from the burning cities and they were still smouldering. However the time when this was happening was a time of unprecedented rainfall, the soot came pouring out of the skies in black torrents. Everywhere it rained was covered in a thick layer of grime, even the poles began to have snow falling on a regular basis and this was grey rather than white. When it wasn't raining and the cloud cover was thin or non-existent the sun beat down on the ice. The darkened surface absorbed a lot more heat than the bright white ice ever could have. The ice caps which had been retreating gradually for over twenty thousand years suddenly started to melt at a previously unheard of rate.

The sea level started to rise, slowly at first but perceptibly. Within ten years of the first bomb the level was up by almost a metre and existing flood defences were no longer sufficient, all over the world the land started to retreat. The rise accelerated, within a further five years the ice at the North Pole was all but gone. The impact of this was not huge as the majority of the ice there had been floating but loss of the ice over Greenland made a significant impact. The sea level was up by nearly seven metres and the Antarctic ice was seriously receding due mainly to the higher sea but by then there was frequent precipitation in this region which began to blacken the ice.

The remaining population struggled to survive in deep basements and tunnels that had been built originally for transport systems sheltering from infrequent bomb blasts and ever present fallout. Against all the odds and this backdrop of terror, Jack was born underneath the former capital city of the country of England which along with another country previously called Wales now make up the state of South Britain. A vast network which had previously been an underground transport system serving a city which was very large indeed even by the standards of the day but unimaginable to people living now. This city was actually fairly close to where we are now and there he had been brought into a terrifying world where a global war had been rumbling on for nearly twenty years. Those were dark days both literally and figuratively, the skies were full of dust from the many bombs that had destroyed the landscape which meant that often virtually no sunlight would be seen for days at a time.

This city was in places less than ten metres above sea level at the start of the war and by the time of Jack's birth many of the deeper tunnels had been breached and were flooded. A lot of the tunnels had had floodgates installed in the dim and distant past but by the time of the war these had been rendered obsolete by the construction of a flood defence barrier on the River Thames on which the city lay. The newest tunnels had been constructed without floodgates and many of the existing ones had been absorbed into the tunnel walls or even removed during refurbishment work. None of the remaining gates were free to move by the time they were needed. While he was still a baby he and his parents headed northwards and up into the hills when the rising sea meant they could no longer shelter from the fallout under the ground there. His father had actually been born in Chelmsford, only a stone's throw from the beach on which we meet but hadn't wanted to risk going back as he wasn't sure whether it was high enough not to flood.

A lot of people had the same idea and when they arrived in the southern reaches of the Pennines they found a community of refugees helping each other out. After a journey of some two hundred and fifty kilometres (Jack tends to talk in an old fashioned measurement called miles of which I have never heard but when he remembers he converts them into kilometres so that I'll understand) on foot in just over a week they were happy to pitch in with this group. A decision that made perfect sense at the time, they believed that there would be a certain degree of safety in numbers but ultimately it was a decision that they came to regret.

For about eighteen months the community quietly got on with the job of staying alive. More people came but their numbers didn't grow as nearly everyone had had some degree of exposure to radiation from the nuclear bombs. This rendered people very susceptible to disease, although the cool climate in these parts kept that at bay to a certain extent even the common cold caused casualties. It started to become apparent that many people were suffering from forms of cancer and slowly they started to die. On a slight positive many of the survivors had the strength of youth on their side, nobody in Jack's community was older than fifty and most were twenty or younger. He was the only child under ten though. They managed to grow crops to sustain themselves and they were also able to hunt for meat, the easiest catches being squirrels which seemed to have seen virtually no reduction in their numbers for some reason. Occasionally they were able to find sheep which had been farmed in large numbers but had all but disappeared in the disaster.

They'd got into a sustainable routine but that was suddenly shattered in the early hours of one morning. All at once there was a bright light in the entrance and the cave in which they were sheltering was thrown into sharp relief. Some of them were pulled roughly from their beds and out into the cold pre-dawn air where they were loaded into a large caterpillar-tracked van, amongst these were both of Jack's parents. The rest, the sick and ailing were shot where they lay in their blankets and sleeping bags. It happened quickly, so quickly that the attackers had not adequately assessed the dwelling before they acted. If Jack had been left alone he wouldn't have lived very long, he was only a toddler but also well hidden at the back of the cave were two teenage girls and a middle aged woman. The three of them lay silent and still through the commotion hoping that Jack wouldn't give them away but unable to risk moving towards him to offer comfort. Luckily he'd actually managed to sleep through the attack and thus began the next chapter of his young life.

These were difficult times for the four of them although Jack was of course none the wiser as this strange life was all he'd ever known. As he grew older he was able to take an active part in their daily lives and with just the four of them to support they were able to have a reasonable amount of free time. Their crops continued to grow and generally the climate was improving which meant they were able to gather the same crop volume from a smaller land area. Their cave was on a southern facing slope and got a decent amount of sunshine. The middle aged woman, Jenny became a teacher to Jack and to a lesser extent to the other girls Lucy and Caia as well. Before the end of the civilisation they had known she had been a doctor, she was a clever and well educated woman and gave Jack a fantastic grounding in academic matters. The practical subjects that were useful to them he picked up naturally as they went along, just as the girls had themselves. He learnt to read from the three books that they had at their disposal, *1984* by George Orwell, a traveller's guide to London and *A Tale of Two Cities* by Charles Dickens. All of them were very battered but they were better than nothing.

Lucy and Caia were fourteen and seventeen on the night when the cave had been raided. They were sensible girls and took their lot with gentle stoicism, looking after Jack as best as they could. All through this period Jenny would go off on expeditions to try and find other people and any trace of what was happening. It made no sense at all to her that all traces of human habitation had seemingly been wiped out, why would anyone do such a thing? This wasn't like a normal war, it was as if its objective were to obliterate the human race. Not a single town or village was still standing anywhere within a couple of day's walk of where they lived, not once did she find any trace of people at all. That is not to say that there certainly weren't any, as logically there must have been since the four of them had contrived to live but any other people were well hidden. There was no evidence of farming, no tracks, nobody else seemed to be hunting and everywhere was dead.

She did however find various potentially useful items from rummaging in basements of destroyed buildings. Tools that they could use to make tending the land easier and something that she thought would be a great prize, a radio receiver that was charged by winding a handle. Exciting as this was it proved to be more of a frustration, after finding it she had carried it with her on all her expeditions and on no occasion did she receive any signal at all. In the end they had managed to adapt the charging mechanism and battery to work with the LEDs from one of the torches they had acquired. Month by month the air was getting cleaner, the rain when it came was almost pure and the sun was no longer hidden behind a haze of soot. The world seemed to be getting safer, when Jack was nine years old they had decided that it was time to head off to see if they could find other communities. They had to find out what had happened.

They headed southwards, this had always been where the majority of the people had lived so it seemed logical that they were more likely to find survivors in that region. If they got nowhere with that line of enquiry they would try to cross the English Channel to mainland Europe to see if anything was different there. To Jack this expedition was a huge adventure, he had never gone anywhere before so whilst the destruction that they saw was fairly consistent the differing landscape made a wonderful change. It soon became apparent to the three of them who had previously seen the lay of the land that the area of land had been massively reduced by the rising sea. They made slow progress as they had no deadlines and took their time trying to find evidence of recent human habitation. Jack was keen to see what remained of London due to his extensive reading of the guidebook although he was well aware that he was likely to be disappointed. He also felt a connection with Chelmsford as he knew that his parents had hailed from there and that if the war had not happened that is where he would be growing up.

After a couple of weeks of gentle walking, they didn't go in a straight line but preferred to zigzag across the countryside to maximise their chances of finding other people, they were walking along the new eastern coastline. As they approached the place where London had once been they could see that nothing remained of this once great city. Even the characteristic meanderings of the River Thames were no more, replaced by a huge estuary more than twenty kilometres wide. After this disappointment they decided to head east along the northern bank of the great river. This strip of land was not much wider than the water as virtually the whole of East Anglia had gone below the sea. According to Jack the landscape at that time was not much different from how it is today, the majority of the rise had already happened by then, he says that the level is no more than two metres higher today than it was when he first saw all that remained of his ancestral homeland.

They spent quite a few days exploring what Jenny decided to call the Essex peninsula walking as far to the east as they could go. This took them a little bit beyond Ipswich, they found nobody. At Colchester they found the largest building remains that they had seen anywhere, Jenny said that before the war it had been a castle but ironically the part that remained, the huge foundations were from a Roman temple and were now over two thousand years old. They made this place a base and stayed there for several days while they scouted around. Eventually they headed off westwards again in search of a place where they would be able to cross the Thames to the south. They paused for a few more hours in Chelmsford where both of Jack's parents had been born and grew up, Jack wanted something from here as a keepsake. Having no memories of either of his parents and not really knowing very much about them he felt that something from there might give him a sense of belonging. After much searching amongst the rubble he was lucky enough to find part of a silver chain, with a little bit of effort they managed to turn one of the links into a clasp of sorts so that Jack was able to wear it around his neck.

They had to go a long way west before the river was narrow enough for them to stand a chance of crossing. The only map they had which was of any use at all was at a very small scale and not very detailed in the back of the London guide book showing the whole of the United Kingdom. Of course they had maps of London showing almost every street but they weren't very helpful considering that the vast majority of the land they showed was by then below sea level and none of the manmade landmarks were in existence anymore. Looking at the map that they had, Jenny thought they had gone further than the place where Reading had previously been before they crossed. It was here that Jack had his first swimming lesson, luckily he was a natural and with plenty of help from the others he made it across the five hundred metres or so. Even at this distance inland the water was tidal and they timed their crossing to coincide with slack water. If they hadn't crossed here they would have had to trek at least another day westwards to reach the places where the river was unaffected by the sea.

Jenny hoped that they would be able to cross the Channel by use of the tunnel as she remembered that the entrance was well inland and she thought high enough not to have flooded due to ingress of the sea. She didn't know about the other side but they all decided that it was worth looking and they didn't think they would find a readymade boat. Also a crossing of the Channel was likely to be a little bit adventurous for them, even given what they'd been through so far, especially if they had to make their own boat. As they headed eastwards once more, this time on the south bank of the Thames Jenny tried to match up the map they had with what they were seeing. This was easier said than done as the map concentrated on cities and major towns which had all but disappeared and crucially didn't have a single contour line marked on it. None of them had spent much time in these parts of the country previously, although Caia had spent several holidays staying in caravans at various places along the south coast. She remembered that the white cliffs were dramatically lower to the west of Folkestone trailing away to gently sloping beaches not much further along the coast. In view of this they decided to continue along the south bank of the Thames as far as they could before heading south to avoid getting separated from their goal by a stretch of water. Nevertheless it was still going to be difficult to find the entrance, there was no guarantee that it wouldn't have been bombed or collapsed of its own accord.

Despite their route planning they'd still had to cross water three more times at Guildford, Maidstone and Ashford. As they carried along their way they were beginning to be demoralised by the fact that they had still found nobody else. They were spurred on by the fact that the troops that had raided their cave in the Pennines all those years ago must have come from somewhere and presumably had gone back to that same place with the strongest members of their community. Logically, since England was so empty of population mainland Europe was a sensible destination and one on which they all agreed, although they'd not really thought about where to head once they'd got there. They were hoping for some kind of sign that would give them directions, getting there was enough to think about at that time. Finally after nearly two months of travelling since they'd left Chelmsford and what they guessed to be about three hundred kilometres they arrived at the site of the main terminal for the Channel Tunnel near Folkestone. They knew this to be the case because there were a large number of railway tracks still in situ and in almost serviceable condition, all traffic had been carried on trains. Unfortunately there appeared to be no tunnel entrance.

They followed the tracks in an easterly direction and found the location where the tunnel entrance had obviously once stood, the mouth had collapsed completely. They followed the remnants of the track and when that was buried continued in the same direction and after walking for a little more than a kilometre found a fairly large crater where the roof of the tunnel had collapsed. It was not a neat hole and was fairly deep, it was a difficult climb down on loose material but after a fair amount of sliding, scratches and the odd bruise all four of them stood on what had been the concrete track bed inside the tunnel. To the west the debris had fallen in such a way that there remained an opening into the darkness of the bore but in the direction in which they actually wanted to head they were not so lucky. The next couple of days had been spent laboriously moving rubble so that they could gain entrance, at first it was exciting but it soon became tedious work. They quickly ran out of space in the crater to pile the rubble and had to remove it from the hole which slowed their progress dramatically.

Eventually they had a crawl way cleared and an entrance of sorts into the tunnel to the mainland, they all crawled through and stood in the darkness. Even with their torch they couldn't see very far at all, furthermore it would probably take two days or longer to get through assuming that they didn't have any problems. They knew that it was going to be a journey to remember, so they decided to rest for a while to recover from their excavation and also to gather enough food together in order to make the trip. They started their journey as night fell, they decided by doing so that they could reduce the stress of what they were doing by tricking themselves into thinking that they were simply travelling by night rather than through a tunnel deep under the seabed.

At first everything went well, there was hardly any dampness at all, in fact quite the opposite was the case. They were walking through a layer of fine dry grey dust which was prone to fly up into the stale air as they walked and made them cough and choke until they dampened strips of cloth to tie over their mouths and noses. The dust didn't help with visibility at all with the torch barely penetrating the gloom but since the floor of the tunnel was smooth and consistently good they decided to walk in total darkness to save them the trouble of periodically winding up the torch. It was hard to judge their distance, they were disorientated by the darkness and the fact that the tunnel changed direction very gently meaning that it felt straight to them as they continued onwards. After they'd been walking for about three hours they thought they must be under the sea so they turned on the torch to see if anything was different. Nothing was, it was still dry although the layer of dust was noticeably thinner.

They continued like this a few hours at a time and then a couple of hours rest, they didn't stop for long periods as they were keen to get through as quickly as they could. They had worked out that they were in the right most tunnel of three, there were access hatches at fairly frequent intervals and even more frequent ducts in the ceiling presumably linking to the other tunnels also. They had investigated one of these hatches, not the first one that they came across as the hinges of the door had been badly corroded and they'd only been able to open it a crack. The second one they'd found no more than half a kilometre further on had opened freely so they knew that there were a further two tunnels to the left of the one they were walking through, the middle one being significantly smaller and having no railway line. The additional tunnels were comforting in that there were alternative passages to follow in the event of coming across a collapse. However they would probably be of no use at all if they found the way flooded since presumably in this circumstance all of them would be affected together.

On they walked and approximately twenty-four hours after they'd begun their journey they were approaching what they thought was probably the midpoint of the tunnels or if not exactly the middle at least a low point. There was a definite dampness in the air, switching on their torch they could see the light reflecting off the water pooled in front of them. A quick taste of the water at least proved that it wasn't seawater although it didn't taste particularly fresh it didn't taste bad either so they filled their water carriers. They had no idea how far the water would go on for but they decided to wade into it, the drop of the tunnel was very gentle so they'd been wading for quite a while by the time that Jack found himself having to swim. They continued onwards and before long they were all swimming, they were able to rest by holding onto wires and brackets fixed to the walls. Gradually the level rose until they got to a point where they were able to pull themselves through the water far quicker than they would have been able to swim by using the overhead wires that had provided the trains that used to run through here with their electricity supply.

It was very hard to tell how far they'd gone through the water as their progress had not been very consistent and their torch had got wet and was no longer working. They were uneasy that they would at any moment come to a point where the water touched the ceiling and if this were to go on for any great distance that would spell the end of their journey. As it happened they needn't have worried, the water came within a hand's breadth of the ceiling but there it stayed for several hundred metres before the airspace started gradually to increase once more. They were so relieved that it took them a while to notice that there was a glimmer of light ahead of them. How far ahead they couldn't tell but it was unmistakeably there. Briefly they entertained the idea of going back but the main purpose of their quest had been to find other people and that was surely what the light meant. They'd got so used to being a group of four alone against the world that they began to wonder whether they should have just carried on as they were in their cave in the Pennines. It was Jack that encouraged the group onwards after their uneasiness and they struck out once more as quickly as they could manage towards the light.

The light got brighter and brighter but still the ceiling of the tunnel remained frustratingly within touching distance. It was another half an hour before they came to the first light, a dim electric bulb set into the wall but they could see the next one and the next and the next. A chain of lights heading off into the distance lighting the whole tunnel, this was an amazing sight to Jack never having seen so many artificial lights in one place. To the others it was even more significant, this meant that somebody was in a far better situation than they were themselves and that somebody could easily turn out to be the same people that had raided their cave that early morning all those years ago. All they could do was carry on and find out. Finally the water level dropped so that the girls and then Jack could wade and then they stood clear of the water on the dry concrete floor of the tunnel, except that it wasn't completely dry there was a damp pathway of footprints leading up the gentle slope in the middle of the railway track.

They followed the footprints calling as they went and listening for an answer but none came which was puzzling but then the path turned to the left towards one of the hatchways and that explained why they'd had no answer. The door was shut and nobody would have heard their calling through the thick plate steel. They knocked but this was equally as inaudible as their calls so with her heart pounding away in apprehension Jenny gingerly turned the handle and they all walked into a brightly lit room in the central access tunnel. There was a long table in the centre with high-backed chairs around it and along the walls of the room there were various armchairs and sofas. Half a dozen faces turned towards them but they were smiling, not angry.

"Hello" said all four of them at once.

"Ah, vous êtes anglais" replied a fairly old-looking man sitting in the armchair closest to the entrance with a grin, "welcome, but please shut the door behind you, were you born in a barn?"

Jack explains to me that this group of people, there were about twenty of them when he arrived ultimately became his family. They were a small group who were hanging on and biding their time to attack the corruption within the system that had destroyed the world as they knew it. They now number many more and he is asking me to join them as he has a very special purpose for me, I'm not necessarily the only person who can do what he requires of me but I'm the best chance that they've ever had and the chances of success with me on the team are very high. Unfortunately events have overtaken us and by the time he gets to the point of explaining his presence on the beach at Chelmsford the Human Rights celebrations are upon us and we've run out of opportunities to meet up. As I leave the beach to wander home at teatime on Tuesday 20th June my mind is racing, I'm pretty sure that I'll go with Jack on Sunday morning but I really wish he'd had time to tell me what he's got planned for me. But of course Jack's not stupid, he didn't really run out of time, he just won't tell me until I'm committed to it. I'll go, after all, what have I got to lose?

Chapter 3

Tuesday 20th June 53

As I walk up the road towards home I'm feeling a little uneasy but I put it down to everything that Jack has been telling me over the last couple of weeks. It's only when I reach the edge of the town that I start to think something is actually wrong. I'd walked past the buildings of the substation in a world of my own, only now do I realise that I'd seen some rights enablers standing just inside the gates which is unusual. Turning into my road I see one standing outside the front door of the house as well and my heart sinks. For a split second I consider making a run for it, but the rights enabler is looking towards me and has definitely seen me and probably recognised me. Also they can track me wherever I go if what Jack says is true and of course I know that it is, there is no point in running or hiding. The only thing I can do is go right up to him and face the music. Those hundred metres or so seem to take an age to walk, in the time it takes me to get to the door I begin to think that something is very strange indeed. Why is he standing outside, surely my parents would have let him in? They must both be in by now as well as Jim. Why did he not just track me down and come and get me on the beach? Then he'd have been able to get Jack too. This actually eases my mind slightly, maybe he's not actually after me, maybe he doesn't know about Jack.

"Let's go inside" he says.

"OK" I say and wait for him to open the door, which he makes no sign of doing so I open it myself and enter. I feel the click as the door unlocks for me, nobody is home.

"You'd better sit down" he says gesturing towards the sofa. I perch myself on the edge and he sits down in the chair opposite, he's not relaxed at all. In fact he looks very anxious indeed, his left leg is twitching slightly, he's finding it difficult to make eye contact and I can see that he's breathing quite deeply. I'm more worried than ever but don't really have any idea what to say, luckily just as I'm about to fill the awkward silence he speaks again.

"There's been an accident at the substation, your mother has been injured and is in the hospital. Do you need a drink or anything before we go?"

"No, I'm fine. How bad is she?"

"I'm sorry but I don't know any more than what I've told you, come on let's get going."

He stands up and moves towards the door, I follow him out into the road, the door shuts behind me and I hear it lock. It takes us less than five minutes to walk to the hospital which is on the edge of the town away from the beach, the western side. Those five minutes seem a very long time to me as all the possible implications of my mum's accident race through my mind, is she badly injured, might she die? It is a relatively large building standing four stories high, only the power substation is taller. Apart from its size, the construction is identical to all the houses being made of large bricks with faces of about thirty centimetres by twenty the clay having being sourced locally and made here when the town was built. As we approach the large entranceway the door opens for us automatically, the rights enabler leads me to the reception desk and speaks to the lady sitting there with a display screen slightly to one side of her.

"Edward Bush, to see his mum Carmen."

The receptionist smiles in an automatic manner without giving anything away and says that she's on the second floor in room twenty-three. My companion flinches visibly at this piece of information and asks if I'd like him to come up with me. I lie, saying that I'll be alright and he watches me walk towards the stairs at the back of the entrance hall with a look of pity, before turning on his heel and heading back outside into the summer sunshine. I climb the two flights of stairs quickly but I don't run, the double doors open and I walk onto the landing, directly in front of me there's a sign that reads *Awaiting Onward Passage*. That explains the flinch and also answers my question; she's bad, very bad. Below the bad news sign there is an arrow pointing to the left saying *20 – 24* and below that another arrow pointing right that reads *25 – 29*, I turn left and room twenty-three is the second door on my right. It opens silently and I step inside.

My mum is lying in a bed directly opposite the doorway, there are two chairs on each side of the bed and a table on wheels at the foot, my dad is sitting on her left and Jim on her right. She is awake and talking to my dad, she breaks off her conversation at my arrival and gestures to the chair next to my brother. I cross the room and sit down giving her a quizzical look. She looks fine, perhaps a little bit flushed and there is a slight sheen of perspiration on her brow, but she certainly doesn't look badly injured. Something is wrong, maybe the rooms on the other floors are full or maybe the sign doesn't mean what I think it means but in that case why did the rights enabler flinch at the mention of the second floor? I sit down next to Jim and look at my mum expectantly; she takes hold of my hands in both of hers.

"Thank goodness you got here in time; I'll be going in less than an hour."

"Going? Going where?" I reply with a slight edge of hysteria in my voice.

"I'll be going to Luxburg for onward passage to the next plane of existence, my time has come. But you'll be fine, Jim will be assigned his future tomorrow, it's just that now dad will too. It's lucky for you that it's happened today, as you'll get your new mum tomorrow, everything will work out for the best."

"But you're fine, you're talking to us, there must be some mistake. What's happening?" I'm finding it hard not to shout by now, but still everyone else is just sitting or lying there totally calm, serene almost. They certainly seem to be accepting of their fate and that's where I'm different, I've never been able just to accept my fate. I feel like I should have some kind of say in what I do, I think I deserve to make my own choices in life. I think everyone should be allowed to make their own choices for better or for worse, I don't believe even for one moment that Europarl is infallible and I know I can't be the only one who thinks this way. I am so cross that I want to punch something or someone, I want to bring down Europarl but I want to make it personal. I want to kick and punch our corrupt president until he begs for mercy and then I want to carry on. I can feel a red mist descending upon me and this strength of feeling worries me but it also feels good in a perverse way that I can't quite put my finger on. I'm not a violent person, I've never had a fight at school (unlike Jim who's had several over the years) and yet at the moment I'd kill any member of Europarl and relish it.

"Right now I'm fine, which is good because it means I get to say goodbye to all of you but I wasn't fine a little while ago. I made a mistake with a circuit breaker at work. I got a massive electric shock, passed out and then had a seizure. I might be alright but the doctors say that when this has happened once there's always the risk it will happen again and continue to happen so it's far better for me to go now."

"It's better this way Ed." Echo both my dad and Jim.

That's it, my head is on the verge of exploding, I've never heard such rubbish. I don't know exactly what happens in the final preparation year at school but I know that Jim wouldn't have been so accepting of this had it happened a year ago. We're taught not to worry about this, in fact I know a boy in my year that went through exactly the same thing about eighteen months ago and he was matter of fact about it, just blindly accepted it. Didn't cry, didn't grieve, was fine, absolutely fine. Then I wonder if there's something wrong with me, I'm going frantic and everyone else is just shrugging it all off. But we have a right to life, it's one of our human rights and yet Europarl is about to terminate a life – yes, I can see through the words, I don't think there's any such thing as the next plane of existence regardless of what all those around me have been led to believe. It's just a trick to make people go quietly when they're of no further use to the state. Either they have no treatment for the seizures, which I think is unlikely, or more probable; a life even in these times of vastly depleted population is cheaper than a bottle of pills. There's only one thing to do now. I can see that all three members of my immediate family are beyond salvation and they're all happy about the fact. They have all found *the final, indispensable, healing change* that it took Winston a whole book and forty years to discover in *1984*. They are not struggling, they have won victory over themselves and they love Big Brother! I however am definitely struggling so must go with Jack, really there was never any question but I am now absolutely determined. For the moment though I must go along with the system, I must bide my time.

"Yes mum, this is the best way." I say quietly and manage to keep the note of angry sarcasm out of my voice. The others all smile and mum squeezes my hands gently and then releases them.

"Ed, I'm so proud of you" she smiles, "you're going to be fine when it's your turn the year after next, you've not got long to wait now."

I feel sorry for all of them but I grudgingly accept that they are happy, or at least they think they are. The next fifty minutes are going to be quite hard for me; I decide that I'm going to need a few diversions to pass the time so I ask if anyone wants a drink. But I'm foiled for just at that moment an orderly comes in with a large jug of water and four glasses, he puts it down on the table at the end of the bed and leaves us to it. I pour us all a glass and pass them around, in spite of the fact that I have less than an hour left to spend with my mum and less than four days with my dad and brother I'm finding it very hard to think of anything to talk about. Luckily the others are talking away as though this is the most natural situation to be in and they either don't notice or choose to ignore my obvious introspection.

Time passes very slowly indeed, I manage to make a trip to the toilet along the corridor last nearly ten minutes. Finally after what seems like an eternity (which of course it actually is for mum) the same orderly comes back into the room, this time pushing a wheelchair.

"OK Mrs Bush, time to go, just get in the chair please."

"It's alright, I can walk" says mum, but the orderly insists that she be pushed in the wheelchair on her final journey, he has to stick to the rules or who knows what could happen. Mum gets off the bed and sits in the wheelchair. We're allowed to go with mum to the train so we follow along the corridor to the opposite end of the building where there is a lift. Despite the circumstances the child in me finds this a bit of an adventure because not only have I never been to the station before, I haven't even seen it or indeed any trains. This is due to the fact the whole complex is underground, it's hard to tell exactly how far underground it is because the lift seems to accelerate progressively for the first half of the journey and decelerate in exactly the same manner for the second so we barely feel any hint of movement at all. Since the display in the lift only shows the four floors of the hospital, a basement and then the station itself there is not enough information to get an idea. Whilst I guess that the orderly might know I decide it would not be appropriate to ask him.

The doors of the lift open onto a wide station platform, about five metres away from us there stands a long train of carriages. The platform ends just to our right but extends a good half a kilometre in the other direction where the front of the train stands at the tunnel entrance. The air on the platform is noticeably cooler than the outside temperature and is actually very pleasant. The train emits a low barely audible hum and I can hear a slight ticking from somewhere underneath it every few seconds. A man approaches from the open door of the carriage directly in front of us, he greets the orderly and then turns to mum and tells her that it's time to say her goodbyes. After that we only have a couple of minutes with mum before the train guard or conductor or whatever he is pushes her into the carriage and that is the last we see of her. The carriages have windows running their full length but they have a very dark tint so it is impossible to see inside, although the chances are that mum can see us.

I'm still in a daze trying to imagine why mum is so accepting of what I'm thinking of as her execution for the crime of having an accident at work. This is all wrong, it shouldn't be happening. I'm just about to make a run for the carriage door that is still open but then I notice there is a viewing gallery behind us running the whole length of the platform about three metres above us. Standing there not more than twenty-five metres away is a rights enabler and he has his gun trained on me. I casually turn away from him trying not to look suspicious and decide not to do anything stupid. My best chance is to hold myself together through whatever tomorrow brings for Jim and dad and make contact with Jack on Sunday after the celebrations are over as we'd agreed. It's almost time for me to start making a difference and it would not be a sensible course of action to get myself shot before I've even started.

Luckily before I get a chance to break down or have any more dangerously dark thoughts there comes from somewhere the blast of a whistle, we hear a hiss of compressed air from underneath the train and all the carriage doors slide shut. A long semi-circular strip of red light surrounding the tunnel mouth changes abruptly to green. The ticking that we've been hearing from underneath the train the whole time we've been here briefly increases both in volume and frequency before stopping completely then the train accelerates into the tunnel mouth accompanied by a hum that gradually increases in pitch with the speed of the train. As the last carriage disappears from view the green light switches back to red and we are left in silence. Now the train has gone I can see that there is a second track in the station and beyond that another even larger platform. There are various crates and pallets stacked up along its length and a large forklift truck stands just in front of us, there is nobody on the other platform. I hear the lift doors by which we entered the station open behind me and realise with a jolt that the hospital orderly, my dad and brother are just stepping in. I quickly walk towards them sneaking a quick peek up at the gallery as I go, I'm relieved to see that the rights enabler has now gone.

The instant I get through the doors they shut behind me and the lift glides smoothly upwards, the indicator shows *Basement* for a second before stopping at *Ground Floor* and the doors slide open. We step out into a wide corridor that leads back to the hospital reception area. The orderly mutters a goodbye to us and goes into a room on the left of the lift leaving us to head home. I can hardly believe my ears when my dad asks me and Jim what we fancy for tea as we exit the hospital through the automatic doors. The sun is still shining and there is hardly a cloud in the sky as the three of us head down the road past the shop and home. It's been no more than fifteen minutes since the train left the station and I wonder how far away it is by now and whether there is anything for mum to see on her journey. I realise that I know next to nothing about the railway, I have no idea how fast the trains travel, whether it's all underground or whether it surfaces once it's clear of the town. There's one thing I can be sure of though, that mum is now further away from Chelmsford than I have ever been. Mind you, that's not exactly difficult as I've never been any further than the beach.

We walk the short distance through the centre of the town where the courthouse stands opposite the shop in silence. Less than five minutes later my dad opens the door of our house and we head into the kitchen. Jim and I sit down at the table whilst dad peers into the fridge to see what's on the menu, so much for asking us what we wanted to eat as there's almost nothing there. In the end he sorts us out some scrambled egg and toast, despite the thoughts cascading around my frazzled mind it goes down very well. As we finish eating I suddenly feel very tired even though it's not even nine o'clock so I say goodnight to dad and Jim and head upstairs. I have a quick shower to wash away some of the day's stress and relish the hot water blasting on my face, this is one thing that I'm definitely going to miss come Sunday. I realise that I don't even know where we'll be going and how we'll be getting there but something tells me that a hot shower is going to be a rare occurrence in the future. I'm asleep almost the moment my head touches the pillow which certainly makes a surprising but pleasant change. Tomorrow is going to be a big day so it will be nice to face it fully rested.

Chapter 4

Wednesday 21ˢᵗ June 53

By the time I wake the sun is high enough in the sky not to be shining on my bedroom window, the clock says eight fifteen, this is the latest I've slept in for a few months. This combined with my early night means that I feel really refreshed after having slept for nearly twelve hours. I decide that for the four days of the celebrations I'll just go with the flow and not get stressed over the significance of what is happening to the remaining members of my family. I get up and go downstairs, I can hear Jim and dad talking in the kitchen. From the tone of their voices they both sound excited and even happy which just adds to the general daze that's been engulfing me since I arrived home yesterday afternoon. I still find it hard to believe that they're happy to let Europarl take total control of our lives without question. I take a deep breath and enter the kitchen.

The small viewing screen on the table is showing the programme for the celebrations, the format of the four days is the same as it always is. The first day (today) starts just before lunchtime when the whole population of the settlement will gather in the town centre outside the courthouse. Obviously those who are on shift at the substation will not be there but for the duration of the celebrations they operate a reduced staffing level as well as halving each shift from the standard eight hours to four. This means that everyone will be able to enjoy at least some of the events, for all the children and those adults who are not working attendance is not optional. Although quite what would happen if someone didn't show up I'm not sure as to my knowledge it has never happened.

The first day concentrates on the community as it currently stands, all of the people who have come of age this year are still with us at this point and there is no mention of anybody's assignments either in terms of their jobs or spouses. It is basically a party lasting the whole day and finishing at sunset or thereabouts, because this is the longest day of the year that is fairly late in the evening. The second day is when the main business of the celebrations starts, it is the day that everyone will be assigned their placements. The people like Jim who have come of age during the year will be told whether they will be moving to another community and if so where, they will also find out the name of their spouses and where they are from. In our community since we have the full population allocated already it is expected that nearly everyone will be moving away unless they have shown a real aptitude for work that is available here.

All of the people who actually came of age yesterday already know that they will be involved with the running of the community and as such will be staying here in Chelmsford. They will be moving into the luxurious apartments that adjoin the courthouse. The other matter at hand on the second day is the reassignments. This is mainly for those people like my dad who have lost their spouses during the course of the year but it also covers those who've not reached the required level of performance in their current assignment. These are usually work-related reassignments with a couple being reassigned elsewhere together along with their children if they have any. Every so often there will be a change of spouses where only one person will be moved, the person who is moved will always leave their children behind. The second day finishes with all the people who are moving away going to the station below the town centre for their transportation.

The third day starts with the welcoming of the new people, this is normally a relatively quiet day here in Chelmsford due to the fact that we are already fully populated. This year however it could be different, if the new settlement really is going to be involved with the electrical power generation facilities there could well be some movement of experienced workers from here to the new settlement which in turn could mean more people arriving here than usual. It could be quite interesting. The second part of the third day is when all the marriages happen and finishes with the wedding reception in honour of all the new couples. Again this is normally not much different from the first day's party since there are usually only a handful of new couples here. The fourth and final day of the celebrations starts with the voting followed by an all day team-building exercise for the benefit of integrating the new arrivals. Then after that everything is back to normal for another year.

Dad and Jim look up as I enter, they are both eating porridge which is a little unusual in midsummer, maybe it's all we've got at the moment as were not going to need much food at home for the next few days since the celebrations are fully catered. It's the main reason that most people look forward to this time of year as the food provided is generally very good, it makes a nice change from the basic provisions that most of us normally have. Dad points to the hotplate, there's a bowl on it keeping warm for me. I pick it up without thinking and almost drop it due to the heat, looking at the almost empty bowls in front of the two of them I realise mine's probably been there for quite a while. I sit down at the table, grab a spoon and start to eat, it's actually very good.

"All set for later then?" I ask.

"Oh yes, should be a really good one this year, what with the new settlement and everything" says Jim.

"I've got to get going for work now" says dad, "so I'll miss the very start, I finish at half twelve. At least I won't have to stand through the awards ceremony."

"Try and find us when you get there dad" I say, "that way we'll be able to sit together for lunch."

"Yeah, stand near the back if you can so I can find you, got to run" he replies over his shoulder as he heads for the front door.

Jim and I while the morning away mainly flicking around on the viewing screen but also chatting occasionally like we used to. There's not a lot showing at the moment on the screen anyway, mainly cartoons for kids and highlights from previous years' celebrations around the country. At about quarter to twelve we head out of the house towards the courthouse. There is already a crowd of people there when we arrive and ease ourselves into a position near the back where we can lean against the wall of the shop and wait. The street fills up rapidly, there is a slightly muted murmur of the crowd, nearly everyone is talking but nobody is speaking much above a whisper.

At midday precisely the front doors of the courthouse open and the governor of our settlement with his wife and the chief rights enabler with his wife come out onto the porch. That precision is open to debate, since the time for the entire country is set according to Luxburg meaning that the sun will not be at its highest point in the sky until nearly twenty-five past. Still there are other inhabited places for which the time is much less consistent with the actual time according to the sun. There is a ripple of applause from the assembled masses then the courthouse doors open again and another group of people emerge. They are the other people in charge of the running of our community all of whom are celebrating their birthdays today. The governor then launches into a long rambling speech about how well everything is going in the country generally and in Chelmsford specifically.

When he finally stops talking he steps back from the podium that has been set up just for today, pushes open the door, reaches in and brings out a small crate. He opens up the crate and then makes a presentation to each of the community leaders, they each receive a small box covered in red velvet. He says something to each person in turn and they smile but nobody opens their box, they certainly give the impression of being quite valuable. As he approaches the second to last person in the line I feel a tap on my shoulder and there's my dad standing next to me. The last box is presented and the governor returns to the podium, he tells us all what a fantastic job his team have done this year and how lucky we all are to have them at the helm. As he finishes the big gates at the side of the courthouse slide open.

He takes his wife's hand as does the chief rights enabler and they proceed through the gates and round to the back of the building followed by all the rest of the town administrators. Once they have all taken their places at tables in a big marquee erected on the lawn behind the building, the bell at the front of the courthouse rings and the general population are allowed to go through as well. There are no set places for us, we simply fill up the places at the tables starting at the front of the marquee in whatever order we arrive at the entrance. There is no crowd surge, everybody just files through the gates calmly like we do every year and Jim, dad and I end up sitting in the third row of tables from the front, the closest we've ever managed to be in spite of starting right at the back of the crowd. There is a flute of sparkling wine at every place for the toast to Europarl and also another glass which we can fill ourselves from huge pitchers of orange juice or water.

Once everyone is seated, finally the governor stands up at the front and taps a gavel twice, the chatter of the crowd instantly tails away. He has our full attention, however there are still a few murmurs from very young children.

"Welcome citizens of Chelmsford, South Britain to our eighteenth Human Rights celebrations. Today we will be celebrating our achievements within our community over the last year. This year we have a record number of thirty-four people who have come of age and of those, two of them were born on the day of the solstice and will be joining my team here. The other thirty-two new adult members of our society will find out their future tomorrow, through the good grace of Europarl everyone is guaranteed their Human Rights. Never again will anyone suffer the misery of being unemployed, of being homeless, of wondering where the next meal is coming from. Ever since the war Europarl has been providing a framework for life that is totally fair, where everyone is able to work in a job to which they are truly suited, where everyone is free from all the worries that faced previous generations. We have never had such a good life in all of human history. So let us all raise our glasses to Europarl."

"TO EUROPARL!"

Glancing around I can see that everyone is hanging on the governor's every word, nobody else appears to have any doubts about what he's saying, only me. After the toast, a group of waiters and waitresses (all members of our local community re-deployed with nobody having to serve for more than one meal during the whole period of celebration) bring out the starter. According to the menu on the table this is *Roast breast of duck with spring onion salad and smoked chilli salsa*. The service is very quick, the meals for the top tables arrive first but within less than ten minutes of the governor being served everyone is tucking in. I've never tasted duck before, it's often like this at the celebrations that we get to eat things that we've never even thought of eating previously. It's also often the case that we never get to try them again as none of these things are in the weekly supplies we are given and not many of them are available to buy in the shop either. The duck is actually very nice indeed, I was expecting it to be like chicken or turkey as those are the only birds that I have eaten previously but the pinkish brown colour takes me by surprise.

There are plenty of bread rolls on the table and I use one to wipe my plate clean in order to savour the juices that remain after I've finished eating. When everyone has finished the plates are passed to the ends of the tables where they are removed to the kitchens, the vast majority of the plates are absolutely empty and many have been cleaned with bread. I refer back to the menu to see what we're being treated to for the main course, it is *Roast loin of venison, spiced red cabbage, cider glazed fondant potato and red wine sauce*. Even the sound of it is making my mouth water but I have no idea as to what venison actually is so I ask dad, he tells me that it's meat from a deer. We see the occasional herd of these feeding on the edge of the forest that grows to the west of the town so it's somewhat surprising that this is not something generally available in our shop since it is available locally and wouldn't have to be brought in with all the other supplies. Whilst I'm pondering this, the dish itself starts to arrive at the top tables.

It takes the serving staff longer to distribute the main course to everyone but it's still only a few minutes before I'm tucking in and really enjoying another food sensation. For the next fifteen minutes or so all that can be heard in the marquee is the clattering of cutlery and that distinctive sound of people savouring a rare culinary treat. Once again the plates are cleared away quickly when everyone's finished eating and the dessert is brought round in short order. This is *Chocolate brownie with cream*, after the delicious first two courses, I feel somewhat let down as I've never been a pudding person but as a fan of chocolate when I can get some I always think it's a bit of a waste to use it in a dish such as this. Nevertheless I eat it and make the most of it. This is the end of the meal and when everyone is finished the people at the head table retire to the courthouse for the afternoon while the rest of us troop outside onto the lawn.

The afternoon is mainly for the children, there are organised games to play while the adults and the older children like me just relax in the sunshine and chat in groups. Unlike many of the other parts of our lives or indeed of these celebrations there is no obligation for anyone to join in, only to attend. It's a last opportunity for me to talk to Jim before he goes off tomorrow and begins his adult life. He does actually seem very excited about the prospect and I begin to wonder whether I'm right to run away with Jack to what will be a life of uncertainty. Yes, I'll be free, I'll be able to make my own choices but if I stay here I will be provided for. I'll know exactly what is expected of me all the time, I will be free of responsibility basically. Right now at the start of our annual festival it does seem like we have a good life and yet only yesterday my mum was removed from it on the whim of Europarl. Europarl fronted by a president who claims to have all the answers as to what is best for us, I know all those who are of age will be voting for our representative there on Saturday but we never see them and we can't be certain that they even exist.

At about five o'clock the governor and the other administrators come out of the courthouse and circulate amongst us all making small talk. At six o'clock the side of the marquee facing the lawn is opened up to reveal a huge buffet of food from which we are all invited to serve ourselves. There is a great selection and plenty of it too, many people eat far more than they should including me. The food is available to us for the whole of the evening although at around half past seven the tables containing what is left are moved away from the open side of the marquee and some are put at each end. This reveals a dance floor and now the party really starts to get interesting, many people start to lose their inhibitions even members of the administrative team sometimes. The fun carries on until late in the evening but people are allowed to leave from as early as eight o'clock and most of the families with young children have left by nine. By the time dad, Jim and I leave just after eleven the party is all but over and we head off home along with quite a few others in high spirits.

Chapter 5

Thursday 22nd June 53

When we wake up the next day it's cloudy and looks as though it might rain, we were lucky that it wasn't like this yesterday as the feel of the afternoon celebrations is never as good when we're all squashed in the marquee. It doesn't matter today though as we'll all be inside the marquee anyway while the new assignments are made and after that finishes the day is free. Just before ten we head off once again to the courthouse, the side gate is already standing open and we are able to join the steady stream of people heading through to the marquee. As we arrive Jim is ushered straight onto a staged area at the front of the marquee which has been assembled since the end of last night's party. Dad doesn't go onto the stage immediately as the reassignments are called individually at the end of the proceedings so I take a seat with him toward the front of the main body of the marquee.

There are chairs on the stage for each of the thirty-four young adults, they are all seated in alphabetical order diagonally across the left hand side so they face the seated crowd in the marquee but they are also facing a desk on the opposite side of the stage which has a chair behind it and another in front. Right at the back of the stage there is a large viewing screen that is showing the time in the top left corner and the blue flag of Europe with its circle of forty gold stars representing each of the states is gently drifting around the bottom. By the time dad and I have taken our places Jim is already seated on the stage, the majority of them are there but a few gaps remain, we can see that Jim is going to be the first assignee. By quarter past ten all the seats on the stage are occupied apart from those at the desk. There is not much talk in the marquee; there is an expectant hush amongst the crowd. At exactly half past the governor steps into the marquee from the side, ascends the five steps onto the stage and takes his place at the desk. He then makes a brief motivational speech.

"In former times people reaching their majority would be approaching an extremely stressful part of their lives, suddenly finding themselves thrust into a world where they have to find their own way. They had the worry of finding a job to support themselves, to find somewhere to live and to find a partner with whom to spend their lives. But thanks to Europarl you have none of these issues, we know your skills and we know your place in our society so without further ado let us begin the proceedings that will launch you into the world at large."

He opens a large folder in front of him and starts by reading out the names of all the people on the stage, as he says each name the person stands briefly before sitting back down. Once this introduction has been done he turns a page in his folder and then calls the first of the names again – "James Bush". Jim stands up and walks across the stage and sits down in front of the governor.

"James Bush, you have worked really hard during the last year and you have done well in all the academic tests that you have been set and you have risen to the challenge of every practical task admirably. You have shown that you will be a very useful member of our community. You will be going to Reims to work in our main transport division; this is a very important job as without our railway network none of the supplies would reach our towns."

Jim really seems to have landed on his feet as working in the transport division is one of the few jobs in the country where you actually get to travel around and see other towns. He could even get to go into Luxburg itself which would really be something. Now we just need to find out about his wife.

"And now what you're really waiting for…" says the governor, there's a slight laugh from the assembled crowd and a nervous chuckle from Jim. The governor touches the viewing screen built into the desk and a picture of a girl appears on the screen at the back of the stage and presumably on the desk as well since Jim doesn't look up. She's pretty but not stunningly beautiful, from the picture she looks quite tall but still a fair bit shorter than Jim which is not surprising as he's already taller than dad and he's not exactly short. The governor finishes "…her name is Nicole Albert and she is from the agricultural centre of Limoges."

With that Jim gets up and returns to his seat on the opposite side of the stage. The governor then turns the page in his folder and calls the next person, Jane Carter, she stands up and walks across the stage and so the assignment process continues.

For the next hour and a half we sit through the assignments of the sixteen year olds and then it's the part that I've really been waiting for, my *new mum*. The governor stands up and comes to the front of the stage and addresses us.

"As you probably already know, this year we have reached a sufficient population level for a new town to be built. Our energy requirements have also increased so the new town will be servicing the North Sea power generation facility the same as we do here. This means that we will need experienced staff at the new plant which is being set up approximately sixty kilometres away in Sevenoaks. Therefore this year's reassignments are much more numerous than usual."

He then goes back to his desk where a second chair has been placed alongside the one that was already facing him and proceeds to read a list of names. He's not wrong there are far more reassignments than normal, he must have read out nearly a hundred including my dad's. The reassigned people are called individually or in couples to sit in front of the governor's desk on the stage, the first two people called are Mr and Mrs Allen who actually live next door but one to us. They and their three children are to be redeployed to the new town of Sevenoaks, once the two of them have returned to their places the next name is called – "John Bush". It is dad's turn. He walks up to the stage, climbs up the steps at the centre and sits down at the desk.

"I am so sorry to hear of your very recent bereavement" says the Governor, "I know this cannot be an easy time for you but to help you through this we are able to assign you a new wife. She is also fairly recently bereaved and has a daughter the same age as your younger son. Your work in the power substation has been exemplary and you have risen to hold a very senior position. So as well as your new wife you are also being reassigned to the new substation, all four of you will be moving to the new town. You will become one of the management staff of the new facility."

The governor displays the picture of my *new mum* on the screen at the back of the stage and says that she is called Anne Paget and currently lives at the transport centre of Reims where she works as an electrician so her skills are a perfect fit. I am in too much of a state of shock to do anything other than glance at the picture, this has thrown a huge spanner right into the centre of my plans. I was due to meet Jack early Sunday morning for our departure but now I'll be sixty kilometres away in Sevenoaks wherever that is. Not a massive distance perhaps but I don't want him to think I'm unwilling when I don't turn up. I can't get a message to him, I'll have to go to him in person but time is going to be tight. When the meeting finishes I'm going to have to run straight to the beach and hope he's there, I don't know how much time I'll have before we're expected at the station and I'll have to pack up my personal things as well. This time yesterday I'd never even seen the station now I'll be travelling on a train before the day is done.

The rest of the meeting is more of the same and time seems to slow right down. We are given food at around one o'clock but I'm so stressed about my immediate future that I eat without even tasting let alone savouring although from previous experience I'm sure it's good. Finally the last reassignment leaves the stage just before four o'clock, the governor steps forward to the centre of the stage once more and addresses us all again.

"That concludes all the assignments for this year. For all of those people who are moving your packing crates are being delivered to your houses as I speak. All your personal effects need to be packed and the crates left outside your houses by five o'clock. You will need to be at the main station entrance by the courthouse by six o'clock. You are now free to go."

When we get out of the marquee we find Jim and then head back home, I try to force the pace a little but dad and Jim seem in no hurry to get back and start packing. As we reach the end of our road I say that I'm going to head down to the beach for a final wander. Dad says that's alright but gives me a strange look. Once they're out of sight I start to jog and a couple of minutes later I'm on the beach again, I run along to where Jack had been camped out and there's no sign of his ever having been there. This is not good, where's he gone? He said he'd be here until Sunday, everything is going wrong, I see my future crumbling before me, in four weeks' time I'll be going back to school for the final preparation. I'll lose my identity and go wherever I'm told, no I can't let this happen, I must find Jack.

I sit down amongst the scrappy grass at the top of the beach and listen to the breakers crashing onto the gravel along the shoreline and wonder what on earth I'm going to do. Then just as I'm on the point of despair I hear Jack calling to me, at first I think I'm imagining it, I look around and then I see him scrambling over the dunes towards me. The relief I feel is immense, he doesn't alter his pace and it seems an age before he grasps my hand and gives it a firm shake.

"Ed" he says, "what brings you here? You're a day and a half early!"

"It's all gone wrong Jack, mum had an accident at work but they wouldn't treat her at the hospital, she's gone. Now I knew when that happened that dad would be up for a new wife today but it never even occurred to me that he'd be moved. I mean *we'd* be moved, we're going to a new town called Sevenoaks. What are we going to do? Can we leave now?"

"Calm down, it certainly sounds like you've been through a lot since yesterday but we can work this out, there's always a way. We can't leave now, we're going to have to change our plans, you'll have to go to Sevenoaks with your dad. If you abscond right now and don't show up for your welcoming ceremony tomorrow they'll come for you and there's no way that we'd be able to escape if they're actually chasing you. It's alright though, we'd have to go past Sevenoaks anyway. Just go and I'll make contact with you there as soon as I can, it may take a while though. Don't worry, everything will work out fine and we have plenty of time. Now hurry back, I should imagine you need to pack all your things ready for your move."

"Thanks Jack, see you soon."

I head off along the beach back towards town for the last time, I've enjoyed this beach, I wonder if there'll be anything like this in Sevenoaks. Most of all I wonder how long I'm going to have to wait for Jack, it doesn't sound like he's in any hurry. It must be quite liberating not to have a schedule forced upon you, to be able to come and go as you please. It's not long before I'm back at the house, I go inside and see a large crate bearing my name sitting on the sofa. I drag the crate upstairs to my bedroom and start to empty my drawers, it doesn't take long mainly because I don't put any particular care into it. I basically tip the drawers into the crate and put the lid on, after all I'm not going to be able to take any of this stuff when I actually go away. Dragging the full crate back downstairs makes a series of satisfying thumps, I drag it through the front door and leave it on the footpath outside.

I go back inside, sit down on the sofa and flick on the viewing screen. It's showing all the assignments for the whole country with a short biography of each person, it's currently running through the Ds, I could rewind it to see our entries but I can't be bothered. In all honesty I feel a little bit deflated, if I'd never met Jack this whole thing would have been an exciting adventure for me but now I've heard of his journey and had a hint of great things ahead for me all I want to do is get on with it and now there's going to be a delay. I suppose I should try and recapture the excitement of the moment and to that end I start to ponder my imminent travel by train. At that moment Jim comes down with his crate, either he's a lot stronger than me or his things aren't as heavy as mine since he carries it down the stairs and out through the door with ease. When he comes back in and sits next to me he's smiling.

"You're all set then Ed?" he says.

"Yes, raring to go, you?"

"Yes, can't wait to get on that train. I wonder how long it'll be before I get to drive one…"

"I reckon it'll be a while but you never know, how hard can it be?"

"Maybe you'll be joining me next year if you're lucky."

"Maybe…"

Just then there's a crash as dad's crate slides down the stairs and hits the front door shortly followed by dad half running and half falling into the lounge. He's out of breath and manages to say between gasps that it was heavier than he'd expected. Jim and I get up and drag it outside for him, it is very heavy indeed.

"Just as well those crates are tough, what on earth have you got in there?" asks Jim.

"Not sure exactly, I just emptied my drawers without paying much attention, I'll sort it all out properly at the other end."

I'm a lot more like dad than I'd realised! At that moment a shadow falls across the window, we all look up and see the lorry that has come to collect the crates pull up outside. The driver hops down from the cab, picks up mine without any difficulty and flings it into the back. He then goes for dad's and it barely moves, with a sigh he presses a button on the side of the lorry and a small lift attached to the back lowers itself to the ground, with a fair amount of effort he slides the crate across the pavement and it drops off the kerb onto the platform of the lift with a metallic thud. Next he picks up Jim's crate with ease and places it on top of dad's before he presses the button to raise the lift, we can hear the straining motor through the triple glazed window. When the lift reaches the top of its travel the platform tilts slightly and with a screech that we are also able to hear from inside the two crates slide onto the lorry's flatbed. The driver returns to his cab and moves up the road.

It's only just after five o'clock so dad nearly missed the deadline, we have nearly an hour to kill before we catch our train. Dad wanders to the kitchen and grabs the last of the food for us to have a bite to eat, it's a slightly odd meal but it's enough to keep us going. After we've eaten we all have a quick scout around the whole house to see if there's anything we've inadvertently left behind but surprisingly we don't turn up anything at all. Even though it's still early we decide to head over to the station, they might open the entrance early and we may as well hang around there as here. It doesn't take long to get to the main entrance and when we get there a few people are milling around the closed gate. Within a minute of our arrival the gate opens and we all walk into the main entrance hall of the station, straight in front of us there is a bank of five lifts all standing with their doors open. We get into the middle one, it is very large and takes a group of about thirty of us swiftly down to the platform.

This lift's doors let us out near the centre of the platform, there is a train in the station standing with its doors open. This is much shorter than the one that took mum yesterday barely filling half the length of the platform and to each side of it there are high barriers raised to stop people falling onto the track. Each of the carriages has a destination display along the whole length just above the window line. The back three of them say Sevenoaks and the first of these is directly in front of us, the front three coaches all have a different destination at each end these being Stuttgart, Nuremburg, Luxburg, Reims, Bourges and Limoges. It's time to say goodbye to Jim, dad gives him a short hug and he heads towards the second coach. Dad and I head straight on into the first Sevenoaks coach and take seats together near the front.

After all the anticipation it's a little bit of a let-down when I'm finally sitting in a railway carriage for the first time. There is a subdued hum that we feel rather than hear, the seats are comfortable enough, trimmed in a hard-wearing grey cloth and they all face in what I assume is the direction of travel. We can see the platform very clearly through the tinted windows just as I'd thought yesterday. By the time we've been seated for ten minutes our carriage is all but full and the doors at each end slide shut with a gentle hiss and a slight clunk. There are fewer people on the platform now so I guess that the train will be leaving fairly soon. Another five minutes pass and then we hear and feel the same ticking noise that we heard from mum's train yesterday despite the fact that it's not been ticking up until now. When the ticking stops abruptly the hum increases in volume and the train starts to move out of the station. It accelerates briskly into the tunnel. The movement is barely perceptible as whilst we're in the tunnel we can't see anything outside at all and there is hardly any vibration to feel.

Suddenly after about three minutes of total darkness we burst out into the early evening sunshine that is now breaking through the cloud of the earlier part of the day. I can now see that we are moving fairly quickly, we are following the shoreline and I can see the high tide water in the Thames estuary glinting in the sun out of the window to our left and the wood to our right. After nearly ten minutes of admiring the view passing by we drop into a cutting and then we're plunged into the darkness of another tunnel. This one I presume is taking us under the river and it takes another ten minutes before we come up into daylight once again. The train is going slower now, I guess this is because we're on a newly laid track that runs into Sevenoaks. My guess is proved right when about ten minutes later we pull into a half-finished station. It looks like it will be underground when it is finished as we are in a fairly deep cutting but nowhere near as deep as the station in Chelmsford. The train stops and the doors open.

We get up and step out of the train onto the platform which has a narrow strip of smooth concrete adjacent to the train but the rest of the area is just gravel. There are no lifts to take us up out of the station, there is a steep slope that looks like it will be stairs one day but for the moment we leave the station by following a curved pathway at the end of the platform that brings us up to ground level. We're standing in what is clearly going to be the centre of the town but all the buildings except for one are not much above waist level. The one building that looks complete is the courthouse, the reason I know it's the courthouse is because it is identical in every respect to the one we had in Chelmsford. A man is standing in front of the open door and we all congregate around him. He waits for everyone to come up from the station before he addresses us.

"Welcome ex citizens of Chelmsford to your new home of Sevenoaks. I am sure that you will all be very happy here. Despite appearances in this area of the town your houses are actually completely finished and are ready for you. All of your crates are already here and have been left outside your accommodation. I will give instructions as to where to find your houses but you'll be able to find the exact unit by looking for your crates. If there are other assignees from other towns sharing with you please leave their crates outside so that they in turn can find where to go when they arrive. You are the first of the assignments to arrive but also the bulk of the assignments. So if you'd like to form a queue in front of me I will endeavour to get you on your way as soon as possible. The information sheet that I give you also details the schedule for the rest of the Human Rights celebrations."

Dad and I are fairly near the front of the queue that forms so it is only a few minutes before dad is holding our instruction sheet. At the top there is a street plan of Sevenoaks showing the town square where we are currently standing with the courthouse, the station building opposite which in reality has barely been started as well as the two big blocks at either end which will comprise the apartments for the people who will run the town as well as the shop. There are four roads that lead off the square on the map, one from each corner but the road heading northeast is just a rough un-surfaced track at the moment, we can see that it ends about half a kilometre away at the large substation building which again is the same as its counterpart in Chelmsford. All the other three roads are finished in a smooth concrete surface and the one that our house is on leads out of the square to the south crossing over the railway line on a temporary bridge that will evidently become part of the station roof eventually. The schedule printed below the map is identical to that which we were following in Chelmsford until we were uprooted midway through. We turn around and head out of the square along our road over the bridge staying well clear of the edge which has no railing or barrier of any description.

"Dad, was everything unfinished when you and mum arrived in Chelmsford?" I ask.

"Oh yes," he says "it was far worse than this. We were all housed in the celebration marquee for nearly two months but that was alright because it was summer after all. The real problem was the inadequate washing and toilet facilities. At least we've actually got our own house ready for us to move in."

"I'll believe it when I see it" I reply.

My worry is unfounded though, when we're clear of the bridge and the stacked building supplies we turn a corner in the road and there before us are two long rows of houses stretching away from us for a good few hundred metres. There are crates stacked outside most of them so we start to scan the name labels. The fifth group of crates on the right are the ones, they're labelled with mine and dad's names as well as Anne and Suzanne Paget. Dad opens the door and walks in, the layout is identical to our old house in Chelmsford and the decoration is very similar. There is a selection of sandwiches laid out on the kitchen table for us but we decide to bring in our crates and unpack first on the off chance that the others will have arrived by the time we've finished. They're coming from Reims which I know is fairly close to Luxburg but I have no idea at all how long their journey is likely to be, also I have no way of telling what time they left either since this would be dependent upon how long the assignment process took in Reims.

I help dad get his crate up the stairs and into his room and we go back for mine, then we spend the next half an hour or so sorting through our things and placing them in our storage drawers. It is nearly eight o'clock by the time we finish but there is still no sign of the others so we decide to eat our food being careful to leave enough for Anne and

Suzanne when they arrive. When we're done we decide to go for a walk around to get our bearings so we head outside and back to the square, as we cross the bridge we notice that the station is empty. When our train came in the three coaches that were bound for Sevenoaks had been uncoupled and left at the platform while the front part of the train had carried on its way. These three coaches have now gone but no other train appears to have arrived yet, the square is also currently empty.

We head down the unmade track towards the substation building, it slopes gently downwards and in no time we're right beside the entrance gate. It's odd to stand by this huge building and hear no noise coming from within, standing this close to the one in Chelmsford you would always hear at least a low level hum but at times of high energy demand it would be fairly loud. But this one is not yet online, dad will be involved in the switch on come Monday so until then we can enjoy the silence. We are far enough away from the town here for all the noises to be natural, we can hear the sea and the occasional sea bird and that's about it. The track does actually finish dead here but the hill continues right to the edge of the Thames, whilst the river is very wide here and tidal it still has a very different feel to it than the beach in Chelmsford does and the smell is different too. We head down the hill, dad is reluctant to go close to the water but he makes no comment when I walk right up to the edge. I walk back up the slope to where my dad has sat down in the long grass and sit down next to him.

"Are you happy dad? I mean the way everything is decided for us, we've just been through two massive changes and there's another one coming soon."

"Ed, we can't change anything. If you try to fight the system you won't survive, I've seen it happen."

"But mum didn't fight the system and she didn't survive either, surely we have to try?"

"No she didn't fight the system, but if she had she wouldn't have lived as long as she did. It is what it is. Come on, let's go back and see if they're here yet"

We stand up and head back up the hill to town, cross the square and back over the bridge, as we cross we hear the hum of a train so we stop and going as close to the edge as we dare see a train arrive in the station at the opposite platform to the one where we disembarked. It consists of only two coaches and while we are standing there we hear a clunk as they separate before the front coach continues on towards Chelmsford. Rather than hang around and trying to meet the rest of our household in the crowd of arrivals we decide to go back to the house where there will be no risk of mistaken identity. There's a hiss of the train doors opening as we walk back to the house.

Dad and I sit down in the lounge with some degree of trepidation. As time passes this only increases until we almost jump out of our skins about half an hour later when the front door opens and in walk my new mum and my new sister. They are obviously mother and daughter and they are both very good looking indeed. Dad says that there's some sandwiches in the kitchen and they both go through, the two of us go outside and bring in the remaining two crates and take them upstairs. When we come back down Anne and her daughter are sitting in the lounge eating. We sit down with them while they finish and then we go upstairs to help them unpack their things, dad helps Anne and I go with Suzanne.

After they're both sorted we go back down to the lounge and start to chat about how we all came to be here. Suzanne or Suzie as she prefers is the youngest of three girls, the other two having been assigned places two and three years ago. Anne lost her husband in an accident, he was working on some wiring in one of the railway tunnels and misjudged the approach of a train. She seems strangely matter of fact about it though just as dad and Jim had been about mum. After a little while we're all talking as though we've known each other for years rather than having just been thrust together. The evening passes in a flash and soon we're all heading upstairs to bed. Dad and Anne head up first, I'm just about to follow when Suzie grabs my elbow and pulls me back. I turn around to face her and she holds out something that looks like a small bent piece of wire. She notices the puzzled look on my face and proceeds to explain in a whisper that it's something her oldest sister taught her to do with an ordinary hair pin, if I place it a certain way round at the bottom of my door it will prevent the lock from activating. She gives me a wink and runs upstairs to her bedroom. I follow slowly up and go into my room, before I shut the door I put Suzie's ingenious device in place as she's suggested out of curiosity.

Chapter 6

Friday 23rd June 53

I had intended to stay awake until midnight to see if the bedroom door really would stay unlocked but after such a day of upheaval I was so tired that I just crawled into bed at ten to and had been asleep instantly. The clock at the side of my bed says it's just after two o'clock when I wake with a start at the sound of the door opening.

"You used the lock blocker then!"

"Yes, it seems to work too."

"Sorry, were you asleep?"

"Yes, yesterday was quite an eventful day, I was tired and I've not been sleeping well for the last couple of months. All those sleepless nights seem to have caught up with me. You don't think it's dangerous to stop the doors locking like that, won't it show as some kind of error when they try to lock it?"

"Me and my sisters did it for years and we never got in trouble, it works on the front door too."

"Are you saying what I think you're saying?"

"Yeah, the front door's unlocked right now, come on, get up!"

"You know they can tell where we are don't you?"

"What Europarl? Yeah, they can. But they have to be looking, I'm sure they've got better things to do. Come on…"

I push the sheet off the bed revealing that I'd not bothered undressing which make's Suzie snigger and I follow her out of the door and down the stairs. Just as she'd said, the front door is indeed unlocked and suddenly we're outside in the semi-darkness. There's a bright almost full moon shining down on us and there is a vague hint of early dawn light on the eastern horizon. I had thought that meeting Jack was liberating but I've never done anything like this before. The thought has never occurred to me to be outside after the curfew, I feel really uneasy as well, especially when Suzie blatantly strides off down the middle of the road in the direction of the town centre. I do my best to shake off the feeling that I'm being watched, only to be caught at any minute and follow her. As we reach the end of the road and enter the town square I realise that I've been holding my breath. There are no lights to be seen in the courthouse so I guess the governor and all his entourage are asleep like we should be.

We skirt around the edge of the square rather than cutting straight across and head down the road that I'd followed with dad earlier. Suzie doesn't even pause at the end of the track and carries on straight down the hill to the water. The tide is in and just short of the edge she slips out of her dress, kicks off her shoes and without breaking her stride wades in still in her underwear. When the water is just above her waist she ducks down into the water and strikes out in an easy stroke. She moves quickly with hardly a splash, when she's about fifteen metres from where I'm standing on the bank she turns around to face me and treads water.

"You coming in then?" she calls.

"I've never swum before."

"Really? But you've lived by the sea all your life, I only had a lake."

"They always told us the sea is poisonous, over the years I worked out that it wasn't but I never tried to go in."

She starts swimming back towards me, when she reaches the shallows she doesn't get out but simply lies there with her head propped on one hand and beckons to me to come in. I take off my shoes and socks then strip off to my boxer shorts somewhat self-consciously as I can feel her gaze on me. I've never spent any time with any girls before except for my mum and that doesn't count. Our way of life keeps the sexes segregated pretty much all the time until you're assigned your spouse and not having any sisters I really know nothing about girls. My sense of fun is definitely beginning to overcome my malaise. I step into the water next to her and start to wade out, as I pass her she stands up and walks with me until we're both in up to our middles. She is very slightly taller than me but her legs are a lot longer than mine, she is really pretty in the moonlight. She demonstrates the basics of swimming to me and I have a go, I cough violently when I inhale a mouthful of seawater and look around expecting to see a rights enabler standing there, but there isn't.

After half an hour or so I am able to swim a few metres, but my stroke is not very elegant and is a long way away from splash free.

I'm also at least twice as slow as Suzie and I suspect she's not even trying to go fast, I'll need a lot more practice. We head back to land, the tide is starting to go out slowly now and I don't want to risk getting swept out to sea, even if I managed not to drown I'd probably get minced by the tidal power generation equipment that we can see in the distance at the mouth of the river. We shake as much water off as we can and then put our clothes back on while we're still damp, I pick my shoes up and walk barefoot on the cool grassy bank. At the beginning of the track my feet are dry enough to get my shoes back on. We reach the edge of the square and see an upstairs light on in the courthouse, my heart is racing but Suzie is predictably not in the least bit concerned saying that even the governor has to use the toilet sometimes. I'm convinced that he's watching us as we walk round the square in the shadows and then up our road to the corner where it turns out of sight. Just before three o'clock I'm back in my bed and the lock blocker is safely stored in one of my drawers, my mind is racing and it takes me quite a while to get back to sleep.

I don't wake until gone nine o'clock, I should perhaps have set an alarm as today's schedule starts at ten so I haven't got a huge amount of time to spare. I shower quickly and remembering that it's the weddings today I hurriedly dress in my best clothes. As I go downstairs I wonder how many others there will be apart from dad and Anne's, it seems likely that there will be quite a few to get through. Arriving downstairs I walk into a scene of domestic bliss in the kitchen, making myself a cup of tea I sit down in the empty seat at the table.

"You must have been tired" says dad, "you're normally awake at the crack of dawn!"

"I had a slightly disturbed night" I reply, grinning.

Suzie kicks me under the table but is also smirking. I grab a bowl, carelessly pour some cereal into it followed by a splash of milk and start to shovel it into my mouth. Dad and Anne get up and head back upstairs to get ready, while we finish our breakfast.

"Are you ready for your next swimming lesson then?" says Suzie.

"What now?"

"No later, silly!"

"We'll have to see, I don't want to get caught."

"We won't get caught, nobody's interested in watching us!"

With that she gets up and leaves me on my own. I finish my breakfast and then wait for the others in the lounge. Before long we're all heading down the road to the courthouse for the welcome. There is a steady stream of people heading in the same direction, many of whom I recognise from Chelmsford, from glancing around I guess that about a third of the people here arrived with me and dad. At a guess that means the total population of Sevenoaks currently stands at about six hundred about half of whom are adults which is much lower than I've been used to. When we arrive in the square though I realise that I was probably wrong, I'd been assuming that the people from Chelmsford would be fairly evenly distributed around the town but all of the people that I recognise are arriving in the square from the same road as us. Everyone is heading for the gate at the side of the courthouse as we did yesterday and it comes as no surprise to any of us when we see the familiar large marquee. We all troop in and are seated towards the middle of the part that has seating. Once everyone is seated my population estimate is just under a thousand all told.

The governor steps onto the stage accompanied by his wife, there are two seats set out for them but only his wife sits down, he remains standing at the front of the stage ready to make his welcome speech.

"Welcome new citizens of Sevenoaks, I trust you all found your accommodation without any issues and that you are all sufficiently rested after your journeys. Today marks the beginning of a new chapter in all of our lives, this new town that will gradually be completed over the course of the rest of the year will be our home from now on. On Sunday the first shifts will begin in the substation and by this time next week all being well we'll be feeding electricity into our national grid. You are all needed for this important work and that is why you have all been chosen to be here. Our country cannot afford people who don't pull their weight and you have all shown yourselves to be worthy of the task ahead. We all have a lot of work to do but it is vital that we succeed as the whole future of the United States of Europe is depending upon us all working to the best of our abilities."

"Normally at this part of the celebrations we would invite the new people onto the stage so that they can say a little bit about themselves but since we are all new here that is not a practical thing to do. Furthermore we have a lot more weddings to perform today than we usually do as the vast majority of you are new couples. Therefore we will be starting straight away with these and we'll all get to know each other during the course of tomorrow. This place in which we now meet has been duly sanctioned according to law for the celebration of marriage. This ceremony will unite all our newly assigned couples in marriage. We are here to celebrate their unions and to honour their commitments to each other. Today all the couples will proclaim their love for one another. We celebrate with them and for them.'

The weddings are done in alphabetical order of the man's surname, dad and Anne are the fourth couple to be called and the first remarriage. The ceremony is short and to the point. After Mr and Mrs Brown have returned from the stage to their places dad and Anne are called to go forward. They walk in single file up to the front of the marquee and climb the steps one at a time and then stand next to each other in front of the governor and he begins their part of the ceremony.

"If any person here present knows of any lawful impediment to this marriage they should declare it now."

I always wonder what would happen if someone said something at this point but I'd never be brave enough to try, I suspect the result would be very bad. This is after all a marriage arranged by Europarl which dictates and administers the law so if there were a *lawful impediment* to the marriage it wouldn't be happening in the first place. Then again there is such a lot about our way of life that works in this way and ever since I met Jack I have been even more aware of it. It's starting even now on only the fourth reading today to be a bit trivial, almost pointless. The governor continues.

"Marriage is a commitment for life, it offers an opportunity for learning and growth beyond all others. Today you will exchange vows of marriage which will unite you as husband and wife, these vows are a promise of a lifelong commitment to each other and to the United States of Europe. Before you are both joined together in marriage it is my duty to remind you of the solemn and binding nature of the vows that you are about to make. Marriage according the law of this country is the union of one man with one woman voluntarily entered into for life to the exclusion of all others. I am now going to ask you each in turn to declare that you know of no legal reason why you may not be joined together in marriage."

The words of the declarations appear on the large viewing screen at the back of the stage just in case they can't remember them after years of attending this part of the Human Rights celebration.

"I do solemnly declare that I know not of any lawful impediment why I John Paul Bush may not be joined in marriage to Anne Marie Paget" says dad only looking at the viewing screen to read his new wife's name. Then it's Anne's turn.

"I do solemnly declare that I know not of any lawful impediment why I Anne Marie Paget may not be joined in marriage to John Paul Bush."

The governor then continues with the next section.

"John will you take Anne to be your lawful wedded wife, to love, honour and cherish her until death?"

"I will."

"Anne will you take John to be your lawful wedded husband, to love, honour and obey him until death?"

"I will."

Now there are just the rings to be given and then only another hundred or so to go. The words appear once again on the viewing screen and the governor hands Anne's ring to dad, he puts it on her ring finger and then says the words.

"I give you this ring as a symbol of our marriage, all that I am I give to you and all that I have I share with you."

The governor then gives Anne dad's ring and she says the same words and finally the governor completes the marriage.

"I now declare that you are husband and wife!"

They return to their seats and the next couple are called forward. I tune out for the rest of the marriages and let my mind wander. I wonder how long it will be before Jack turns up, I also begin to wonder whether I want to go with him after all. Right now I actually find myself pondering the possibility that all this is the best course of action, that Europarl are actually acting in the best interests of the nation. Then I check myself and realise the real reason behind these stray thoughts is sitting next to me right now, I don't want to leave right now because I want to get to know her. There's something about her that draws me in, she's so forthright and different. I wonder if she'd come with me but I'm really not sure how to broach the subject, I think it's best not to say anything until I can speak to Jack however long that may be.

By the time we have a lunch break and are passed around sandwiches to eat I have lost track of how many we have got through so I have no idea how much longer we are likely to be here. To say that the wedding ceremonies are monotonous is somewhat of an understatement and never before have I had to sit through so many. In a way it's a pity that dad's was so near the start as it added a little bit of light relief to sit through one where I actually had a personal connection. After everyone has finished eating and we are settled once again the governor returns to the stage, his wife is not with him this time, she obviously got bored or has something better to do, I for one can certainly relate to this. The first couple of the afternoon session is called and it is with a feeling of dread that I realise that we are only up to the letter *G*.

As afternoon turns to early evening the last couple is called to the stage to the accompaniment of an almost imperceptible collective sigh. We are all tired, stiff and extremely bored but everyone is listening to this one in anticipation of the end and the chance to get out of here and stretch our legs. It is just before half past seven when Mr and Mrs Yates leave the stage as husband and wife but that is not the end of it, we still have the wedding reception to attend, but this part could be fun. A buffet meal is now is being set out at the back of the marquee and then there will be music and much the same kind of party as we had on the first night of the Human Rights celebrations which now seems such a very long time ago. I think this time I could have a willing dancing partner though.

The governor makes a short speech marking the end of the weddings and invites us all to tuck in, he steps down from the stage where his wife re-joins him having come back in during the last marriage and they head towards the buffet together. There is a scraping of chairs and there is a scramble for the food, luckily there is plenty to go around. When people have filled their plates they move chairs around and sit in small groups talking and eating. I sit with Suzie, dad and Anne, the chairs are all grouped around the edge of the marquee leaving the central area clear as a dance floor.

After about twenty minutes or so the music starts, this is the signal for all the newlyweds to take to the dance floor for the first dance. The song that is played is always the same and according to rumour dates from before the war, this is never officially acknowledged of course but it's so unlike any of the other music that we have that it seems fairly likely. It is called *Can't Help Falling In Love* and is sung by someone called *The King* which seems a very strange name, I have known people whose surname is King but I have never come across anyone called The. At the opening bars of the song the relevant parties stand up and make their way onto the floor, dad takes Anne's hand and leads her right into the centre and they start to move in time to the music. The song only lasts about three minutes and then the people who were making a token effort return to their seats but the others stay on the dance floor for the next song. Surprisingly this includes dad and Anne, it is at this point that Suzie gets up and drags me onto the floor as well.

This is something that I've never really done before as I've never known any girls as we are separated at school so I've never approached anyone for a dance on these occasions and I've certainly never had anyone approach me. She is a fantastic dancer predictably enough, she is so good that she brings out the best in me and I don't feel at all awkward. After we've started dancing we only leave the floor every now and again to have a quick drink and the odd bite of food from the buffet to keep us going. Time passes very quickly and it seems much earlier than it is when the last song fades away and the previously dimmed lighting suddenly returns to full brightness. Blinking in the glare and slightly disorientated by a ringing in our ears we look around to find dad and Anne and then head towards them. As we approach they stand up and we all head for the exit together.

When we get back to the house we all head straight up to bed, it is after midnight so normally the front door would be locked by this time but it still lets us in before locking behind us. Whether the door would always let people in who are outside after the usual locking time or if it's a special dispensation because of the occasion has never really crossed my mind before but it does now. When I enter my room the lock clicks behind me as I close the door, it's only as I cross the room that I realise that I've left the lock blocker in my drawer. With a sigh of resignation I go into the bathroom, splash some cold water on my face and clean my teeth. But the front door is locked anyway so it makes no difference, I undress leaving my clothes in a messy pile on the floor and crawl into bed. Maybe it's just as well as

I feel quite tired and my face has barely touched the pillow before I've fallen asleep.

Chapter 7

Saturday 24ᵗʰ June 53

If I jumped last time the door opened in the middle of the night it really takes me by surprise this time. I'm sure I heard the door lock, straight away I'm in a panic and my still half sleeping mind is imagining rights enablers storming into my room to take me away. There is a little bit of light coming through the crack of the curtains and a slight glow from the clock beside me which says nearly three o'clock but all I can make out is a silhouette walking towards the bed. Then when she sits on the edge of the bed and greets me, my anxiety turns to relief and immediately to puzzlement.

"How on earth did you get in here? The door was locked."

"I used the parental override."

"How did you do that and if you can do that why did you give me the bent hairpin?"

"The bent hairpin is easy and works every time, it's a lot harder to trick the parental override and it doesn't always work."

"Is there anything you don't know about bucking the system?"

"Not much, budge over a bit."

With that she slips under the covers next to me which takes me by surprise, there's not much room, I can feel the heat of her body radiating into me and it's not an unpleasant feeling. In fact it's a very pleasant feeling indeed, she turns to face me and I can feel her breath on my face, even though I can't really see her I know she's smiling.

"So what do you want to know?" she asks.

"About what?"

"Bucking the system, I've been doing it all my life. But you're very easy to lead astray."

I'm now wondering whether to mention Jack but I think better of it, after all I've only known this girl for a couple of days and despite the fact that she's currently lying in bed with me I hardly know her at all.

"We'd better get to sleep if we're going to be any good in the team exercises later on" she says suddenly.

"You're not going then?"

"I can't, I only know how to override the locks from outside, besides you don't really want me to go anyway!"

With that she turns her back towards me, puts her right arm under the pillow and settles down to sleep leaving my mind racing. After about ten minutes I think that she's asleep but I'm wider awake than ever, her hair is tickling my face.

Eventually sleep finds me and when I wake up she's gone, it's nearly eight and I actually feel reasonably rested and ready for the day ahead. I get up, get dressed and go downstairs somewhat surprised to find that I'm the first person up. I grab a couple of slices of bread and pop them in the toaster and make a cup of tea. I've finished my toast when dad and Anne come down, I say good morning and leave them to themselves heading back upstairs to clean my teeth. Before entering my room I look the door up and down, there's no obvious marks or features to indicate how to trick it into overriding the lock.

The team building day starts at nine o'clock and by twenty to all four of us are out of the house and heading back to the centre of the town. We head through the open gates at the side of the courthouse and round to the lawn at the back on which stands the marquee. There is a queue at the entrance and we join it, when we reach the front we are given a team badge printed with our team number and first name. Dad and Anne are in a different team from me and Suzie, we head to our designated areas of the marquee. There are half a dozen others in our group when we join it, two boys and four girls who all look about our age, their name tags reveal that they are called Thomas, Michael, Katherine, Ella, Rebecca and Sarah. By the time everyone has arrived our team consists of twenty people in total, ten boys some of whom I know from school and ten girls, again I recognise some of them and we have established that we are all roughly the same age, fourteen or fifteen. These team building days always follow the same pattern but the actual activities and tests vary from year to year. Sometimes we are told what we have to do and other times we have to work it out for ourselves, all the teams usually do all of the activities but sometimes not. Once all the teams have greeted each other and settled down the governor steps up onto the stage and welcomes us.

"Good morning everybody, I hope you are all fully rested and ready for today's challenges. There will be a mixture of physical and mental activities but the key thing that you need to remember is that you should work together as teams. Each of you has your own skills and you will need to communicate with each other to ensure that the best person on the team is assigned to each of the tasks. If you are able to do that then you will be strengthening our community to overcome any challenges that the future may bring us. But apart from that this is also going to be fun. You may now open your team instructions."

There is a rustling of paper as the envelopes are opened, Michael has ours as he was the first person in our team to arrive. He pulls out a sheet of paper on which there are printed instructions, we all look at him expectantly but he doesn't read them out, just stands there with a puzzled expression on his face. We all crowd in to look at the paper, it's gibberish, recognisable letters but there aren't any recognisable words or rather there's the odd one here and there but they don't make any sense. It's obviously a code, hopefully not too complicated or we could be stuck here for a while. There's a hum of people talking in low voices as everyone in the marquee tries to solve the puzzle. Suddenly I notice that there is a list on the back of the page, until now we've only been looking at the sea of letters swimming around the front of the page but to my mind the list looks a lot simpler and could provide a clue.

I take the paper from Michael and turn it over to study the list, it hits me instantly. There are twenty words each with a capital letter, they must be our names. Sure enough the fifth word in the list reads Rfqsef, it's my name Edward, each letter has just been replaced with a different one so as long as the code on the other side is the same this should be easy enough. I point out my discovery and then everyone looks for their names and we write out the code on the envelope. Between the twenty of us we have twenty-one letters of the alphabet, the only letters missing are *F, G, P, Q* and *Y* and we can tell that these are represented by *D, H, O, T* and *W* although it's not obvious which is which but we should be able to solve our instructions without too much trouble. Several other teams are ahead of us though; they've worked out their instructions and have already left the marquee. Quickly we work through the instruction sheet replacing the letters and before long we know where we have to go.

We haven't got to go far for our first challenge, altogether there are eight separate places to go but the list only gives the locations and no indication at all as to what we'll be doing at any of them. The third location is shown as being for a double session of two hours, the fourth is the marquee so it's a fair bet that will be lunch which may or may not involve a challenge, it varies from year to year. The last is also the marquee so this will be some kind of debriefing followed by supper. We all leave the marquee together heading down the lawn away from the buildings of the town and towards the river. At the end of the mown grass there is a thin row of trees about three or four deep forming a boundary at the edge of the courthouse grounds. Right in the middle there is a narrow muddy track that leads between the trees; we follow it in single file and come out at the top of the river bank.

About half a kilometre away to our left we can see the power substation rising up and only a few metres to our right there are two men standing next to what looks at first glance to be a pile of firewood. Looking a little more than fifty metres beyond the men we can see a row of twenty targets attached to straw bales each with five concentric circles, white on the outside then black blue and red with a yellow one in the middle. The pile of firewood must be bows. On closer inspection however it's definitely a pile of firewood. The men approach us and introduce themselves as Fred and Adam. Fred explains that our task is simply to make a bow each from one of the pieces of wood in the pile. The wood is yew which apparently is ideal for making bows as it is very hard but nice and flexible and has a nice straight grain so that it can handle the tension. All we are required to do is carve our bows with the knives provided, there are strings readymade and there are three arrows each which appear to be made out of metal, probably some kind of aluminium alloy, so we haven't got to worry about making those. Even so it's going to be tricky to complete the challenge in the time available, we have until ten o'clock to make our bows and each fire three arrows at the target and hopefully make a decent score for our team. Three arrows each gives us a best possible result of six hundred points, I suspect that we won't be anywhere near that.

The pieces of wood in the pile vary in length between about one and a half metres and two, they also vary in thickness, Adam suggests that we choose a piece that is roughly as tall as ourselves. He picks up a bow that is hidden from view behind the woodpile and shows it to us explaining that it's only rough but he made it in only twenty minutes. It is roughly his own height, the centre part of it has been worked only slightly so that it is easy for him to grip and there is a small groove to guide the arrow, it has been roughly tapered towards each end where there are fairly deep grooves to hold the string. He turns away from us and taking an arrow from a wooden box on the ground fits it to the string, draws it back and lets the arrow fly with a twang. It goes right into the middle of the leftmost target with a dull thud, putting the bow back down he points to the knives and tells us to get started. I take a medium sized piece of wood from the pile that is slightly longer than my height, collect a knife and sit down. Suzie joins me with her piece and we all start work.

While we all carve at our pieces of wood Adam and Fred circulate and offer advice. After about fifteen minutes some of the pieces are starting to look very good, mine however is causing me problems as there is a knot in an awkward position that I am struggling to carve to the right shape and I'm slightly worried I might cut myself. Suzie's effort on the other hand looks almost finished. Sure enough no more than a couple of minutes later she gets up to collect a string which Adam helps her to fit. Everyone looks up to watch her take her shots, she approaches the shooting line and fits an arrow to the bowstring, she struggles to pull it back fully and her first arrow goes into the ground a couple of metres short of the target. Undeterred she picks up a second arrow and this time manages to find the strength to draw the string right back, there is a frown of concentration on her face as she lets the arrow fly and this one hits the target just inside the outer white circle scoring us a single point. By the time she takes her third shot she seems to have got into the swing of things and the arrow flies cleanly towards the centre of the target and scores an almost perfect nine. All in all not a bad start.

Another minute or so passes with us all whittling away with our knives and then three of our team finish at the same time, two of the boys Michael and Cameron and one of the girls Jane. Fred and Adam help them with their strings but the notch at one of the ends of Michael's bow has been carved too deep and when the string is fitted it splinters off so he's going to have to redo that end once the others have shot. Jane and Cameron collect three arrows each and take their bows to the shooting line, Jane goes first and we all cheer when her first arrow goes right in the centre of her target to score ten points but it turns out this was just luck as neither of her remaining arrows even hit the target. Cameron then raises his bow and fits his first arrow, he draws the string back effortlessly, releases it and scores four points. His second arrow scores five and with his last one he manages to score seven, the best combined score so far and the most consistent.

Four more of the others including Michael on his second attempt have gone before I'm happy enough with my bow to get the string fitted. I approach the line with my three arrows, I find it surprisingly hard to draw and I can feel the muscles in my arm twitching slightly with the strain as I look along my arrow trying to sight where it will go. When I am happy I let it go, the string rubs slightly against my left forearm which hurts a bit and knocks the arrow slightly off target but I score a respectable eight. I take my second arrow and repeat the process changing my grip on the bow to avoid hurting myself on the string again, the result is that the arrow is off target to the left this time rather than the right but I score another eight which actually puts me joint first with just two arrows since nobody has yet beaten Cameron's score. Even though I know I'm doing quite well this only serves to increase the pressure, I can sense that everyone is holding their breath in expectation. Finally I let the string go for my last shot and it seems as though time itself has slowed down, I watch the arrow fly towards the target in slow motion and it hits the yellow section but I can't see whether it's a nine or a ten, then Fred holds up ten fingers with a grin. I've done it, twenty-six points out of a possible thirty.

I go back and sit next to Suzie while the others finish off and by the time everyone has had their turn we have a grand score of two hundred and seventy-three which impresses both of the instructors. I'm only slightly disappointed that my individual score wasn't the highest, Nicholas beat me by one point with three nines. We almost ran out of time as it's now almost ten and we can see the next group appearing through the trees, Michael retrieves the instruction sheet from his pocket and looks to see where we need to go next. Given the time we're all hoping we haven't got too far to go, item two simply says to follow the river bank past the substation with no indication of distance. As a group we walk along next to the river passing the place where Suzie and I went swimming the other night, as we approach the substation we can see one of the teams heading up the grass bank towards the track back to town, presumably the people who were doing our next task previously.

As we clear the substation we can see a small river or large stream flowing into the Thames estuary about two hundred metres further along, it is about three metres wide at the point where there is a rickety bridge made out of wood freshly cut from trees tied together with rope. Our next task is going to be building a bridge by the looks of it. Again there are two men standing by the bridge and as we approach them they introduce themselves as James and Andrew. They invite us to sit on the ground in front of us and explain the challenge to us. We have to build a bridge across the stream which apparently is called the River Darent, there is a small pile of hand tools saws mainly but there are also a few knives, a spade and there are ropes, lots of ropes. The bridge that the previous group constructed is actually quite good when we look at it up close and I suspect that its presence will tempt us into copying the design rather than starting from first principles.

There are two basic rules for the task that make it slightly harder to achieve, we are not allowed to go in the water and we are not allowed to have any pieces of wood spanning the whole distance. When the structure is complete we have to cross the stream using our creation in a single file but we must link hands whilst crossing so whatever we build is going to have to take the weight of at least six of us at once. Of course being a younger and therefore lighter team we have a slight advantage here. The land on either side of the stream is totally covered with trees which in the main stand about four or five metres tall with fairly slender trunks. Before we begin James and Andrew show us how to do a selection of lashings and knots but stress that they are happy to help further once we have started in earnest. There is a large pad of paper and pencils for us to sketch our design before we begin work.

One of the boys, Alexander is first to pick up a pencil and he draws a somewhat ambitious sketch given the available time that consists of a platform with an a-frame on one side with one of the diagonals set into the ground on each side of the stream. The crossbar is mounted at a suitable height for a handrail with ropes wrapped around this and the edge of the platform. Finally he draws a third almost vertical beam meeting the top of the a-frame and going into the water and touching the bed of the stream on the other side of the platform. We all look at his design with approval, it's good and looks like it should be strong enough and what's more it looks nothing at all like the previous team's effort. We decide to go with this design and Alexander becomes the team leader for this challenge. We need three tall trees with reasonably thick trunks to build the a-frame and a fourth one for the vertical. The platform itself can be made from thinner trunks and we will vary the positions at which the joins are to make sure it's strong enough. We are just about to set off to start cutting and gathering the timber when one of the instructors, James clears his throat and points out that our design breaks one of the rules in that we have a single piece spanning the whole structure, the crossbar of the a-frame. Alexander changes the design so that the crossbar is made of four separate pieces paired either side of the diagonals with each side having an overlap of about half the whole length. It's a compromise but should be strong enough as long as our lashings are good.

We pick up some saws and head into the wood, there is a good selection of trees but there are quite a few ash trees that will be ideal for the main large pieces as they are nice and straight. The actual platform can be made with almost anything as we won't need any individual pieces that are any longer than three metres. We choose our main structural trees first and work together to bring them down using a rope to ensure that they fall in the direction we want. Once we have those back at the construction site we split up with some of us including me and Suzie collecting the smaller pieces needed for the platform and others under Alexander's guidance building the a-frame. There is a fair amount of stripping of side branches required but some of these can be used in the making of the platform. We decide that the best way to get it across the stream is to build the a-frame and then tip it over the water with the vertical post already attached. This decision brings us a small design change whereby we brace the vertical post back to the base of the a-frame at each side. This will also have the advantage of supporting the platform as well as enabling us to slide it across.

Time passes very quickly but by the time the a-frame is complete we have finished collecting the wood for the platform and are over half way through its construction. We have twenty minutes left when we stop and get into our positions to tip the main frame across the stream. Alexander is slightly worried about the length of the vertical post as we are not absolutely sure of the water depth. He wanted to cross to the middle of the first team's bridge to measure but obviously this wasn't allowed so we guessed as best we could by dipping long branches into the water. We all pick the whole structure up together and position it so that the foot for this side of the stream is adjacent to the small hole that we've dug for it to slot into. There is a rope attached to the top of the a-frame and half of us take the strain on that while the others grasp the frame itself to begin the tipping process. There is a sticky moment when it reaches the point of no return slightly earlier than we expected so we weren't quite ready on the rope but we manage to stop it from falling uncontrollably and all is well, we have the main frame in place. The vertical pole is not touching the bed of the stream but this is only because the other side of the a-frame is not in a hole yet, the fact that the structure hasn't bent at all to enable it to touch the bottom is testament to its strength.

We send our lightest team member, Cassie across with the spade tied onto her back to sort out the other side while the rest of us concentrate on finishing the platform. She digs the hole right next to the foot of the frame, by the time she's finished we've completed the platform and we have less than ten minutes to go. She gives the foot a good hard kick and it settles into its hole with a slight creak. We then feed the platform across to her and she gingerly crosses back so that she can process across with the rest of us in line with the rules. Then Alexander leads us all across, it creaks under our weight but stands firm, a triumph of construction. The next team is arriving as we cross back over the bridge to head off to our next activity, dad and Anne are in this group and we are able to exchange a few words as we pass.

The next location is right on the other side of the town so we're running a little late when we cross the town square and head up the road past our house. We reach the end of the road where there is a large open space with patchy grass covering it. There is another team standing there with a couple of chaps who are wearing camouflaged clothing who are presumably the instructors for this activity. For a moment some of us wonder whether we've come to the wrong place as the other team are making no move to leave but then we realise that as this activity is filling a double time slot it's logical that it will involve two teams. There is a big crate on the ground behind the two instructors and next to that is a big pile of camouflage gear and a small pile of plastic goggles. The two instructors are called Sam and Harry and they explain that we are going to be *paint balling*. This is not something that I've heard of before and everyone else in both teams seems to be none the wiser. We will each be given a paint ball gun which is loaded with a plastic ball containing paint fired with compressed air. We are each handed a camouflaged overall, each one has a number on the front and back from one to forty. Once we have them on we are also given a pair of goggles each and they proceed to explain the objective and rules of the game.

We will each be given a card with a number printed on it, that is the number of our target. We are only allowed to shoot the person with that number on their overall. We will be given half an hour to head off into the woods surrounding the open area then a klaxon will be blown and the game will begin in earnest, the boundary of the game area is marked with an orange plastic tape. We will have to hunt down our target and shoot them, once we have successfully shot our target we take the card from them for the person that they are currently hunting and that becomes the survivor's new target. The casualty then returns here with the cards of any targets that they might have taken already. The winning team is the team that has the most cards at the end of the game, that being either when there is only a single person left or when the time runs out at one o'clock. Harry opens the crate and removes one of the guns, he shows us how to load the paint balls, how to prime the gun and then he tells us all to put on our goggles. He also puts on his own pair as does Sam, he then demonstrates shooting it by pulling the trigger and firing it at Sam's left leg where the paint makes a large splatter and Sam curses under his breath. He emphasises that no matter what happens we are to keep our goggles on at all times.

We are told to form a line and one by one we are given a target card, a gun and a bag containing a dozen paint balls and sent off on our way. My target is number sixteen but I have no idea who that is, my own number is twenty-three. As I walk across the open ground I load one of the balls into my gun but I don't prime it yet, I'll wait until the klaxon goes and do that then. I head into the woods quickly and start to check out the lay of the land, the trees are about the same size as the ones we used to make our bridge. The relatively small size of the trees means that there is not much in the way of canopy cover so there is quite a bit of undergrowth. Unfortunately this mainly consists of brambles and stinging nettles so my intended plan of hiding somewhere on the ground is not particularly appealing now. It is clear that not many people have been through these woods before so the path that I've taken is worryingly obvious.

Time is ticking away and I'm lost for a strategy, there appears to be a small clearing a little ahead of me so I battle through the brambles and stand on the thin grass to look around. There is a clear path running through perpendicular to my own entrance route and splattered paint from a paint ball attack on one of the trees presumably from the last session. I walk along the path away from the painted tree looking around carefully for the location from which the shots were fired, the paint balls don't travel a great distance so when I think I've gone too far I turn around and head back to the clearing. Almost straight away I see some faint scuff marks on the pathway and adjacent to them is a large hollow in the ground with a huge bush covering it almost entirely. I slide myself into the hollow and gently brush the scuffed ground with my sleeve to eliminate the marks. From where I'm crouching I have an excellent view of the clearing but I'm pretty sure nobody can see me, I settle down to wait.

I've not been in my hiding place for long when I hear the klaxon sound to indicate that the game has begun. Soon after that I hear people moving around in the woods and the odd shout but nobody comes anywhere near me to start with. Then all of a sudden a girl that I don't recognise comes crashing along the path within a metre of where I'm lying, number thirty-two runs into the clearing. I'm too busy watching her trip and land flat on her face that I don't notice Suzie standing right next to me until I hear the sound of her gun firing. Her first shot hits number thirty-two right in the middle of the back, she then walks into the clearing to get her target card, luckily the girl seems alright, she gets to her feet and heads off the battlefield. What happens next is not what I was expecting but actually not altogether surprising, Suzie turns around and heads straight back to where I'm hiding and slides in next to me.

"Who are you hunting?" she asks.

"How did you know I was here? I thought it was a really good hiding place."

"It is, I only noticed you because I stopped right next to you to take my shot. My next target is seventeen."

"I've got sixteen. I reckon we'll probably see a few people using this path, I think I'll just wait here and see what happens."

"Mind if I join you?"

"You already have, but no I don't mind."

As it happens I was right, we do see a lot of people come along the path through the clearing and not a single one of them spots us. Unfortunately neither of our targets comes anywhere near us, we're just thinking that time must be running out and pondering a different strategy for the last few minutes when we hear the klaxon again. The battle is over. We crawl out of our hiding place and head back to the open ground where we started off. The cards are counted, I was not the only person not to achieve a *kill* and one of the other team managed four but in spite of this our team just manages to scrape a win. We all head off towards the marquee in the town centre, both teams and the instructors, it's lunchtime and I think we're all ready for it.

Chapter 8

As we enter the marquee it's apparent that we are amongst the last to arrive back, there is a general sound of chatter and eating so it would appear that there is no challenge this year. There are tables all along one long side laden with various dishes of food that can be eaten with fingers, bowls are piled at a few places so I don't have to wait very long to get a few sandwiches and other nibbles. Most people seem to be sitting in their groups at long tables dotted around the central area each with twenty chairs but there are also a few people in smaller groups of two or three. I decide to follow the expected behaviour and sit down at the table where some of our group are already seated, Suzie joins us sitting down next to me and before long we're all chatting together as we eat. I must admit to myself that I am actually enjoying myself and I wonder whether I really want to throw this away to join Jack and his group. I've not given him a second thought since I left him on the beach the other day until now and I do feel a pang of guilt. There's no reason to of course since he's not currently here so I'm not affecting any plans he might have made, not yet at least. It's funny how people can change one's outlook, until I met Jack I'd not really thought there was a possibility of leaving and now I've met Suzie I'm contemplating staying once again. But she's so rebellious, I wonder if she'd come with me, would Jack be happy with that? I wish he'd hurry up and get here, I really need to talk to him.

We all finish our lunch well before we are out of time even though most of us go back for several extra plates full and our talk turns to speculation as to the nature of the final activities and challenges this afternoon. None of the things we've done so far today are repeats of anything I've ever done before so I really have no idea what to expect, nevertheless we all chat about some of the challenges that we've faced in previous years. Since the vast majority of our group are from Chelmsford we have a lot of shared experience. Before long there begins to be a movement of people from the marquee and we decide as a group to head off to our next location. We don't have far to go, heading out of the gate by the courthouse we turn left onto the square and then go along the road in the north-eastern corner. Once clear of the houses there is a grassy field about two-hundred metres square and covering the whole of the area are various obstacles, this looks like it's some kind of assault course but unless there is more elsewhere it's hard to see how completing this is going to take a whole hour. As usual there are two instructors but this time they are both women, they introduce themselves as Mandy and Dawn and proceed to explain the task ahead.

There is a rucksack for each of us and there is a pile of large stones next to them. Mandy explains that the weight of the rocks is the same as the weight of our team, just over thirteen hundred kilograms and our challenge is simply to take all the rocks around the assault course in the shortest time possible. The pile is surprisingly small but each stone is presumably fairly dense, it would be possible to load them all into the rucksacks in one go but that would render the task impossible for any normal person to complete. This is going to be the hardest activity yet and it will be made harder still by the fact that we have just eaten. Realistically I can't see myself carrying any more than twenty kilograms around that course and some of the others, especially the girls won't even be able to achieve that. We are probably all going to have to go around four times. Each of the obstacles is numbered so the sequence is obvious and goes around the field in a clockwise direction finishing to the right of where we're standing with a waterlogged tunnel emerging into a muddy pond. There is a large set of scales to weigh the stones as we deposit them in a metal crate. Dawn tells us that there is a baseline score for moving all the stones to the end of the course in the available time, if we are quicker the score will increase and if we don't move all the stones within the time limit then the score will be reduced in proportion to the weight of the stones not on the scales.

At precisely two o'clock we all put our rucksacks on and start to load stones for each other. The stones are of various sizes but most of them seem to be around five kilograms, I end up with five stones in my pack as do most of the boys but Nicholas is obviously very strong so he ends up with eight. The smallest girl on our team, Clare can only manage two of the smaller ones but most of the girls take three and both Suzie and Victoria take four. Once we're all ready we set off at a jog to the first obstacle which is a plain brick wall standing about two metres high that we have to get over, some of us bunk the others up and once they're on top of the wall which is plenty wide enough to be able to sit on they pull the rest of us up. We all jump down the other side and then we're single file as we balance along a log. I miss my footing and slide off to one side, luckily without injury, I'm about to carry on when one of the instructors, Dawn tells me to go back to the start of the log. This is going to be hard work if we have to complete each obstacle perfectly. Next there is a mud filled ditch to swing across on ropes, there are five of them so we all make quick work of this with only William ending up in the mud although he's not made to swing again and allowed to carry straight on to the next obstacle.

This is the hardest yet, a large rope net to climb up to a height of something like five metres from the ground and then down the same the other side. The holes in the net are a really awkward size not large enough to allow our feet to poke through so we have to rely on our hands more than we'd like. The slope of the net the other side makes it possible to slide down without too much trouble or risk of personal damage. Once down we're at the first corner of the field and a quarter of the way through the course, the whole of the next side is clear of large apparatus and consists simply of a hundred metre run across varying surfaces starting and finishing with grass. There is a stretch of deep pea shingle into which we sink quite badly immediately followed by a wade through water which at its deepest almost reaches my crotch and some of the smaller members of our team are waist deep. As the water shallows we can feel the ground under our feet trying to remove our boots and the final stretch is through thick mud, we are then at the next corner. Most of us are out of breath by this stage but nobody seems to be struggling just yet although we are not much more than five minutes into the task.

Along the next section we are single file again as we climb three metres up a ladder to a small platform where we have to cross a bridge made up of three ropes, one to walk on and two for handrails. Luckily the distance is relatively short and it doesn't twist too much, there's always the threat of a fall of course and some of our team are obviously not enjoying this section. When we reach the second platform we have to pick up a short length of rope with a hand grip at each end and a reinforced centre section that we hook over a long length of rope to slide us to the ground. This takes us to the final corner of the course, the last side is the worst for people who don't like getting wet. This consists of a long stretch of muddy water with alternate low walls that have to be climbed over and tree trunks just below the surface which have to be ducked under. It culminates with a totally submerged tunnel that is about half a metre in diameter and is about five metres long. This is nasty and it is with a great sense of relief that we unload our rocks into the weighing crate. Short lived of course as we now have to load up and go round again, amazingly though we have already shifted over half the weight of rocks. None of us are able to take anywhere near what we took on the first go so at least some of us are going to have to go a third time.

We all start for a second time but is becomes apparent that some of our team members aren't going to make it. As people drop out exhausted we share the extra rocks out amongst those of us that are left and by the time we reach the last side for the second time there are only thirteen of us still going and I am carrying six stones, one more than I had on the first attempt and I can really feel the weight dragging me down. The final effort through the water of the tunnel is nearly all I can bear and I'm gasping for breath as I break the surface at the end. We've been much slower on the second pass and we only have a little over twenty minutes left. It's starting to look like we won't finish but the remaining pile is really quite small so we all load up again, Katherine, Cassie and John who were amongst those who dropped out re-join us to load up as we start for the last time. This time there are no further dropouts and we finish the course with nearly two minutes to spare, we are all far too worn out to celebrate much and we are all very aware of the fact that we still have another two or possibly three challenges to face before the day is done. As we leave we walk through a specially designed tunnel where we're sprayed with water to clean the worst of the mud from us and then dried off with a combination of warm air and infrared lighting. It sort of works, there are still a few traces of mud on us and I can feel that my feet are still slightly damp but by and large I'm clean and dry.

The next task thankfully is not very far from where we are now as we are pretty tired but it seems a bit of an odd one as we are actually heading to one of the houses. When we arrive the door is standing open and we head into the familiar building. It's obvious when we step inside what we're going to be doing, there is no furniture or fittings of any kind in the place and no floor covering. A man and a woman are standing in the centre of the lounge wearing paint splattered overalls, on the floor next to them is a pile of similar protective clothing, some painting pads and tubs of white paint. All the walls and ceilings of the house are the beige-pink colour of unpainted plaster, we're going to be painting. At least it's not an energetic task after the assault course. Jeff and Jenny brief us, it's not a race, quality of work is more important than how much we actually manage to do in our allotted time. We put on our overalls and each collect a paint pad and a tub of paint and under the direction of Jeff and Jenny we spread ourselves out through the house in groups of four to begin work. I am in one of the bedrooms with Ella, Evie and James. James takes the bathroom leaving the main bedroom to the girls and me. The paint pad has an extensible handle to allow us to paint the ceiling but as I'm taller than both of the girls I take this job and leave them the walls. I start in the corner by the door and work my way along the wall, the paint covers very well in a single coat and it is surprisingly relaxing and therapeutic as a task. It doesn't require much exertion or thought.

I'm about three quarters of the way across the ceiling when James enters from the bathroom and announces he's finished in there. I suggest that he starts from the opposite side of the ceiling and works back towards me, by the time we meet the girls are all but finished on the walls as well. As we only have ten minutes or so left we decide to relax a bit and the four of us finish off the walls together very slowly and then head back downstairs to find the instructors. We are not the first in the lounge, one of the other groups is already there and painting the large wall. There is no room to join in but it doesn't matter because at that point Jenny informs us that it's now time to head off to our final challenge. The others come downstairs and we all head out of the front door and back to the square, the last activity is on the lawn of the courthouse behind the marquee. The marquee is shut when we get there so we have to go around the side rather than through it and sure enough there are the usual two instructors for this challenge standing on the far side of the lawn next to a small gazebo. The gazebo has closed sides so that we can't see what is inside and there is a large green tarpaulin on the ground in front of the instructors, scattered across this are various wooden building blocks in different shapes.

The two instructors tell us their names Sasha and Isabelle and invite us to make ourselves comfortable on the tarpaulin, we all sit down gratefully as we're still fairly tired from the exertion of the assault course challenge. Sasha explains that inside the gazebo there is a structure that is made out of all the same pieces that are spread out across the tarpaulin, all the pieces will be used. Each member of our team is allowed to go into the gazebo once for up to thirty seconds, how we use that time is totally up to us but the person or people inside are not allowed to talk whilst they are there, the task is simply to build an identical structure outside. We decide to send two people in together to start with and see where we go from there. John and Katherine enter the gazebo first, when they come out thirty seconds later they explain that the structure we are building is model of the main Europarl building in Luxburg. It stands about half a metre high, about three metres wide and a metre deep, John starts to sort through the blocks that are scattered across the ground and puts them into piles according to what parts of the building they are. Meanwhile Katherine points to two identical cuboids which form the symmetrical ends of the building and we all help to drag the heavy pieces into place then the three giant archways between them that form the main entrance.

As the shape of the building is very well known to all of us we are able to get a reasonable amount of the large pieces into place before we have to send anyone else into the gazebo. It is the small detail pieces that are the challenge and especially those around the back of the structure since the vast majority of the pictures we see of this elegant building show the front elevation. After half an hour we have the whole of the main structure in place and also the distinctive glass pyramid roof that stands in the centre above the arches covering the main parliamentary chamber where the upper house sits. We even have the tiered seating in place underneath the four triangular pieces of clear plastic but now we start to lose our momentum. There are only five of us that have not been inside the gazebo yet, me, Jane, Luke, Sarah and William, everyone else has used their thirty seconds. We still have a fair number of small pieces and they're mainly unique which makes them difficult to find in the structure, all the repeating pieces that form the facade were put in place a long time ago. We lay out all the remaining pieces around the building in the places where we think they're most likely to go and then it's my turn to enter the gazebo.

I spend my thirty seconds frantically trying to remember the pieces that we have left over and see where they are positioned but it's quite hard. When I'm called out I approach our model and pick out five or six pieces straight away and position them successfully but then it starts to go wrong. I notice one or two other pieces that look wrong but I don't know where they should actually go so instead I try to make sense of some of the other pieces, there aren't many left now only about twenty or so and we still have a reasonable amount of time left. While I'm still struggling with what I saw we send Sarah in for her look and when she comes out she is able to position a handful of the remaining pieces immediately as well as moving the two pieces that I thought were wrong along with another that she's identified. We're on the final run now so to keep the momentum up we send in the last three of our team in quick succession to make a final push. Within another five minutes we have the last few parts in position and we're all fairly happy with the result. There are still a few minutes allotted to this task but rather than risk making last minute changes and possibly getting ourselves into a mess we decide to leave it as it is and head back to the marquee.

Despite being right next to it we're not the first team to arrive back at the marquee, a small section near the middle has been opened up to allow us to enter without going round to the main entrance on the other side. There are two other teams already inside sitting at the same large tables that were used at lunchtime, we take one near the stage and sit down to wait for the summing up to begin. There is a steady flow of returning teams from the time we sit down but not everyone has returned by the time that the governor enters and mounts the steps to the stage. He addresses those of us that are here saying that he will wait until everyone is back before starting and proceeds to sit on a chair behind the microphone stand. After another quarter of an hour all the teams and instructors are seated within the marquee and the governor stands at the microphone.

"Good afternoon everyone, I hope that you have all enjoyed today's activities and that you all performed to the best of your abilities. There was a variety of tasks both mental and physical and whilst not all of the teams took all the same challenges similar attributes were tested and the scores for the teams will be weighted according to various factors to make the final scores fair. Please help yourselves to food on the tables at the back of the marquee whilst we await the final scores, I'm sure you must all be very hungry after all your exertion during the course of the day."

There is a scraping of chairs as people head towards the buffet, the food is as usual varied and delicious. I help myself to a very spicy stew which tastes delicious but makes my lips sting and my eyes water and when I hastily drink a whole glass of water it actually seems to make things worse. Suzie is laughing at me whilst she eats exactly the same dish seemingly with no problems at all. I decide to cut my losses and go back for a fresh plate of something less challenging, I am absolutely starving and if I persisted with something difficult to eat I may not have time to eat enough. As we eat there is a bustle of activity on the stage with all the instructors sorting out sheets of paper where they are sitting at a table to one side. I think the final scores will be announced very shortly and there is an air of expectancy around the tables. One of the instructors now has all the papers in his hand and walks over to the governor who takes them and approaches the microphone.

"The moment we've all been waiting for is here, I have the final scores and I am pleased to say that you have all done very well indeed. Even the lowest placed team has a very respectable score and I am very encouraged that you are all going to be able to make a success of this new settlement of Sevenoaks. This has been a fantastic start and I know that we are very well placed to begin our work on Monday."

He then proceeds to read out the names of the people who collected the instructions for each team in reverse order of score, each team is told to stand before he reads their scores. He gives the scores as percentages and the team with the lowest score in thirty-third place has a score of fifty-nine percent. By the time he's read out twenty names the scores are up in the seventies and our team has still not been called, we're beginning to get excited. I've certainly never been in a team that's done this well before although I remind myself that there are far fewer teams here today than I have been used to in the past. Dad and Anne's team were in fifteenth place with sixty-eight. Slowly he reads through the scores up to fourth place and still we've not been called, at that point he stops and says that the remaining three teams are to come up onto the stage for the presentation. We all get up and head to the front, one of the other teams is made up of newlyweds so they are not much older than us and the other team are a mixture of adults and younger children. Once we are standing in our groups on stage the governor continues with the scores, our team is in third place. We are each given a small bronze coloured medal on a ribbon that is placed around our necks depicting the Europarl building on one side and the face of the president on the other. The other two teams are given the same but silver and gold respectively for second and first.

After the presentation we are free to go, Suzie and I head towards dad and Anne who congratulate us rather embarrassingly and we all head off out of the marquee towards the house. We are all quite tired despite the fact that it is not much after six o'clock. Dad and Anne head straight up to bed despite the fact that they don't have to work until Monday, tomorrow is Sunday and will probably be a slow lazy day after the excitement of the last few days. My mind wanders to Jack once more and whether I should tell Suzie about him and my plan to leave with him but instead of seizing this moment I tell her that I am very tired and with that I head upstairs leaving her alone in the lounge. She gives me an odd look as I go and I wonder whether I'm doing the right thing by stalling like this. It's possible that Jack could be here tomorrow but I think it's more likely to be another day or two, I'm very aware of the fact that I've become close to Suzie in a very short time.

Chapter 9

Sunday 25th June 53

Due to being very early to bed I'm awake not long after first light, my bedroom in our new house faces west so I don't have direct sunlight streaming through the window here. My clock shows just after five o'clock, the door is locked so there is nothing I can do except wait. Time drags for nearly an hour until I finally hear the door lock click open at six, I get up, put on a dressing gown and go downstairs. Suzie is sitting at the kitchen with an empty bowl and plate in front of her and on the opposite side of the table there's a small pile of toast.

"Good morning," she says, "I thought you'd be up early after such an early night!"

"I was, but I didn't stop the door from locking."

"What are we going to do with you eh? Eat your breakfast and get dressed, I thought we could go and explore, see what there is around here."

"Alright, that sounds like a plan. I suppose the front door's not locked."

"Of course!"

With that she gets up from the table and runs up the stairs saying that she's off to clean her teeth. I spread some butter and jam on a couple of the slices of toast and start tucking in. I'm not actually that hungry after the last few days of huge meals courtesy of the Human Rights Celebrations so two slices is more than enough. I put the remaining four in a plastic lunchbox to take with us, I head back up to my room and hurriedly get dressed and pick up my small backpack that I normally use for school. When I get back downstairs Suzie's back in the kitchen, raiding the cupboards for supplies and putting them into her own identical backpack. I take a selection of what she's got on the table and start to fill mine, after a couple of minutes we're ready to depart. Sure enough the front door is unlocked despite the fact that it's still before seven and we retrieve the lock blocker as before allowing the door to shut and lock behind us.

We decide to turn away from the centre of the town and head up the road to the place where we were paintballing yesterday. It's quiet and we can hear birds in the woods, there wasn't much evidence of them when we were crashing through the undergrowth with our guns. We take the path that leads through the clearing where we hid during the game and follow it through the woods beyond where the plastic tape had been marking the boundary for the paintball game. The woods are fairly dense although the trees where we are seem no taller than any of the others around here. Whilst initially we were following a trodden pathway we are soon battling our way through undergrowth, some of which is prickly. We see quite a few squirrels which don't seem to take any notice of us at all and the occasional rabbit that runs off as we approach even though we're not making that much noise.

All of a sudden the wood seems to thin out, the trees are much smaller and then in the space of no more than a hundred metres we're standing in a clearing. This however is not a normal clearing that can be found in any wood, this is very large and there are distinctly rectangular shapes within the area where the undergrowth is much lower than elsewhere. We glance at each other both realising the significance of our discovery and feeling a certain sense of unease, this must be the site of a town from before the war. This is probably the original town of Sevenoaks from which our settlement presumably takes its name. It might only be a small part of the town as the whole area is not much larger than our current settlement and populations were so much greater in the old days. We follow some of the shapes whilst looking out for signs of anything interesting on the ground, it's quite exciting even without seeing anything recognisable but then I find something really interesting. It's just sitting there on the ground, a small bright red thing glinting in the sunshine.

I call to Suzie as I pick it up, I've not seen anything like it before, some of the red paint is flaking off its surface revealing corroded metal. It's no more than ten centimetres long and has the melted remains of four black plastic wheels attached. It looks a bit like a small version of the lorries that deliver our supplies, a small model of some kind of vehicle, it could possibly be a toy. I put my find into one of the small pockets in my backpack and start looking for more things. During the course of the next hour or so we crawl around on the dusty ground looking for more things but we don't find anything else, or at least nothing that is instantly recognisable as something manmade. We move back into the edge of the woods and sit on a fallen tree in the shade to have a drink. I'm just putting my drinking bottle back in my pack when Suzie frantically whispers that someone's coming, turning around I look to where she's pointing. There is a figure striding across the clearing vaguely in our direction, I'm almost sure that it's Jack. As he gets closer I can see that I'm right, I tell Suzie not to worry and call out to Jack. He turns towards us but obviously can't see us so I step out into the open and Suzie follows suit, once he can see us he walks straight towards us.

"Hello Ed," he says, "who's your friend?"

"This is Suzie, she's sort of my sister now. I'm glad we've bumped into you like this, I wasn't sure how I was going to find you."

"That wouldn't have been a problem, I'd have been able to find you alright, especially as you seem to be a bit of an explorer anyway. It seems you've found a kindred spirit, that is really good news because it means that Europarl haven't been looking at your movements because they'd never create an assignment that puts two wanderers together. They've learnt that lesson the hard way a few times over the years!"

I can see that Suzie is a little confused by the conversation between me and Jack which is understandable as I'd not mentioned him to her at all, I suggest that Jack might like to introduce himself properly. The main reason for this is that I don't want to give away anything that Jack doesn't want to. I needn't have worried however, Jack gives her a very brief life story before going straight on to why he's here now and how he's hoping that I will be joining his cause. At this point I'm watching for her reaction to this information as well as waiting to see if Jack will suggest that she come as well. Instead Suzie takes the initiative at this point and asks Jack outright if she can come too, Jack isn't fazed by this in the slightest and agrees that this would be a good idea. He then follows this up by saying that we have quite a long journey ahead of us for which there will be a certain amount of preparation. The most significant thing is that he will have to remove our chips, this could be quite painful depending upon where they are. He produces a small box from his pocket, this is a multi-purpose device but it will be able to locate our chips.

He starts with me, the usual place for it to be located is in the upper arm but they are sometimes in a foot or even bottom depending upon the medical staff in attendance at the time of birth. He scans my left arm from top to bottom without success and moves on to my right, again without finding the chip. He runs it over each of my feet still without a result and then over my bottom, I ask him if he's sure it's working to which his response is that sometimes the chips move around in the body. In the end after a couple of minutes scanning my whole body he finds it on the right side of my chest when the scanner makes a gentle bleep, we guess that it probably started off in my right arm but has migrated there over the course of my life. At least it's not in one of my feet as this would be likely to make walking long distances uncomfortable and the cut might be prone to infection, this would make our journey potentially harder than it's already likely to be. Touching an icon on the screen of the device changes the sensor setting to reveal the depth of the chip in my flesh which reads as nine millimetres, it is quite a relief to me that it's not especially deep. He then moves on to Suzie and finds her chip instantly right in the middle of her left upper arm. The initial jollity soon wears off when we discover that her chip is much deeper, in fact it would appear that it's almost touching the bone.

We're now potentially at the point of no return, Jack says that he has all the necessary things in his pack to remove our chips now if we're happy with that. We'll then have to carry them around with us until such time as we leave which he suggests should be tomorrow evening. This will give us a whole night before we're noticed as being missing, we'll then confuse the trail further since there will be a train in the station when we leave upon which we'll be able to plant our chips. This train will be leaving for Luxburg at five o'clock on Tuesday morning so it will give the impression of our having stowed away on that. It's looking as though my fifteenth birthday tomorrow could be a major turning point in my life. Suzie and I glance at each other, we are both extremely nervous but it is also very exciting, however we both agree that this is something we need to do. I wonder how my dad and her mum are going to take it; it's obvious that we can't risk leaving any sort of a note for them. Realistically we'd both be leaving quite soon anyway and I don't think they'd get into any kind of trouble due to our departure, I've never known anybody to run away like this before though.

Jack looks pleased with our decision; he removes his backpack and puts it on the ground. He pulls out a small package and shows it to us, he explains that it's a special tool that his organisation has developed specifically for the removal of chips. It is in a sterile package, the problem is he only has one with him so he'll need to clean it as best he can between the two operations, he has special wipes to do this but there is a slightly increased risk of infection for the second user. He says that he'll remove Suzie's first and then mine since mine is not as deep. The tool is a split needle with a special grabber in the middle and a lead to connect it to the device he used to scan us. The needle is pushed into the skin in the correct location; the display screen will indicate when it is in the right place. When it reaches the chip this is also shown and the grabber can then be activated and the whole thing gently withdrawn, he makes it sound very easy.

Before he opens the package he tells Suzie to roll her sleeve up, once she has done this he cleans her arm with one of his wipes, then it's time to go. He slips the needle out of its plastic cover and plugs the lead into his device, the needle looks very big now it's just about to be stuck into someone's arm. Suzie looks away, luckily the location information is displayed on the screen without any sound so she doesn't know when the needle will be pushed in. Jack gets it in the correct place and then firmly but slowly pushes it in, she gasps slightly as he activates the grabber and I can see by the look on her face that it is much more painful as he slowly pulls it out. There is a slight trickle of blood on her arm which he cleans away with a wipe and then tells her to hold it over the hole in her arm which she does. He then shows us both the chip, it is a tiny metal pellet about two millimetres long and smaller than half a millimetre in diameter. He hands it to her telling her not to drop it, then he wipes the needle clean, puts it down on top of its packaging while he searches in his backpack again. He takes out a small piece of cloth, ties Suzie's chip into it and tells her to keep it in her pocket from now until we leave.

Now it's my turn, I undo my shirt so that Jack can stab me in the right place. I take a deep breath and hold it as I watch him push the needle in, it hurts but isn't unbearable. Noticing that Suzie has turned away again, I gasp in pain as he withdraws the needle, the chip has come out sideways. Jack laughs slightly as he reveals they sometimes do that, grumpily I take a wipe from him and gently clean my small throbbing wound. Jack ties my chip into another piece of cloth and I put it in my pocket, he then cleans off the needle again with another wipe, unplugs it, puts it back in its packaging and stores it once more in his backpack. He hands us each a small sticking plaster which we put on before readjusting our clothing. Jack gestures across the clearing and asks if we've been exploring it and whether we've found anything, I take the small red vehicle out of my backpack and show it to him.

"Ah yes, a toy car, that's quite a good find. Most boys would have had quite a few of those before the war, of course nearly every family had at least one real car in those days, personal transport for a whole family. A little while before the war started cars were run mainly on oil-based fuels but these were in increasingly short supply. In fact oil was the cause of quite a few wars in the past and the extreme taxation on such fuels was one of the major causes of the riots that triggered the start of the war. It's a pity but at that time they were actually starting to find alternatives that really might have worked if the world hadn't changed so suddenly. Of course the technology hasn't actually been lost, it's just that it's not available to the general population anymore, the MEPs all have cars. Then of course there are the lorries that service all the settlements, they're pretty much the same, they all have motors powered by electricity generated on board using a hydrogen fuel cell. Of course that technology is very old indeed, people were experimenting with fuel cells in vehicles about a hundred and fifty years ago. The real problem has always been getting the hydrogen, it still is now but with such a small population and such a large power generation facility it's possible to produce enough by electrolysis. Of course this is no help to me, my car runs on batteries."

"You've got a car?" both Suzie and I both ask together.

"Yes, it's not here though, I can't get it across the English Channel. I've got it hidden near the tunnel mouth on the other side, the batteries are charging from the railway's supply, unless of course it's been discovered. I hope not though because if it's not there we'll have a very long walk indeed, our base is up in the Alps about six hundred kilometres from there as the crow flies. I've got a map from before the war in my pack, let me show you."

He pulls out a well-worn and slightly crumpled sheet of paper and opens it out on the ground. It's very different from the maps that we're used to seeing at school, the land area is much larger but that isn't the main difference, it's absolutely covered with names of towns and cities. Jack explains that these are only the larger places since the scale of the map is quite small, it includes Chelmsford but not Sevenoaks for example. Many of the larger cities would have had populations greater than the whole population of the United States of Europe, which is totally mind-blowing to both of us. He's marked the current coastline onto the map himself and it shows just how much land has been lost to the sea. He explains to us that a fair bit of the land in the northern parts of mainland Europe had been reclaimed from the sea before but remarks that it's going to be many centuries before we're struggling for space to live again even if we ever get there.

"So shall we do some archaeology, see if we can find anything else to go with your toy car?" suggests Jack.

"Do you think we'll find anything else?" I ask.

"There aren't a lot of things around unless you take the time to dig but we might be lucky again. Look…" he says, pulling a chain that's round his neck out from inside his shirt, "I found this in Chelmsford the first time I went there. I've worn it ever since, sentimental old fool that I am. It gave me a connection to my parents as they came from there and in the absence of anything actually belonging to them it seemed the next best thing. But it took quite a bit of searching to find it and that was a long time ago, it's not as easy nowadays unless you have the right equipment." With that he produces the scanner from his pocket that he used to find our chips and reconfigures it by touching the screen in various places. "Metal detector!" he says and then points diagonally across the clearing. "If we follow the edge of where the road used to be we should be able to find something interesting."

Jack walks slowly along the line that he'd pointed out whilst holding his scanner out in front of him. Now he's told us it's quite obvious that it is indeed a road, we follow behind him, it's not long before the scanner makes a beeping noise. Jack says that whatever it's found is over a metre deep, it's not worth digging as he only has a small trowel in his pack so it would take ages. We carry on across the clearing and just before reaching the halfway mark the scanner bleeps once more. This time it's less than ten centimetres deep, Jack reaches into his backpack and pulls out his trowel. He starts to dig taking a couple of full trowel loads out and then gently scraping after that to avoid damaging whatever it is. When he finds the object it's a little bit of a disappointment, it's a coin, unfortunately it dates from very shortly before the war meaning it was made out of mild steel and then plated. This means that it has rusted quite badly over its years of interment, Jack says that he thinks it's probably a ten Euro. There had been a period of high inflation in the years immediately preceding the war and ten Euros had gone from being a note that could actually buy something worthwhile, like the toy car that I found or a loaf of bread, to being the smallest coin that wouldn't even buy a single sweet in the space of a couple of years.

"They used Euros before the war?" I ask.

"Oh yes, it's one of the many causes behind the riots that were catalysts of the war. They used Euros in many of the countries in mainland Europe but here in Britain they'd held on to their old currency until very shortly before the war. The government of the day made a very sudden decision to enter the Euro, there were calls for a referendum on the issue but they'd decided it was too risky, they were not likely to get the result they wanted regardless of how they worded it. A lot of people were angry, they felt disenfranchised and betrayed."

"Really, over something as trivial as money?"

"Well yes, but it's actually quite an emotive issue and people felt very strongly about the erosion of their national identity, that was the culmination of a lot of changes over the years. The problem with the Euro was that it was doomed to failure without a common taxation regime across all the countries that used it. Quite a few people, even some of those in positions of power were predicting that the single currency would ultimately cause a war but it didn't seem that likely to the majority. It's such a pity they were wrong because that war has changed the world forever, far more than any war before."

I find it hard to understand fully what Jack is talking about as we now live in such controlled conditions, we have no inflation, there's no need for it. The wage for a job is the same regardless of what job you do and it's the same every year, that wage can buy the same things at the same price every year, it seems normal to me. Jack continues to tell us about how things used to be, he seems so knowledgeable about these things that it's easy to forget that he didn't actually live through those times himself. But of course he grew up with people that did, in many ways his childhood was much harder than my own. I'm actually quite worried about what life is going to bring us in the future, but Jack is very reassuring and Suzie is very enthusiastic so there is a burning excitement growing inside me too. Things are going to be very different from now on, but I can see that freedom from our rigidly controlled state is going to bring with it a huge responsibility, we will have to pull our weight rather than toe the line. We'll have to prove our worth rather than simply do as we're told.

During the course of the afternoon we share the food we brought with Jack and work our way right along both sides of a couple of roads with his scanner. We find a few interesting items including a few more coins most of which are the same rusty mess as the first one we found but we also find a couple of the larger coins that were made out of more durable metals so when the dirt is polished off we can actually see the markings on them. We also find a gold ring which looks like it used to be set with a stone of some description but looking around we find no trace of it. The most interesting find of all is a large plastic sign, we only find this because of a rusty metal pole that is fixed to the back of it, the sign is green and there are traces of white writing. We are able to read some of the words including *Westerham A25* and *Hastings (A21)*, despite the fact that Sevenoaks is not marked on Jack's map and neither are the two places on our sign, both of the numbers are clearly marked as roads, so we are able to work out more or less where we are standing.

After we've helped Jack pitch his tent on the edge of the woods Suzie and I head back to the house shortly after five o'clock. We've decided that given our now imminent departure we should try and spend a relatively normal evening at home. We both answer in a non-committal way when dad and Anne ask if we've had a nice day and what we've been up to. Anne prepares a very nice evening meal for the four of us which we eat in a preoccupied silence. There is certainly a feeling of tension around the table but I don't know whether it's just because I'm harbouring a guilty conscience. After we've finished eating and cleared the things away we go into the lounge and watch some of the highlights from the Human Rights celebrations which are showing. That passes the time until we're ready to head up to bed, I am actually very tired so I'm quite glad. After a quick wash I jump into bed and I'm asleep almost before my head touches the pillow, tomorrow is going to be a busy day and probably my most interesting birthday ever.

Chapter 10

Monday 26th June 53

I'm awake early which is good because it means that I might be able to manage to sleep later on this afternoon to set me up for a night's travelling. I forgot to use the lock blocker so it's just over an hour before I can leave my room, come what may I must remember to use it this evening at bedtime or it could make things a little more difficult than it's going to be anyway. I am fifteen years old today and this evening I'll be starting a new and very different chapter of my life. I get up and cross the room to the desk and sit down, the touch screen doesn't activate, I tap the screen gently and still there's no response. I wonder whether we're having a power cut, they're rare but happen every so often when there is a large demand for power in Luxburg. Glancing at my bedside clock I can see that the power is on, the touch screen isn't working, then I remember that I no longer have my chip inside my body. Picking up my trousers from the pile on the floor I take the piece of cloth out of the pocket, I don't go over to the desk but instead I gently throw the cloth across the room so that it lands on the touch screen. The touch screen activates!

So much of our infrastructure is reliant on our chips, it seems so obvious now but until I met Jack less than three weeks ago it had never crossed my mind. I decide to take a shower, after today it's probably going to be quite a while until I can enjoy hot running water. In fact it strikes me that I have no idea as to the conditions under which Jack and his cohorts live, this is perhaps something I should have thought about before now. I take off my bedclothes and step into the shower, this reveals a recurring theme, the water doesn't run. With a sigh I wander back to my desk and pick up my chip, back in the bathroom I place it on the floor next to the shower and step inside again with same result. I pick it up and take it inside with me and the shower starts. After I've finished enjoying the hot running water and dried myself off I retie my chip inside a clean spare handkerchief putting it in my pocket as I get dressed.

With it there my touch screen works as it would normally, as it activates I take a look at the map of the country. It shows all the settlements and their populations, sometimes you can see them change as people are born or die but nothing is changing at the moment. I scroll southwards to see just how far we're going to be travelling on foot before we reach Jack's transport. It's about seventy kilometres to the south coast, then about fifty kilometres following the line of the tunnel underneath the sea. That is when the bulk of the journey will start, I'm looking forward to travelling in Jack's car. I can't be sure exactly where Jack's settlement is, as of course it's not marked on this map and I can't remember the exact position from his map yesterday, the closest settlement to where we're going seems like Lyon. It doesn't look anywhere near as far on this map as it did on Jack's old paper map, probably because of the lack of towns, cities and roads nowadays. It certainly seems like the world was a more interesting place before the war.

I hear the door unlock as the clock in the corner of the viewing screen ticks over to six o'clock. I head downstairs as I know dad and Anne will be up very shortly as they're due in for the first shift at their new place of work at seven o'clock. I grab some bread and start to make toast for everyone, the first person to take a piece is Suzie but Anne and dad are down almost immediately afterwards. Dad wishes me a happy fifteenth birthday, although birthdays are not especially significant to us unless you happen to be born on the summer solstice of course but we do tend at the very least to acknowledge the passing of another year. Effectively the Human Rights Celebration is a celebration for the whole community for all occasions, it is after all everyone's wedding anniversary so it may as well be everyone's birthday too.

Once dad and Anne have left for work Suzie and I start to work out our plans for later on today, we think it's going to be sensible to travel light so we're going to take only our school backpacks. Neither of us have many personal items because nobody really does, what we don't know is what to do about clothing. We're both happy to take a bare minimum, just the clothes we're wearing, a jumper and a couple of changes of underwear for whilst we're travelling but that is assuming we'll be able to get more clothes when we arrive wherever we're going. If clothes are going to be hard to come by then it makes sense to squeeze a few more into our packs, we decide to go and see Jack this morning to find out the best course of action. As we helped him pitch his tent he shouldn't be too difficult to track down. We finish our breakfast and both head back upstairs to get dressed. It's now after seven and we figure that Jack is likely to be awake given how light it is so we head off up the road and through the woods.

When we arrive at Jack's tent we see that he's not there at the moment, there is however a small fire burning on the ground just in front of the opening. He's probably out searching for some breakfast so we sit down on the ground to wait. After not much more than ten minutes he appears out of the woods, tied to his belt are two dead pigeons and a catapult. He's carrying a third bird and is plucking it as he walks towards us, the feathers fluttering away in a gentle breeze. He greets us with a smile and proceeds to pass us each a pigeon to pluck. This isn't something that I've ever done before and it's harder than it appears but we both soon get into the swing of it. Meanwhile Jack has pulled a knife out of his pocket and is gutting his bird and preparing it for cooking, he wraps it in some large leaves from a pile on the ground that up until now I'd not noticed, securing them with two small sharpened sticks and placing the package carefully into the fire. He then takes Suzie's plucked bird and starts preparing that one in the same way.

"So Ed and Suzie, are you all set for later?"

"Well not really," I reply, "we're not sure how many clothes and things like that we need to take with us. Where we're going, where you live, do you have plenty of supplies or are we only going to have the things we bring?"

"Of course, very sensible to ask, I realise I've not told you very much at all about how I live but things haven't gone quite to plan but we have plenty of time right now."

He puts the second bird into the fire alongside the first and takes mine to prepare before he starts to tell us about where we're heading.

"We have a large base in what was once called the Mont Blanc Tunnel, my group had to leave the Channel Tunnel due to Europarl reopening it for their own purposes. We'd lived quite happily there for a few years and our numbers had increased steadily both by people joining us and also births. Mont Blanc seemed a sensible destination as it moved us further away from Luxburg but not so far away that we couldn't still be in touch with what was going on. When we got there we found a group similar to us already installed and when they welcomed us with open arms we knew we'd made the right decision. Now there are nearly ten thousand of us all told, several times the size of one of your settlements and we have a lot more older people. We don't believe in sending people *to the next plane of existence* when they reach a certain age or on a whim."

"It's a long tunnel but we've outgrown it over the years, we still have many of our lodgings there but we also have expanded out on the Italian side away from the prying eyes of Europarl. We have remodelled the entrance on the French side where Chamonix used to be to make it look less obvious. With regard to supplies we're better off in some respects and worse off in others. We don't have to waste effort supporting a huge ruling elite that persists in living in the way they did prior to the war of their own creation. This means that everything we do is done for ourselves but we don't have the resources for the huge factories that produce all your manufactured goods. We have either to make our things or obtain them from Europarl, we have agents in Luxburg that keep us abreast of developments there and bring things back that we particularly need as and when they are able to do so. In answer to your question, you only need to pack for the journey, but anything you particularly want to bring won't be a problem as long as you can carry it yourself."

"Great, that's what we wanted to know. So what is my place in your scheme, why have you come all this way to find me?"

"I'm sorry Ed but I can't really tell you until we get back, you can make all the difference to us. You will enable us to infiltrate Europarl in a way that has never before been possible, you're not our only hope but you're the best hope we've ever had. But more than that I can't say at the moment, it's not my place to tell you, but I can promise you that you will have everyone behind you to help and you will be fully prepared for everything that you need to do."

"Okay, I suppose I'll just have to wait and see. What about Suzie?"

"There's a place for Suzie, there's a place for everyone who wants to come, active recruitment is very rare for us although you're not the first, but anyone who wants to come is always welcome. You're sure you want to come Suzie?"

"Yes, I'm sure, I haven't really got much of a choice now my chip is in my pocket instead of my arm!"

"I could put it back in for you if you like."

"No, I'm fine thanks!"

"Good, now I suggest you leave your house as soon as you can be sure that your parents are asleep then come and meet me here. I'll make sure I'm all packed up and ready to go. What sort of time do you think you'll be able to get here?"

"It's hard to tell," I reply, "it could be as early as ten o'clock but obviously it won't be any later than midnight because of the locks."

"Yes, the locks, you'll need to stop the door from locking so that you can get out, I can show…"

"I know how to sort out the locks!" interrupts Suzie.

"Impressive, did you work it out yourself?"

"No, my sisters showed me but I did work out how to trick the parental override."

"Now I'm even more impressed, I think you're going to be quite an asset to our team young Suzie."

Jack deftly turns over the packages that are cooking in the embers of the fire and then proceeds to tell us about the journey on which we will embark before the day is out. He says that we could get to the Channel Tunnel in two days if we push it but three is more realistic. Then another day to get through the tunnel, that is potentially the most dangerous part as whilst he knows the bulk of the schedule via his hand-held gadget there are often trains that don't appear on the schedule. You hear them coming for quite a while but it is very difficult to judge the direction from which they're coming as well as the point at which you have to get into a safe area, also the safe areas are a fair distance apart. He explains that there used to be three tunnels, one for each direction of travel in addition to a continuous access tunnel.

When Europarl came to reinstate them, the tunnels were even more flooded than they had been when Jack made his first crossing and it would have taken a long time to pump them out. What they did have however was a setting derivative of silica gel that they had been using for reclaiming land before the war. The scientists calculated that just filling the smaller central tunnel with this substance would not drain the other two completely. Putting large quantities of this into one

127

of the outer bores would reduce the level in the other two tunnels sufficiently that subsequently filling the central access tunnel would empty the final tunnel completely of water. Sacrificing the convenience of the two extra tunnels allowed them to open the third within a week for tracked vehicles although it was several more months before the railway was open again. Since the trains can clear the tunnel in less than ten minutes it doesn't cause a problem with regard to trains running but it does mean that our journey through might be more difficult than it otherwise would be.

Once we're through the tunnel the journey should be a bit easier as we'll be in Jack's car, unfortunately it will not be much quicker as the batteries only give it a range of about three hundred kilometres at any decent speed before it will need to be recharged. Basically this means that we'll be able to do the first three hundred kilometres of our journey through the State of France at over a hundred kilometres per hour where the terrain allows us. We'll then have to stop and connect the car to the railway's electricity supply to recharge. Once we set off again we'll have to get the remaining distance on a single charge as the railway doesn't head in the necessary direction, this means that we'll not be able to travel any faster than seventy kilometres per hour if we want to have a hope of getting anywhere near our final destination. This is especially true as we'll be climbing quite steeply towards the final stages of the journey and the location of the roads that we can follow adds over a hundred kilometres to the journey.

There is now a delicious smell coming from the fire and Jack says that the birds are ready, using a couple of sticks he picks up each of the wrapped packages and removes them from the dying embers. Pulling out the sharpened sticks the crispy burnt outer leaves crumble away, the innermost leaves on each package are still intact and when they are each unrolled and placed on top of a fresh one from the pile serve as a plate. Jack hands us each a bird and begins to tuck into his, they are perfectly cooked, succulent, they're not at all dry and have a lovely flavour to them. We eat in silence for several minutes; we don't mention that we've already eaten; besides it would be very difficult to refuse something that smells so nice. Even after the last few days of delicious food for the Human Rights celebrations this simple meal seems special, perhaps because of its simplicity or perhaps because of its clandestine nature.

Once we've each devoured the bulk of our food and start to pick at the bones, Jack suggests that we shouldn't spend too much time with him today. We should try to have a fairly normal day to avoid raising any suspicion before tonight's departure. I struggle to think what constitutes normal, the last few weeks have been such a whirlwind of unusual activity. Besides the fact is that we've not even been in Sevenoaks for long enough to establish any routine, today is the first day that our parents have been back at work. There is also other work going on, we can hear the rattles and crashes of construction in the distance resuming after the festival. I wonder vaguely how long the settlement has been under construction and how long it will be before it is complete. In the end we decide that it would probably be considered fairly normal to pass some time watching the men at work, it might be interesting and shouldn't get us into any trouble.

We bid Jack farewell and agree to meet him back here as soon as we can leave the house tonight. We walk back through the woods towards the town, as we reach the end of our road we see a group of youngsters playing on the grassy area adjacent to where builders are working on a new block of housing. When we get close enough to be recognised Michael who was in our team yesterday calls to us. There are a few familiar faces from yesterday amongst the crowd and we pass the rest morning kicking a ball about and just being children, this is likely to be our last opportunity to do so. We head back to the house for some lunch mainly because all the others do the same rather than out of hunger. As neither of us is particularly in need of food we decide to pack some into our packs for the journey. After that we finish off our packing with the few personal things that we each have and a few items of clothing and toiletries. Once our packs are ready we head to our beds to try and get some sleep in order to be fresh for a night's walking. Making sure that I have set an alarm for a quarter to six to ensure that I'm awake for when our parents return from work, I slip between the sheets and find it surprisingly easy to nod off.

Chapter 11

It doesn't seem like I've been asleep very long at all when the alarm goes off, I'm slightly disorientated so I don't realise immediately that it is in fact the door bell and not the alarm. Looking at the clock it's a few minutes before three o'clock, something is wrong, as I jump out of bed I hear footsteps on the hallway outside, the door opens and Suzie runs in with a look of alarm on her face.

"What is it?" I ask.

"There's some rights enablers at the door, they've rung the bell four times now and I don't think they'll wait much longer before they just come in. What are we going to do? They must know what we're up to."

"How can they know what we're up to? We don't really know what we're up to ourselves!"

"This is no time for joking, we've got to get away, we're going to have to leave right now."

"But if we use the emergency door it'll set off the alarms and then we'll really be in trouble, I'm going to answer the door and try to get rid of them. No, I've got an idea, do you think you'd be able to give me a black eye?"

"A black eye?"

"Yes, punch me in the eye then we can say that I was going to answer the door and tripped, that will explain why it took us so long. Just do it and let me do the talking."

"Alright you asked for it!"

With that she swings at me hard, harder than I expected, so hard that the back of my head also hits the wall. I briefly see stars and then start to recover, I tell Suzie to go and answer the door and I lie down at the top of the stairs. Suzie opens the door at the precise instant one of the two rights enablers opens it and he stumbles over the threshold, he doesn't look at all happy. Then he looks up the stairs, sees me and asks if I'm alright.

"I've felt better, I was resting on the bed when you rang the bell, got up too quickly and fell, I suddenly went dizzy. I guess I'm lucky I wasn't on the stairs."

"You've got a nasty bruise, were you knocked out?" he asks.

"I don't know…" I reply looking at Suzie who quickly responds.

"I was in my room and heard the thump, he was unconscious the whole time you were ringing the bell, I didn't open the door until he came around."

"We'd better get him over to the hospital to be on the safe side, looks like you're going to be the first casualty."

"What are you here for anyway, has something happened?" asks Suzie.

"No, it's not important, it can wait until Edward's been checked over. You'd better come to the hospital too." Says the rights enabler and proceeds to call the hospital.

The other rights enabler leaves after a brief discussion with his colleague in a low voice so that we can't hear what they're saying. Moments later a porter from the hospital arrives with wheelchair, I sit in it when I am told and we make the three minute journey to the hospital which is on the same side of the town as our house. All the time my mind is racing, trying to work out how we're going to extricate ourselves from the awkward position into which we've got ourselves and I can see from the expression on Suzie's face that she is doing the same. At least we now only have one rights enabler but even so there's no way that we'd be able to escape right now. I'm sure a better chance will present itself at some point once we've arrived at the hospital, I just hope that we're going to be able to find Jack without too much trouble as we're going to have to get away completely as soon as we can. There is still the possibility of course that we've unnecessarily jumped to a conclusion and that the rights enablers' arrival at our house was completely unconnected with our plans but that doesn't seem particularly likely indeed.

It is clear that the hospital building is far from complete, the outside is unpainted and has no signage at all and the brief glimpse I get of the windows on the top floor reveal them to be nothing more than holes in the walls, no frames and certainly no glass. The main doors slide open in the usual manner and the reception area (identical in every detail to that in Chelmsford) is complete. Because of the nature of my admission we don't even approach the desk, the porter wheels me straight along a corridor on the right of the entrance and into room two. The porter pushes me over to the bed and tells me to lie on it, he leaves the room saying that a triage nurse will be with us shortly. The rights enabler then looks at us both in an odd way that I can't really place, as if he's weighing up something in his mind and then leaves the room without saying a word, shutting the door behind him. The room is facing the back of the hospital and at the end of a short lawn we can see the edge of the woods the other side of which we caught up with Jack. He's probably no more than half a mile away from us right now.

The window doesn't open since the whole building is air-conditioned and the glazing panel consists of three pieces of glass. We have no idea how long we've got until the rights enabler will return, he's probably gone to get a drink but could just as easily be chatting up the receptionist, also we know that a nurse will be here very shortly. We need to escape within the next couple of minutes, I think that it's going to be better to risk a quick look out of the door rather than smashing the window since we have been given no reason to suppose that we are in custody. Suzie goes over to the door and when she discovers that it's locked finds out the answer to one of our questions, we are definitely being detained. I get off the bed and look at the window frame, it's exactly the same as the ones in our houses, secured from the inside rather than the outside, we just need something to prise the clipped-in glazing bead out of its channel.

There is nothing in the room apart from the bed, two chairs and a small wheeled table, none of these have any parts that could be used. The table could probably break the window but people would surely come running immediately, time is moving on. We are both starting seriously to consider the drastic option of breaking the glass when I glance at the floor in the corner. The plastic floor rises up the wall all around the room for ease of cleaning, in that corner it has peeled away and is revealing a thin metal clip that is supposed to hold it in place. I dash over to have a closer look, kicking at the clip loosens it but I can't pull it clear of the wall, I kick it again and again until finally it drops off the wall. I pick it up and with a bit of effort I can slide it behind the glazing bead at the bottom of the window which then pops out completely as I gently twist my tool. The side beads come out just as easily but I have to stand on one of the chairs to remove the top one and the action is slightly more awkward as the end of my tool is restricted by the ceiling. I tell Suzie to bring the other chair over and she stands next to me, she puts both of her hands against the top of the window as I lever the glass panel out from the top, then we both pull. It is very heavy and we struggle to get it down without dropping it but the moment we have, we're out of the window and running.

As soon as we're hidden amongst the trees we stop to have a quick look behind us, nobody is after us as yet. We run through the wood as quickly as we can but there are no pathways in this area, the brambles scratch at our legs and bodies tearing our clothes and cutting us but we ignore the pain. All of a sudden we burst out the other side onto the clear area where the old town of Sevenoaks had once been. We've been heading in slightly the wrong direction, we can see the place where Jack was camping is about half a kilometre away to our right. We run as quickly as we can and cover the distance in a few minutes, as we approach Jack appears from the edge of the wood having heard our breathless arrival. After the initial surprise he listens as we explain what has just happened and quickly works out an escape plan, his backpack is ready to go, we're going to be travelling far lighter than we'd planned. After ensuring that we both have our chips he hands us each something that looks like a small piece of black plastic, we're to chew the plastic until it goes soft and sticky and then wrap our chips in the resulting goo warning us that it tastes quite nasty.

He's not wrong, it is absolutely foul and it's all I can do not to gag, what's more it takes quite a bit of chewing to achieve the correct consistency. Jack then puts his backpack on and we head off away from the settlement toward the railway line. We are making a reasonable pace because he says there is a train that is going to pass by in no more than five minutes and we need our chips to be on that train to give us some breathing space. It is almost certain that we've been missed by now, the local rights enablers will probably not be able to locate our chips outside the settlement but as soon as the situation is escalated to Europarl they'll be able to locate them within fifteen minutes. All of a sudden we're at the edge of the railway cutting, we've both got our chips wrapped in the sticky plastic, we're only going to get one shot at this so it has to be good. We each scrabble around for some small pebbles about the same size and weight as our plastic-encased chips and have a couple of practice throws aiming for the middle of the track. It's not too hard but even so only about half our shots hit the target but then we can hear the tracks humming and the train appears. Luckily it is going relatively slowly but even so we don't have time to think, just aim, throw and hope for the best.

I see mine land in the middle of the roof of the first coach, Suzie is not so lucky, we can't see where it lands, but once the train has disappeared from view there is no sign of it on the ground. Jack takes his scanner out of his pack and scans the area of the track in front of us, there is no signal so it must have stuck to the train somewhere. His scanner is not powerful enough to pick up the signals from the train; it is already too far away for that, so anyone searching for us with any luck will be tricked into thinking we've stowed away on a train heading for Luxburg. Right now we need to put as much distance between us and Sevenoaks as we can, unfortunately the train is heading in the same direction as we need to go. Jack puts his scanner away and we scramble down the embankment then over the railway track, we can still feel a slight vibration from the train even though we can't actually see it as we cross. It's fairly hard to get up the other side as it is steep and since this is a new section of track to serve the new settlement there's nothing growing on it to get hold of. As soon as we get to the top we enter the shelter of the wood.

It's difficult to make quick progress through the trees but we daren't risk walking along the railway line where the going would be much easier. Despite the seriousness of our situation Jack is still able to point out the types of tree that we see as well as much of the undergrowth. I realise that he's doing it to try and lighten the mood but I am very aware that we are at real risk and after a while it starts to grate on me. Luckily Jack is a fantastic judge of peoples' moods and he stops before I need to say anything. We walk on in silence for a while, we are about half a kilometre away from the railway but we will be following it all the way to the great tunnel. We make as quick progress as the thick ground cover allows, there isn't really anything much in the way of paths as nobody ever walks through these woods. We do make out the odd track made by wild animals, Jack points out deer tracks as well as foxes and badgers.

At about nine o'clock we hear the sound of some bats flying around in the failing light, because the trees are fairly dense it's starting to get quite dark in the woods. We decide to sit down for a short rest. It's an awkward time for us to travel because it's getting hard to see the way through the wood and not trip but out of the cover it's still completely light. Jack suggests that the best plan would be to wait where we are until it's dark enough not to be spotted walking along the edge of the railway line. Every now and again we hear a train pass, but they're going at their usual speed, there's no suggestion of anything going past slowly, looking for us but we don't want to expose ourselves to any unnecessary risk now we're actually travelling with a purpose. Jack takes his old map out of his pack and lays it out on the ground, he then points to a town labelled Tonbridge and says that we're probably a little bit southeast of there. He explains that his multi-function scanner would have been able to tell us exactly where we are to within a few metres before the war but the satellites that used to provide this function were destroyed or their transmissions were disabled, they can't tell which.

As we sit there, Suzie and I start to feel a little bit cold, because of the way we left we have no extra clothes and we aren't exactly wrapped up warmly. Night is really starting to fall and since there is no cloud cover the temperature is dropping slightly. Jack reaches into his pack and takes out two small silvery packages and hands them to Suzie and me explaining that they're blankets. We take them dubiously given their very light weight but once they are unfolded and we have them wrapped around ourselves, they are surprisingly effective. We sit quietly in the gathering gloom, listening to the noise of the bats and insects. After about half an hour we hear a train go past, Jacks says that this train is the one that is heading into Sevenoaks onto which we would have planted our chips had today gone to plan. We wonder what sort of an effort has been made to try and find us and whether our deception with the chips has already been discovered. Jack doesn't think it likely that they would have made an unscheduled stop of the train, but they would have been quite likely to have done some kind of a search whilst it was on the move. That's assuming of course that they have been able to track down a signal from our chips anyway, the tracking isn't always totally reliable.

According to Jack, now that train has passed there shouldn't be any more trains until it returns to Luxburg at five o'clock. We get up and start to make our way towards the railway line, we make very slow progress as under the cover of the tree canopy it is very dark indeed. With hindsight we should have got closer to the edge of the woods before we stopped, it does at least provide evidence that Jack is not infallible and we all have a bit of a laugh whilst we shred our trousers and scratch our legs on unseen brambles. After a battle of almost twenty minutes we arrive at the edge of the wood, we are only a few metres from the edge of the tracks. It is now quite close to sunset, the sky to the west beyond the woods from which we have just emerged is a fabulous orange with a few wispy, red streaked clouds. From where we are standing we can't see the sun itself as it is hidden by the trees, meaning that we are completely in their shadows. We would be quite hard to spot as we walk in single file along the edge of the area that is cut back by the railway engineers every few months, the grass is no more than ten centimetres high and there is the odd small tree sapling that has shot up since the last cut but nothing more difficult. It is not long before we are warm enough to fold away our blankets again and are able to maintain a very good walking pace for several kilometres, we can also follow our progress on the map to a certain extent. Jack explains that where we reached the railway line was almost exactly the point at which it starts to follow the route of the original high speed railway line that was engineered to serve the Channel Tunnel when it was first built all those years ago.

Whilst Jack's scanner device is no longer able to get our exact position, it is able to work as a pedometer to work out the distance we have travelled. Jack says that it took him nearly a year of travelling with it before he was able to get it totally reliable in its ability. As we travel on the sun sets behind us, we are travelling far more eastwards than southwards at the moment because the tunnel that we need to reach is situated at pretty much the narrowest point of the Channel for obvious reasons. It was a huge step forward in tunnelling technology, there had been other attempts previously that had never got very far at all. Its completion had led to many complicated tunnelling jobs being done particularly within cities which had previously been thought to be far too difficult.

There is no moon visible in the sky at the moment but there is very little in the way of cloud cover and since there are no manmade lights to be seen anywhere, the light from the myriad stars is just about sufficient for us to be able to see our way. The going is made slightly easier when the track is on an embankment since we are able to walk along the gravel-filled drainage channel at its foot which makes a good path. The arrangement is slightly different where there are cuttings as the drainage channels are adjacent to the lines in the cutting itself. We carry on through the night and as the light of dawn begins to appear on the horizon ahead of us, Jack says that we've travelled over forty kilometres from Sevenoaks and that we're over half way to the tunnel. It won't be long now until the first train for Luxburg is on its way so we make our way back into the wood. We find a decent place to rest for the daytime, only about a hundred metres or so away from the train track and cover ourselves over with our blankets once again.

Chapter 12

Tuesday 27th June 53

The wood is very much alive with the noises of wildlife as the morning sunlight begins to filter through the canopy. After a night of walking and yesterday afternoon's quick escape we are tired but Suzie and I are not used to being out in the open air, we both struggle to sleep for any more than a few minutes at a time. Jack, however is out like a light, he is sleeping deeply and almost silently, oblivious to the sounds of nature all around, although he stirs slightly every time a train goes past. Considering the small population in these parts the trains are surprisingly frequent, barely an hour goes by without one passing. Our minds wander in our sleepy state as to why they might be going past so much, although if there were any other settlements that we didn't know about it would seem likely that Jack would have mentioned them. Eventually we both manage to sleep for a few hours awakening to the crackling sound of a fire that Jack is tending with his back to us.

He turns round as we start to fold our blankets up, from the direction of the sunlight glinting through the tree cover we can tell that it's a little after midday and even in the shade it is very warm indeed. On the fire I can see a fairly thick sheet of something that looks like plastic but isn't melting in the heat, on it Jack is frying some eggs. I wonder whether to ask where they came from but decide not to, they're quite small though. Jack, ever the mind reader sees the look that's crossed my face and says that they are actually chicken's eggs just like we're used to having. Before the war chickens were kept in huge numbers and many of them managed to escape, there are now fairly sizeable populations in most of the woods and their eggs are easy to find. Of course they're largely fertilised so you have to hope that they're as fresh as possible as they're a little bit unappetising once the embryo has started to develop.

He removes his frying sheet from the fire and passes us each a fork and we tuck in, they taste delicious and fresh but I still can't help thinking about where they came from. This is odd as I've never really thought too much about where my food came from in the past and I've not been squeamish about it in any way, even when we prepared and ate the pigeons yesterday I didn't think twice. I suppose that from now on it's going to be much more obvious as we'll be getting our own food by hunting, gathering and probably growing our own, life is going to be very different from now on. There was plenty to go around and we all feel full, as we polish off the last few mouthfuls our thoughts turn to the continuation of our journey. Jack says that we've got about thirty kilometres to go until we reach the tunnel mouth, which we could cover in five or six hours if we were walking along the side of the track. The problem is that to travel that conspicuously right now is potentially risky so walking along the edge of the woodland is going to be a safer if slightly slower option.

We decide to set off now and find somewhere to rest up near the tunnel before making our way through this evening.

Jack stamps out what's left of the fire, not that there's much as he's judged the amount of wood required for cooking breakfast perfectly. We weren't far from the edge of the wood so it takes no more than a couple of minutes to make our way out. Just as we break cover we hear the sound of an approaching train so we duck back behind some brambles and watch the train pass on its way to Sevenoaks or Chelmsford or both. As soon as it's out of sight we re-emerge and start to make our way along the edge of the woods, whilst the sun is still fairly high in the sky, the trees are sufficiently tall for us to be in their shadow so our going is much the same as it was yesterday afternoon. We are all a little more relaxed now than we were yesterday, we've got no ideas as to what if any search is happening in our honour, it would seem incredible to imagine that our chips would not have been found by now. I think about Jack's scanner and ask if he could set it up to scan for people's chips so that we'd have some kind of warning if someone were to be on our trail. Jack says that it's a good idea and sets it up accordingly, he's not certain of the range in this mode but thinks that it should be somewhere between one and two kilometres.

When the next train approaches his scanner starts bleeping slightly before we hear the tracks hum so it makes us jump, then we pull ourselves together and back into the undergrowth. Once it has passed we continue on our way but no more than ten minutes later it bleeps again, this time there is no hum of the tracks straight after. We stop while Jack tweaks the settings to try and find a direction and distance for the signal, it seems to be coming from straight ahead of us and is about thirteen hundred metres away, whoever it's coming from doesn't appear to be on the move at the moment. We decide to go into the woods so that we can approach the signal with a hope of not being seen. It is really hard going as there are no tracks whatsoever through the undergrowth here but at least this time we are not running so we are able to pick our way without scratching ourselves too badly. As we get closer we start to spend long periods of time holding our breath without realising it, the person is still not moving and we are now within two hundred metres of them.

Keeping as low as we can we creep towards the railway line not really knowing what to expect. It could be someone working on the line perhaps but surely there'd be more than one of them, people never work on the line alone. It could be someone looking for us, but again surely there'd be more than one. Although there could be a whole search party split up over a large area, but if that were the case surely they'd be moving. It is all very puzzling, we even wonder whether it could be someone else running away, but in that case they're not running very fast. Unfortunately the part of the track from which the signal is coming is in a fairly deep cutting so we can't see anything at all from the edge of the wood. There is a fairly tall tree right next to us with some decent low branches so I decide to climb up to get a view of the line, it doesn't take long for me to get as high as I can in the tree without making it bend over. I now have a clear view of the railway track in the cutting but I can see nobody. I make my way down and tell Jack and Suzie, Jack tells us to wait here while he goes down to check it out. Suzie and I sit and worry while Jack breaks cover and scrambles down into the cutting. Two minutes later he's back carrying a familiar looking piece of black plastic.

"I can't believe I've been so daft, all that worrying over nothing, it's Suzie's chip!" exclaims Jack as his head appears at the edge of the cutting. "Let's get going, we've wasted plenty of time!"

He passes the chip back to Suzie and says she should pop it in her mouth to make it sticky again as we should try and put it on the next train that goes past. I can see the look of revulsion on her face so I offer to do the honours much to her relief, the flavour isn't any better the second time. He turns off his scanner as the constant bleeping is more than a little irritating. This raises the interesting possibility that nobody has bothered looking for us at all, they should have been able to find the chips fairly quickly. We've been missing for over twenty-four hours now and we certainly left Sevenoaks in a very unorthodox manner. We have a brief break from this train of thought when we hear a train's approach, the cutting here is not as deep as it was where we collected the chip but it is still deep enough for me to be able to get a good shot at the train roof without much risk of being seen. I stretch out on the grass at the top of the cutting, take the disgusting piece of plastic out of my mouth and take aim. The train comes into view and after a moment of panic where it sticks to my fingers I manage to launch Suzie's chip at the train's roof and score a direct hit right in the middle of the third coach which according to its destination board is heading for Stutgart.

Once the train has disappeared I get up and re-join the others, we then go back to walking along the edge of the wood and puzzling over what could be going on with regard to a search. Whilst it's true that there's no school at the moment so we wouldn't necessarily have been missed officially, my dad and Suzie's mum couldn't fail to notice that we've not been at home in spite of the fact that neither of us have taken anything with us. They would surely have raised the alarm and then there's the question of why the rights enablers were knocking at the door that afternoon. We both reacted in an extremely guilty fashion and then the way we broke out of the hospital, it seemed like our only hope at the time but now I'm beginning to wonder if we were actually in any trouble after all. It seems incredible that they would ignore the fact that we removed a pane of glass from a window though, even if we didn't actually do any damage. Of course there were plenty of windows at the hospital missing their glass anyway and even their frames so it's just about possible that it wasn't seen as peculiar. We all begin to relax once again as we carry on our way to the south coast.

We journey onwards heading for the mouth of the tunnel uneventfully, shrinking into the woods as the occasional train goes by. Not long after six o'clock we are approaching the tunnel mouth, we're just thinking about finding a place to settle down for a rest before the crossing when Jack's scanner starts bleeping again. This time is different though, it's not the mass of bleeps from an approaching train and it's not the single signal that we got from Suzie's chip either. Jack adjusts a few settings and announces that there are at least six people a little bit more than a kilometre away which he thinks means they're guarding the tunnel mouth. This is bad, it probably means they're expecting us, it also explains the lack of people searching for us if they knew where we'd be heading. The whole of our journey is dependent upon us being able to get through the tunnel, as long as we can get in without being seen we should be able to get through without difficulty as it is not lit and the headlights are unlikely to reveal us as the trains are very fast.

According to Jack the tunnel mouths on both sides are normally unguarded, apart from the first time that he made the crossing when he was a boy he has been through the tunnel over twenty times through the years and in all that time he has only ever come across someone guarding one of the entrances on one occasion. It would seem fairly conclusive that these six people are waiting for us and if that is indeed the case they're quite likely to stay there until they catch us. This gives us a real problem as there is no practical way of getting across apart from the tunnel, it may be possible to find a small boat hidden away somewhere. It would of course be possible to build one ourselves but it would take a while and none of us relish the prospect of about forty kilometres at sea on a cobbled together raft. We could perhaps get onboard one of the trains in order to go through the tunnel but unless there is a problem with the running schedule it is unlikely that a train would stop before entering.

We need to get into a position where we can actually see the activity around the mouth of the tunnel, maybe then we'll be able to formulate some kind of plan. Jack calls up the map on his scanner and shows us roughly where we are, we had stayed on the south western side of the railway track as we followed it in a south easterly direction. Unfortunately we stayed on the same side as the track curved round to the east and this has put us on an area of flat ground to the south of the tunnel entrance meaning that we'll be fairly easy to spot. If we cross over the line we can head up the hill and break cover in a position overlooking the entrance, we could even work our way around and above the entrance itself. Picking our way carefully through the undergrowth at the edge of the woodland we slowly head deeper amongst the trees, the going gets harder as we start to climb the hill. It takes us just over an hour to make our way round in a large semicircle to a position north of the tunnel opening. The trees and undergrowth peter out a little way down the slope, we lie down and edge forward so that we can see the clearing in front of the tunnel.

There are two rights enablers standing either side of the entrance looking vacantly along the railway line, there are also two fairly small tents. As there are no other people visible they must be inside these tents, Jack guesses that the six people are three shifts of two so that they can guard the tunnel twenty-four hours a day until we are caught. Whilst we are watching we hear the sound of a train approaching, as it comes into view it is clearly slowing down. The guard that we can see remains standing exactly where he is, a little bit close to the train for comfort but he turns his head away from it and shields his eyes with his hand as it passes him. The train is travelling far slower than its normal speed as it passes into the tunnel mouth, possibly only fifty kilometres per hour. That is slow for a train but it's still very fast considering the idea that is going through my mind. If we can get into a position directly above the track we may be able to jump onto the roof of the train as it goes in, we won't have very long to do this especially as there are three of us. There is also the issue of the overhead wires that could easily brush against us, that thought is very worrying but as long we don't touch anything else at the same time it shouldn't be a problem.

A quick glance at the others tells me that they're thinking the same as me, that it's probably worth a try. We're not going to be able to get into the tunnel on foot with a constant guard, we can almost be certain that the guards are indeed waiting for us so they're not going to go away any time soon. We don't really have an alternative, it does create a second problem however, that of how we are going to get off the train again. There is also the question of where we get off the train as well, whether we should get off as soon as we're past the guard and in the tunnel while we're still travelling relatively slowly or take advantage of the train to take us all the way to the other side. Carefully we crawl backwards into some thicker cover and Jack consults the train schedule, the one that just passed was not actually listed. The next two trains that are listed are both heading the wrong way but then there are two more going the right way, the second of these and the last one until tomorrow will be entering the tunnel about a quarter past midnight. This means it will be dark, or at least what passes for dark at this time of year making us less likely to be seen, on the other hand it also means that our target will be harder to see.

We get our special blankets out again and make ourselves as comfortable as possible, it seems sensible to try and get some sleep now for a few hours in the hope of feeling fresh and rested for our next death defying adventure. I can't say that I'm particularly looking forward to riding on the roof of a train and I'm hoping that it's going to be a one off experience. Even now that we're further away from the guards we can still hear them talking every now and again but we can't actually make out what they're saying. Before he closes his eyes, Jack sets an alarm for midnight as we don't want to risk missing our train. At eight o'clock I still haven't fallen asleep and I hear the guards changing shifts. Jack is sleeping soundly and it looks as though Suzie is too, I close my eyes try to clear my mind but it is hard because the last few days have been far more fast-paced than anything I've ever experienced before.

Chapter 13

Wednesday 28ᵗʰ June 53

When Jack's alarm goes off at midnight I wake up with a jump, it's right by my ear and both Jack and Suzie are looking right at me and grinning. Jack reaches over to switch off the alarm and pick up his scanner in one smooth movement. They already have their blankets packed up so I follow suit and then we make our way back to our vantage point overlooking the track, there are still two rights enablers standing guard either side of the tunnel mouth. If the train is on time we have a little less than ten minutes to wait, we decide that the best plan is for me and Suzie to jump first, together, one of us on each side of the overhead wire. We take our positions at the edge and slowly start to prepare mentally for the ordeal ahead. Once the two of us have jumped Jack will then follow, assuming there is still enough train left, we're hoping that it will be one of the longer trains.

Despite our nervousness at the imminent risk we're about to take those few minutes pass surprisingly quickly. Suddenly the headlights of the train are visible in the distance, sure enough it is slowing down on its approach just as the earlier one did. Time now seems to slow down, the noise of the train seems deafening even though it's no noisier than any other train. Suzie and I stand up and move right to the edge so we're standing in plain view of the guards if they decide to look above the tunnel portal. Just as the headlights are about to disappear into the tunnel we drop smoothly down. It's about a two metre drop, as my feet hit the roof I bend my knees and allow myself to fall forwards, I actually feel the train sliding underneath me before I come to a stop just before the end of the first carriage. I look to my right and see that Suzie is right next to me just before everything goes dark, we grab each other.

We're now in the tunnel of course, we look towards the slight hint of light from the entrance in the hope of seeing Jack's arrival on the roof of the train but we just don't know if he's with us or not. The sound of the train echoing around the tunnel and the constant rush of air makes it almost impossible to speak to each other. We can sense the acceleration of the train, it's subtle but relentless and lying on the roof we really get a sense of speed. Luckily we're not being dragged along the roof, which is something I had feared. Still holding onto Suzie's hand I edge my way towards the back of the train, she guesses correctly that I want to go and look for Jack. In next to no time we're at the end of the first coach and our first obstacle, however the coaches are fairly close together and the flexible tunnel that connects them is only just below the level of the roof. We have to go one at a time but it is easy to cross to the next carriage, I go first and then help Suzie to follow me.

We find it easier to make our way along the second coach, the third coach has an extra obstacle however in the shape of the pantograph. The base of this is wide enough to make it extremely awkward to get around, especially as we don't want to risk touching any part of it just in case. There is a fairly constant blue flickering of sparks from where it touches the overhead wire so we are actually able to see where the edge of the coach is. We both go round the same side and hold tightly to each other as we slide past single file. Where the edge of the roof curves down into the wall the effect of the wind is much greater and we both have a few slips and scares. We both feel greatly relieved when we get around it and head back to the centre of the roof, we are now perched at the end of the third coach. It is only after we've done this that it dawns on both of us just how dangerous jumping onto the train roof could have been, if we'd landed on the electrical pickup then the results could have been really bad. Then we're even more worried about what may have become of Jack, if he'd jumped straight after us then he could well have been near this position on the train.

We carefully make our way onto the fourth carriage and at this point we see the light of a torch a flickering at the other end. I call out to Jack but get no response, carrying on towards the back of the train we meet him pretty much at the end of the coach. Jack actually landed on the fifth coach but twisted his ankle quite badly, he doesn't think it's broken but can't be sure. It feels as though the train must be travelling at its full speed now so there's no way that we're going to be able to get off until it slows down again which might not be until it actually makes a stop at a settlement. There are no lights at all in the tunnel but Jack's torch is fairly decent so we can see each other without difficulty, he tries training the torch on the wall of the tunnel to get some idea of our speed and even our location. There are occasional painted markings on the concrete walls but whilst we can see them we are travelling too quickly to be able to focus on them. The battering of the wind is constant and we are all lying flat on the roof as close to each other as we can get to minimise the risk of falling off. Even though our heads are practically touching it is still very hard to hear each other even when we shout.

After almost twenty minutes of this we are still not out of the tunnel, since the trains are able to get through the tunnel in about ten minutes it follows that we are travelling at less than half speed. The sense of speed we are feeling is increased by our circumstances but we are all expecting the end of the tunnel to be approaching soon. Even when Jack turns off his torch we are unable to see any hint of the exit, but of course it is still dark outside anyway. We are all disorientated now but it certainly seems as though we are climbing, then all of a sudden the train starts to slow down quickly. The driver has not applied the brakes but it feels as though there is no longer any drive, we are coasting. This is both good and bad news. If our experience at the other end of the tunnel is anything to go by then it probably means there are guards on the French side as well, but the fact that we are slowing down means we might have a chance to get off without killing ourselves. There is no way that we can risk jumping off the roof, according to Jack the ground around the exit is flat so we'd have a fairly long drop with a real risk of broken bones. Instead we make our way to the end of the coach and lower ourselves into the gap between two coaches adjacent to the connecting corridor. With three of us all on one side it is a very tight squeeze but our feet are not much more than a metre off the ground, there are various places where we can hold on and in hindsight it would have been a better place to spend the bulk of the journey.

No more than a minute after we are secure in our new position we feel the air is much cooler and there is a difference in the sound the train is making. As soon as we've noticed the difference the train breaks out on the other side, we seem to be going much slower on this side than when we jumped onto the train. We are even able to notice a rights enabler standing only a metre and a half away from us with his back to us. Because we are near the middle of the train and it probably won't begin to accelerate again until the back is clear of the rights enablers, we bide our time and don't risk jumping off straight away. We don't want the train to pick up too much speed before we get off but we need to minimise the risk of being seen. There is plenty of undergrowth on our side of the train as well as trees and bushes, unfortunately they are still about ten metres away from us when the train begins to pick up speed once more. Without thinking too much about it we each in turn jump clear with me going last, collapsing onto the ballast and rolling into the drainage gulley.

We are still too close to the rights enablers for comfort, there are two of them just like on the other side but we are too far away from them to be able to see which direction they are looking. There is no indication that they have seen us, but even in the relative darkness we would be fairly easy to spot if they look in the right direction. Keeping as flat to the ground as possible I see Jack starting to ease his way towards the edge of the cleared area, I can see from the way he's moving that his ankle is causing him quite a bit of pain. Suzie also starts to edge sideways and I follow all the while keeping an eye on the guards to look for any movement that might mean we've been spotted. Suzie is the first to reach the undergrowth and disappear, I reach the same spot a few seconds later. We both make our way through the edge of the wood to the place Jack is heading and wait for him, we pull him into our hiding place by his arms. There is sweat beading on his face and he is breathing heavily, we take his back pack off and turn him over to lie on his back. We get the blankets out and cover him up whereupon he gratefully closes his eyes to an almost immediate sleep, then the two of us make ourselves as comfortable as we can. We are very tired so a couple of hours rest will do us all the world of good and we are far further on our journey than we ever expected to be at this stage.

It is after dawn when I wake up, there is a vague sound of a train somewhere in the distance and getting further away so I guess it was that train passing that started me waking. The other two are still asleep, Jack has turned onto his side and his legs are no longer covered, in the light of day I can see his foot is at a strange angle, I'm no doctor but it looks broken to me. I decide to leave Jack and Suzie and have a scout around, first of all I creep to edge of the clear area by the railway line and look towards the tunnel mouth. The guards are still there, standing either side of the track but they are glancing into the darkness every now and again, it's obvious that they were not expecting us to take the train and it seems as though we've got away with it. Unfortunately Jack has paid for our escape with quite a bad injury that could easily cause us real problems for the remainder of our journey. In the daylight I can now see two tents the same as those on the other side, there is also a small plume of smoke rising from a fire just in front of them. I ease myself back into the wood and return to the others.

When I get back they are both awake, Jack has his boot and sock off and Suzie is looking at his foot with a fair degree of revulsion on her face. His foot is twisted to the side at an odd angle, now his boot is off it is very easy to see that the joint is dislocated, there is a lot of swelling as well. Jack is biting down hard on a stick to combat the pain but he removes this as I approach and says that Suzie has been trying to reduce the dislocation under his instruction but has not managed so far. It is quite likely that if we'd done it straight away before we slept that it would have been less difficult but as blood has had a chance to pool from the damaged tissue this makes it slightly harder to do. Jack says with a wry grin that if he'd had a vial of a suitable anaesthetic in his pack, he could have injected this into the pooled blood which would then have made the operation considerably less painful for him. I kneel down on the ground in front of his foot, Suzie takes a firm hold of his lower leg and he puts the stick back between his teeth.

As instructed by Jack, I get hold of his foot with both hands and pull it straight out with a slight twisting movement. There is a lot of resistance and looking at his face I can see that he's in terrible pain which is really distracting. I close my eyes and move my left hand so that I can feel the gap at the bottom of the tibia where the talus, a bone whose name I was unaware of until just now needs to sit. Now I'm feeling the problem rather than seeing it and I can't see the pain on my patient's face, my mind clears, I pull again and this time I feel the bones move and with a muffled click it pops back into place. At the same moment I feel something hit me in the face and hear Jack scream, I open my eyes, Jack has bitten through the stick and it was the end of this that hit me. Looking down at his foot I can see that it is now pointing in the right direction, he is also able to move it. It's clear though that he is not going to be able to put his boot back on, the swelling is impressive and never before have I seen such an angry bruise.

Then Jack whispers urgently that we have to get moving quickly, we are not far away from the rights enablers' camp and they will certainly have heard his scream which could easily prompt a search. He says that there's the remains of an old road from before the war that makes its way through the woods near here, his car is hidden just off this road where it is quite close to the railway line. It is a purpose built garage with a power supply stolen from the railway to enable the charging of its batteries. Normally he would simply walk along the train track to get there but right now that would guarantee our discovery, we're going to have to struggle through the woods again. He glances towards the sun that is glinting through the foliage and then his watch before showing us which way to go. He's limping quite badly as we set off but we soon find a branch that is ideally shaped to serve as a crutch. Rather than try to pull it from the tree and risk damaging it, Jack has a small chain saw in his pack which he unrolls, wrapping it round the branch he deftly saws it off in next to no time.

Even with the aid of his crutch Jack is significantly slower than he was on the other side of the Channel, he remarks that he is perhaps a little on the old side for this kind of adventure. After about a quarter of an hour of struggling through the woods we suddenly break out onto the road, Jack points to the left and says that his car is about half a kilometre that way. We are so relieved at having a decent path to follow for a change that we forget to be on our guard, we only realise our mistake when a bang echoes amongst the trees, there is a flapping of birds suddenly taking flight and Suzie drops to the ground with a gasp. Before we get a chance to react there's another gunshot, luckily this doesn't hit any of us, quickly Jack and I drag Suzie off the side of the road and back into the cover of the bushes. There is a small but growing patch of blood on her left trouser leg half way up her calf, quickly Jack pulls up the trouser leg to inspect the damage. She's been lucky, the bullet has nicked the side of her leg, it's only a small wound but it's bleeding a lot, he gets Suzie to apply pressure to the would whilst he rummages in his backpack for something to use as a bandage. She is recovering from the shock by the time Jack has tied a strip of cloth around her leg.

Time is ticking, we don't actually know how far away the rights enabler who shot at us is, but he knows exactly where we are. The only hope for us now is to get to Jack's car before we get caught, we've come such a long way so quickly so I guess our luck couldn't last indefinitely. We're relatively close to Jack's car now, probably no more than three hundred metres but that is going to take a while to cover through the edge of the wood. In the end we decide that the best course of action is to break cover again and make a run for it, it's going to be painful for Jack and Suzie but there is no real alternative. If I had experience of driving then I could go and retrieve the car and come back to collect the others but this is not really an option, it could easily end in disaster. Jack takes his scanner out of his pocket and brings up some options that relate to his garage and his car, then holding it carefully in his hand he breaks cover and starts running as fast as he can along the road. He's not very fast but no shot comes, once he's gone about a hundred metres Suzie follows, she's quite a bit quicker and is soon catching him up. After another few seconds I make a dash for it, I can hear my blood pumping as I run up the road expecting a shot to ring out at any moment. Then I see Suzie and Jack disappear off the side of the road and a few seconds later I'm at the same point. As I turn off the road, out of breath, I'm probably imagining it but I'm sure I hear a bullet whiz past my head.

Jack and Suzie have both stopped about five metres from the edge of the road, there are some tracks on the ground where Jack's car has been driven in but they just stop a couple of metres from where we're standing and they're not easy to spot unless you're looking straight at them. Then a large section of the ground rises up with a slight hiss, until it opened there was no sign of it at all and there down a gentle slope under this camouflaged cover is Jack's car. It is remarkably similar to the toy that I found the other day, even down to how battered it is but it's not red, well not entirely. It looks like every panel is a different colour, nevertheless it responds to Jack's controller by flashing two orange lights on the front. He then limps round to the back of the car and picks up an electrical lead from the ground, unplugging the connector he rolls the remaining length of flex up and puts it into a hatch at the back of the car. There are two seats in the front accessed through a door on each side and behind them are another pair of doors giving access to a bench seat that could just about take three people but would be more comfortable for two.

Jack suggests that Suzie gets in the back so that she can stretch out a bit to ease her injury, he gets in on the left side at the front where he sits behind a small wheel and I get in next to him. He clips his scanner into a cradle behind the control wheel and it lights up with information about the car, remarking with relief that the batteries are fully charged. He moves a lever that is next to the control wheel from a position marked with a *P* downwards to a position marked *D*, then pressing a control that is on the floor we begin to move forwards up the gentle slope out of the garage. The moment we are clear of the door it begins to shut and it has closed completely by the time we reach the road. We turn left, there is a rights enabler just on the point of reaching us from the right, instinctively I duck down, Jack presses the control as far to the floor as it will go and the car takes off as though it's been stung. We hear a few shots from the rights enabler's gun, there are two loud thumps in the car, a bullet has come through the back window and out the front leaving a small hole and a trickle of molten plastic on each.

The car is quite a bit louder than the trains are, this is due largely to the poor quality of the road making it crash around, but we are moving quite quickly and the rights enabler is soon reduced to a dot in the distance. After that Jack slows the car down slightly to a speed that will get us to the last place that we can charge the batteries as quickly as we can and still make it there. According to the display on his scanner we are travelling at a hundred and twenty nine kilometres per hour which seems an odd speed to me, Jack spots the quizzical look on my face and taps the corner of the screen of his scanner and the display changes, it now says eighty, our speed in miles per hour, his preferred measurement. He also sets the car to maintain the speed itself which means he can then stretch his legs out a bit, he still keeps hold of the steering wheel, this would once have been unnecessary as the car used to be able to follow the roads itself according to a pre-set route but the roadside equipment that allowed this is no longer working.

It takes us quite a while to begin to relax a little bit, the road is in a surprisingly good state considering it has not been maintained at all since before the war started. It used to be a lot wider than it is now however, the local flora has been reclaiming it very slowly over the years, it would once have carried three lanes of traffic in each direction but now it would be somewhat awkward if we were to meet a vehicle coming towards us. Although avoiding the vehicle itself might be the least of our problems depending upon its origin. There is no sign of any chase, but then again there wouldn't be as all of the official travel within the country, at least outside Luxburg itself is by rail. It seems amazing to me that eighty years ago there would have been hundreds or even thousands of cars running on this same surface, this road would have seen more travellers in a day than there are people living in the United States of Europe now. The sheer scale of what we have lost is huge and it makes my head ache just to try and think about it.

Chapter 14

The car is quite a relaxing way to travel, especially compared with our journey through the tunnel on the roof of a train but even when comparing it with my official journey by train from Chelmsford to Sevenoaks the extra convenience more than makes up for the slower speed. Even so after two hours of the journey it is beginning to lose a little bit of its appeal, we have covered over two hundred kilometres and only have another eighty or so to go until our enforced stop to recharge the batteries. There has not been much change in scenery for this part of the journey although Jack assures us that there will be significant differences towards the end of our journey as we start to climb seriously. Here in the lower lying lands the whole area has reverted to being a huge forest in the space of less than a hundred years with nobody chopping down trees.

The road used to be the main motorway from Calais to Reims according to Jack's old paper map and it will be just beyond there where our route starts to head away from the railway. In the rush of our escape I'd not thought very much about anything other than our immediate predicament but now my thoughts turn to my brother Jim. We're getting closer and closer to where he is minute by minute, where he is settling into a new job in the transport division. It's possible, but unlikely that he could have been on the train which brought us through the channel. Suzie is asleep curled up on the back seat but I wonder also what she thinks of this journey back to where she called home until the other week. At that moment there is a curve in the road which has on the whole been fairly straight, we are now only a few kilometres away from Reims and we can see the outline of the settlement in the distance. There is a junction on the railway here with one line turning towards the east to Luxburg and the state of Deutschland and the other line heading southwest towards other settlements in the state of France.

This part of the journey is going to be the hardest for the car as we have to leave the road to get around the settlement, we can't just drive straight through the middle. Although I can't see what they'd be able to do about it if we did, but after our antics with the rights enabler we are probably expected. Since we have been in sight of Reims Jack has slowed the car down to not much faster than walking pace, he is looking along the side of the road for a track. Suddenly he stops, the lurch throws Suzie off her seat and she wakes up with a gasp. Jack apologises and then turns the car off the road into a gap between two of the largest trees, there is only just enough space for the car to fit between their trunks and there is a horrible scraping noise against both sides of the car as it forces the branches out of its way. Just as I'm wondering how long we're going to have to travel in this rather awkward manner we reach a small clearing and Jack stops the car, he suggests we all get out to relieve ourselves and stretch our legs.

Out of the car it is quite a warm day, there is an abundance of bird calls in the trees and it is a pleasant place to be. Once we are all back at the car Jack points to the far corner of the clearing where there is a fairly innocuous forest track. This he says is a pathway that was cleared by a team of his friends over a period of several months to allow them to get their vehicles around Reims in a subtle way. It runs for about five kilometres, taking us well to the east of the settlement where we will have to drive across the railway line and then there is another shorter track through the forest which will take us out onto the remains of another road heading southwards. The charging point for the car is at the beginning of the second track just after we've crossed the railway line, he makes it all sound so simple. Before we set off again Jack sits down and has a good feel of his foot, the swelling has lessened a great deal but he still can't put his boot back on. He also has a quick look at Suzie's bullet wound, it has stopped bleeding and scabbed over, it's not causing her too much pain now.

We get back in the car, this time Suzie goes in the front with Jack, once we are on the track it becomes clear just how much work has gone into it. It is plenty wide enough for the car, in fact there were places on the old road where there was less clearance. The trees that were chopped down to clear the way have been cut up to form a foundation, meaning that there are not many plants growing in our path and those that are there are small enough simply to drive over. Nevertheless the ride is quite bumpy and we aren't able to travel even at a quarter of the speed that we were previously. It takes us about twenty minutes to reach the end of the track and Jack stops the car again, the arrangement here is the same as where we left the road in that the car will have to squeeze its way out between two large trees. The location for the railway crossing has been chosen well, the track is at the same level as the surrounding ground, there are however, two separate lines to cross. We are going to have to move some of the ballast around so that the car can make it across.

There is half an hour before a train is due which Jack thinks is not long enough to move the ballast around and cross, there's no point in moving the ballast around before the trains pass as they would shake it out of position, so we sit down at the edge of the woods where we are still well hidden to wait. There will be another two trains within the space of fifteen minutes before there is a long enough window of opportunity. The trains pass by exactly according to schedule and then Jack takes a shovel from the back of the car and heads out onto the line telling us to stay put. We watch him shift some of the granite chips to form small ramps on either side of each of the four rails, when he has finished he comes back to the car, puts the shovel away and we all take our places. He eases the car between the trees, this is an even tighter squeeze than last time but we make it out and onto the ballast which crunches under the tyres. We make it across one of the tracks but as we reach the second there is a loud crash and the car stops abruptly.

We can still hear the motor humming but the car isn't moving, Jack tries to reverse with no luck, the sound of the motor is faltering now so he switches off the power and we all get out to see what's happened. There's nothing immediately obvious but when I kneel down and look underneath, it looks as though a panel underneath the car has come loose and jammed on the rail. My arm is not long enough to reach the cause of the problem and there is not enough clearance to slide underneath. We need to lift the car up but we aren't strong enough, despite the fact that it is made of fairly lightweight materials such as aluminium and plastic it still weighs the best part of two tonnes because of the batteries. We've only got about quarter of an hour until another train is due so we're going to

164

have to think of something quickly or our journey is going to end right here in disaster. Then an idea comes to me, if we retrieve a couple of the logs from the track, a short thick one and a longer thinner one we'll be able to lift it up.

We head back into the woods and start scouting around for suitable logs, it doesn't take long to find something to use as a lever, the trunk from a silver birch that is about four metres long and about twenty centimetres thick. I drag it out to the car with Suzie while Jack continues looking for a pivot. By the time Suzie and I return to him he's found something that will do the job, we roll the remains of a tree stump out of the woods and over to the car. With the tree stump a little way away from the side of the car and in the middle, we manoeuvre the long trunk over the stump and under the sill of the car and once it's in far enough we all pull down on the end. The car lifts slightly and very easily but then it stops without its wheels even having lifted off the ground. We're all putting our full strength into pulling the tree trunk down fully aware of the time ticking away and then all at once there's a bang and the car jumps up in the air, the trunk slides out from underneath the car throwing us all onto the gravel. The car drops to the ground like a stone, I get up quickly and run over to take a look underneath, calling to the others that it appears to be free.

Jack gets into the driver's seat and tries to switch on the power with no luck, the vehicle is dead. There must be no more than five minutes until the train is due. Jack says that we're going to have to push it off the line, he releases the brake and gets out of the car again. We all line up together at the back and start to push, the ballast slides around underneath our feet and it's very difficult to get any kind of purchase. Eventually after what seems like ages it slowly starts to move but we need to get it moving at a decent speed so that the front wheels will jump the final rail. It hits the rail which jars us all but we keep on pushing and the front wheel is clear, then almost immediately the back wheels hit the first rail of the second track and we don't have enough momentum to keep it moving. We are all starting to panic but forcing ourselves to remain calm we rock the car against the rail and with a great effort we get it moving again and this time we build up enough speed to get the car completely clear of the rails. It picks up speed and too late we realise that it's not heading towards the gap in the trees, we stop pushing but it carries on until it stops with a crunch against a large oak tree.

The car is now completely clear of the track but would still be blindingly obvious to anyone on-board a train, I double back onto the track to retrieve the stump and Suzie follows my lead dragging the trunk clear. Jack suggests trying to use the log to lever the car clear of the tree, we ease it underneath again and this time it goes according to plan. With a scraping sound the car slides away from the tree and is now pointing straight into the gap between two trees. We take our positions at the back once again and with a final effort we ease the car out of sight and collapse onto the ground exhausted, less than thirty seconds later we hear the train hurtle past. That was a little close for comfort. We lie on the ground for a few minutes to recover from our exertion before Jack retrieves his scanner from inside the car and uses it to open the hidden garage and charging point. The camouflage is excellent, the opening is less than five metres from where we are and there is no sign of it at all until it begins to open. We then begin the process of pushing the car into the garage which although a lot easier than pushing it off the railway track still takes us a little while.

Once Jack has switched on the lights we can see a lot more clearly, the shelter is basic but dry. The roof is made of corrugated aluminium with the moving part propped open on two huge gas struts. There is a small workbench at the back which holds a few basic tools and the charging device for the car but that seems to be all, it doesn't look as though we've got anything with which to re-commission the car. However Jack retrieves a connector lead from amongst the tools and plugs one end into his scanner and the other into a socket in the back of the car, this allows him to run a series of diagnostic tests on the car's electrical circuitry. Unfortunately the results are inconclusive, all the minor systems appear intact but there is no power getting to any part of the car, this means either catastrophic failure of the batteries or the main cable has been broken in some way. Either way, we're not going to be able to continue our journey for a while but if the batteries are severely damaged we've got a very long walk ahead of us.

Whilst the majority of vehicles that were designed to run from batteries allow for relatively easy access to such things, Jack's is a different kettle of fish. His car was designed to generate electricity via a fuel cell at the front connected to a cylinder containing hydrogen at the back. When it was converted for use with batteries these two locations were filled up with small batteries in multiple layers to maximise the available capacity. There are also some under the back seats, realistically the only way to gain access is from underneath the car which means we have to lift it up, we don't have a jack other than our logs which none of us particularly want to risk again. Then I see that there's a rope on the ground at the back of the garage, I ask Jack if he thinks the opening part of the roof will support the weight of the car. He immediately realises what I am thinking and picks up the rope and passes it underneath the back of the car so that it hooks under the wheel arches. He then sets the entrance closing by pressing a button set into the wall and when it is shut we tie the loose ends of the rope tightly onto the main load-bearing beam of the hatch that runs between the two struts. Then the moment of truth, pressing the button opens the hatch once more and whilst it opens significantly slower than it did previously it lifts the back of the car smoothly off the ground.

We have plenty of clearance to get underneath and we can instantly see the problem. The aluminium plate that had been guarding the underside of the batteries at the front of the car which had got caught on the rail has been forced backwards. This has got wedged into the main cable that runs from the batteries at the back of the car to the other batteries and motor at the front, the whole area is melted from where it's welded itself together and from the look of it, to the track as well. The batteries will be completely discharged as a result of this, we now have to hope that they are going to take a charge once we have repaired the damage. It's at this point my stomach gives a loud rumble and we remember it's been quite a while since we last ate anything other than the cereal bars that had been in a storage compartment in the car. Jack has a trick up his sleeve, or rather at the back of the garage, hidden behind the workbench is a small freezer which he opens and offers us a choice of lasagne or chilli con carne. We just need to gather some firewood, no hunting needed.

When Suzie and I return Jack already has a fire going, he sniggers a bit at the quality of the wood we've brought back, but nevertheless adds it to his wood pile. Unfolding his frying sheet he carefully wraps the still-frozen contents of the plastic container and then places it onto the fire. A really nice aroma quickly starts to waft around and I can feel my mouth watering. The freezer is always kept stocked up for people using this charging point as it is frequently visited unlike the one where Jack had left his car while he was visiting South Britain. It's not long before Jack has dished up the chilli con carne and it is very nice, despite the fact that we are all ravenously hungry we savour our food but after a while we have to turn our attention back to the car and getting back into action. We head back into the garage, Jack picks up a large crowbar and goes underneath the car. He hooks it behind the guard plate and pulls it away, there is a screech of metal on metal and then with a loud clatter it drops to the ground. Now it's away from the car we can see that the main cable is quite badly damaged, it's been very hot and all the insulation has melted away, however the actual cables are still intact albeit thinner now than they should be. Jack is eager to assess the condition of the batteries so he quickly wraps each of the cables with some plastic adhesive tape and plugs the charging cable into the charger on the workbench.

After a tense few seconds Jack says that the batteries appear to be taking a charge, now we just have to wait, it's going to take just over twelve hours for a full charge. The batteries themselves would be perfectly alright being charged much faster than this, but the charger is restricted on the amount of current it can draw from the railway's electricity supply, they have to make a balance between the risk of discovery and the rate of charge. Jack closes the door and the car lowers to the ground, once it's down we untie the ends of the rope and coil it back up. Jack retrieves some sleeping bags from the back of the garage along with some rolled up foam mats and joy of joys, a small cushion each. We lay out our beds on the floor next to the car, after nearly two days of travel we are all tired and it feels like the greatest pleasure possible to slide into a warm sleeping bag on a padded mat and pillow with a full stomach. Once we are all tucked in Jack switches out the lights, it is not pitch dark because there is a constant glow from the screen on the charger but no light comes in from outside. It's four o'clock in the afternoon but our heads have barely touched the pillows before we all fall into a deep sleep, the safest that we've had for a while.

Chapter 15

Thursday 29th June 53

When I wake up I feel the most rested that I have for a while, it is a little lighter in the garage than when we went to sleep, this is because Jack is standing at the workbench looking at the battery charger and has turned on one of the lights. Suzie is still asleep and snoring gently, I ease myself out of the confines of my sleeping bag and wander over to Jack absentmindedly rubbing the sleep out of my eyes as I go and then flinching where the bruise from my three day old black eye is still a little bit painful. Jack turns as I approach the bench, he smiles but I can tell there's something not quite right.

"What's up?" I ask.

'The batteries are not as fully charged as they should be, they've been charging for just over eight hours now and they're not even half charged. What's more the charging rate has slowed right down, I think that the short circuit and total discharge has caused damage to them."

"So what can we do?"

"We could wait a bit longer to see if they continue charging but from past experience of these batteries I would say they're not going to achieve much more than half their capacity no matter how long we leave them going. The other option is just to set off now and see how far we get, if we take it really slow we should be able to get over half way but no matter how slow we go we're not going to make it all the way. Whatever we do we're going to be walking at least a hundred kilometres."

"I think we should set off now but let's see what Suzie thinks when she wakes up."

Just as I say that we hear Suzie stirring from her sleep, quickly, she gets up and joins us at the back of the garage. After Jack has explained the situation she agrees that we should get going now, especially as it's currently not long after midnight meaning that we can put some distance between ourselves and inhabited parts under cover of darkness. We pack our bedding away, Jack unplugs the charging lead, takes another readymade meal from the freezer (lasagne this time) and puts it in the back of the car to give us a dinner later on. Jack sets the door opening and shuts off the lighting and we all pile into the car. At the press of Jack's foot on the accelerator the car eases out of the garage and as soon as we're clear the door begins to shut once more, out of the garage there is a clear sky above us and even amongst the trees there is a reasonable amount of light from an almost full moon filtering through the canopy. We are able to see the track though the wood without using the lights on the car so this will save our batteries a little.

Jack drives the car at sixteen kilometres per hour which predictably enough is a nice round ten miles per hour, the display shows that our range is a little under five hundred kilometres. This isn't bad if it's true, the total distance remaining for us to travel is now less than six hundred kilometres. After less than ten minutes we have left the track behind us and are heading almost due south on what remains of the old road from Reims to Troyes. We wouldn't have been able to go anywhere near as fast on this road as we did on the first leg of our journey because it's in a much worse state with frequent encroachment of the forest undergrowth and even some relatively tall saplings to drive around, but still we seem to be travelling ridiculously slowly. Running without lights means that we don't see any of the potholes that are frequently present although because of our relatively slow progress most of the time we are not badly jarred by them.

At this speed the car's motor is very quiet so we are able to hear all the squeaks and rattles that were masked by its hum up until now, Jack says that it's a tribute to British engineering that it's still around over eighty years after it was built. The car in which we are riding was made in 2019 just before the start of the war, although his praise for British engineering is slightly misplaced it seems, as the company and its design were both Japanese, it merely having been assembled in the northeast of England. Another precursor to the war had been the gradual erosion of manufacturing from Europe and other large consumer nations to places where labour was cheaper and exchange rates were favourable. This meant that there was an ever shrinking demand for unskilled and semi-skilled labour which contributed to the civil unrest. Once upon a time there had been a vast and thriving manufacturing industry for such things in Britain and indeed all across Europe. It had taken the promise of land being sold at agricultural rates for the factory to be set up there and it was pretty much only by luck that it became the manufacturer's European base for electric vehicle production. By the start of the war there was a small but growing market for electric vehicles although the vast majority still ran on fossil fuels but these were becoming increasingly expensive to refine. Of course as it turned out they needn't have worried, having said that a fossil-fuelled car wouldn't be much use to us now.

After we've been travelling for a couple of hours we've left Reims about thirty kilometres behind us but it has now become apparent that our battery situation is nowhere near as good as we'd thought when we set off. Our range indicator is now showing only two hundred kilometres remaining, the possibility of a few days walking to complete our journey has turned into an absolute certainty of a very long walk indeed. Despite the fact that Jack's scanner device was originally manufactured as a mobile telephone he is unable to use it to speak to anyone at his Mont Blanc base. This functionality relied on a network of masts that used to cover the densely populated parts of the world which would pick up the relatively weak transmissions from all the mobile phones in the area and transmit them to the required destinations. This entire infrastructure has long since disappeared.

Jack's original device has, however, been modified to allow it to work as a simple transmission and receiving device to connect with other such modified devices. This means that when other people from his group are within range, they can be used in this way, also the absence of millions of similar devices cluttering up the airwaves means that the range is significantly greater than used to be possible as long as they stay away from Luxburg. Take one of these close to Luxburg and they start to go crazy. As if to prove the point, at that moment it starts playing an irritating little tune. Jack presses a button on the steering wheel, the tune stops abruptly and Jack greets the caller.

"Hi Jack, all going to plan then as you're on your way back?" says a man cheerily.

"Well, we've had our ups and downs but Edward is with me and a friend of his too, it's not been plain sailing and we've got a problem now. We're over three hundred miles from home and our batteries are dying, we had a sudden discharge caused by a short circuit and they've been badly damaged. Anyway, how come you're in range?"

"I'm just on my way to Luxburg, but I've got an idea, I'll be at the Reims charging point in about an hour, if you turn around and meet me there we can swap cars. Mine will need a charge to get back to Mont Blanc but at least you'll get all the way back."

"Sounds good but, we've been on the road two hours and we've gone barely twenty miles, I've been trying to conserve enough juice to get us home!"

"OK, you turn around and if I catch you up I'll give you a tow."

"Great but we'll get back in no time now, see you in a little while then. Bye."

The line goes dead, Jack stops the car and does a somewhat awkward about turn on the narrow road. Andy, the man who called is another one of their field operatives and is a good friend of Jack's, they've worked together frequently. Andy is a whiz with batteries and all things electrical or electronic, he'll be able to remove the dead cells from the battery packs which are causing their inability to hold a reliable charge. Jack accelerates the car quickly and soon we're zipping along as quickly as we can on the poor road surface, it's fairly uncomfortable but after a little more than half an hour we're back where we started with the batteries almost flat once again. This time Jack eases the car as far over to the side of the garage as possible to make room for a second vehicle, he doesn't bother to plug this car in as there is little point until Andy has worked his magic on it. We've only been in the garage about quarter of an hour when we hear the distinctive approach of another electric car. A minute later Andy's parked up and is greeting Jack warmly.

Jack introduces Andy to me and Suzie and when he sets eyes on me he breaks into a broad grin and then says to Jack that my photographs don't do me justice and that the likeness is uncanny. He stops talking abruptly when he notices Jack's alarmed look and embarrassedly sets to putting his car on charge. The plan is now that we'll all wait here while Andy's car charges up and then we can be off, this one is even more battered than Jack's and is in fact older still. Despite this it is technically superior, its battery system is a far better installation than in Jack's, this means that on a full charge we'll be able to get all the way back to their base without having to hold back at all. The only downside to this plan as far as we're concerned is that we'll now be hanging around here for over sixteen hours; the increased capacity means an increase in charging time. The wait is worth it of course as we'll easily make it all the way back inside a day, we'll be able to set off about nine o'clock this evening and all being well we'll be at Mont Blanc well before breakfast time.

The downside for Andy is that he now has to fix Jack's car and head off to Luxburg in an inferior vehicle but he doesn't seem too bothered by this. I can see a certain amount of relish in the way that he opens the hatch at the front of the car and starts prodding around inside with a couple of probes attached to his standard-issue mobile telephone, one with a red wire and one with black. He works quickly but carefully, checking each individual cell and isolating any damaged ones from the circuit rather than physically removing them. After no more than half an hour he has checked everything that he can through the front hatch and needs to get underneath to check the rest of the front batteries, so far out of the fifty-nine cells that he has checked only two have required isolation. Jack has already pulled out the rope that we used before and we proceed to set up our makeshift hoist once again, opening the door lifts the car cleanly off the floor and Andy crawls underneath with his tools. He's only been there a couple of minutes when all the lights go off, the only light in the garage is coming from the doorway and the dawn sky filtering through the trees outside. Jack jokingly asks Andy what he's done, but he quickly checks the charging equipment by the workbench which reveals the worst, this power cut wasn't caused by anything he's done.

The most likely scenario is that the power to the railway line has been cut for some kind of maintenance work, if this is the case then we just have to wait for it to be restored. We have no way of telling how long the outage could last, it might be only one of the two tracks affected, in which case it won't be causing too many problems for Europarl so it could be out for quite a while. If this is the case, depending upon where the workers are, we may be able to connect our supply to that of the other track. There is of course the possibility that it's our power lead that has been discovered, in which case we're in deep trouble. The only thing to do is go and have a look. Without power the only way to shut the door is to wind it down with a handle, it takes quite a while but we don't want to risk going away from the garage and leaving it open so we each have a go at turning it. It won't shut completely as the handle is inside and we have to leave a small enough gap to reach it, even so the place is almost as well hidden as usual.

We all approach the edge of the railway line carefully, listening for any noises but not hearing anything other than birds calling and the slight rustle of the trees blowing in the breeze. Indicating for the rest of us to stay put, Jack pokes his head out of the cover of foliage and proceeds to ease himself out of the undergrowth completely. He only goes far enough away from the trees to see along the line and then comes back, whispering that there is a group of four people on a maintenance truck at one of the poles holding the overhead wires on the line closest to us. That explains why the power is off, they are about half a kilometre away. Jack says that from his quick glance there appear to be a few drop wires missing, these are the wires that support the contact wire to the catenary wire. He can't see anything else that is obviously wrong and they are not close to the pole into which our power supply is connected. With any luck they'll simply replace the wires and be on their way, however it's quite likely that they'll check other wires at the same time.

We all lie down out of sight at the edge of the wood and ease ourselves into positions where we can see the railway line but remain hidden, we can't actually see the people working but we can now hear them faintly as well as the hum of the motor as they move their truck our way. We wait patiently and before long the voices become louder as they work their way along the line towards us and we are able to pick out the odd word. I have a really odd feeling that I can't quite place but the moment that the crew come into view I realise what it is, Jim is in that crew laughing and joking with his colleagues. I don't know how to react to this information, I'm just about to break cover without thinking but luckily Jack grabs me with a surprisingly firm grip and frantically asks me what I think I'm playing at. I point out Jim to the others and quickly explain in a whisper that he's my brother. Looking properly at the group it would appear that there are two older workers teaching Jim and another apprentice. Jack quietly but forcefully says there's no way that I can risk going to speak to him, it's not as if he's in any imminent danger either so it would be very foolish to jeopardise my chance of actually making a difference for so little return. Of course I know he's right, but it doesn't make watching Jim any easier.

For a little more than an hour we watch them getting closer, during that time one train passes in each direction along the other line, both of which are running fairly slowly and sound their horns as they approach the crew. Then shortly after the second train passes, they reach the support pole next but one to that which our power supply connects, they pack away their tools, sit down on a bench running along one end of the truck and head off in the direction of Reims. It's another half an hour before the power supply is restored, Andy returns to his working on the damaged batteries after he's checked that his own car is charging correctly once more. Jack takes me and Suzie off for a bit of instruction on the ideal wood to use for a cooking fire and how best to build it. We come back each with arms full of dry dead oak sticks about the thickness of our thumbs, a fair amount of hawthorn for kindling and some papery bark peeled from a silver birch to get it going.

Under Jack's guidance Suzie and I build a square fire of oak sticks with the rest placed to one side for easy feeding once it's going. In the centre the hawthorn twigs are placed on top of the birch bark, making sure that we have a suitable place to light it. Jack offers me a lanyard from his pocket keeping two pieces of metal together, one is a silvery coloured rod and the other is flat with a serrated edge a little like a hacksaw blade. I look at him blankly and he explains that it's what he uses to light fires, taking the flat piece of metal he strikes it along the rod and releases a shower of sparks. I take it from him and holding the rod close to the birch bark I strike it several times, the bark soon catches and all the kindling soon follows suit. With a bit of judicious blowing the whole thing is nicely ablaze and it's not long before we can start heating the lasagne that Jack has retrieved from the back of his car along with another package of the same from the freezer.

By the time the food is ready to eat Andy has finished checking all the batteries at the front of the car as well as those under the back seat and has made a good start on the ones at the rear. He joins us sitting around the fire just as Jack is dishing up, the lasagne is every bit as good as last night's meal and it certainly fills a gap. Jack fills Andy in on the trials and tribulations we've endured on our journey and also about the times he spent with me and Suzie before we left. We both talk about our experiences living within the regime and the little things that we have done to subvert the system, admittedly this latter is mainly Suzie's input as until I met her, the sum total of my deviance has been the odd sneaky walk along the beach and the salvaging of various unidentified objects washed up. Both Jack and Andy are obviously avoiding any mention of anything to do with their group, they both talk about their experiences before joining the group. We're already aware of how Jack came to be there although he fleshes out the story of his journey a little more.

Andy however is much younger than Jack and was actually recruited to their organisation right here where we are currently sitting. Nearly ten years ago he had been stationed within the main transport division at Reims for seven years and during that time, due in large part to his technical ability when it came to all things electric had risen to being in charge of monitoring the entire railway's power distribution. He had noticed an inexplicable drain on the system which he'd isolated to a section of the westbound track a few kilometres to the west of the depot. Over a period of several weeks he'd sent out various work groups to try and identify the problem to no avail, in the end he'd gone out himself, alone, outside his working hours. After several hours of frustration he had discovered a cable spliced into one of the cable posts, it was so well hidden that the only way he could follow it was by scanning the ground for a signal. In the end he'd arrived at the garage and found it occupied by Jack, who was struggling with an electrical problem.

Jack's quick thinking and persuasive manner had got Andy onside, Andy had been happy to help Jack out with his problem. He also looked into the problem that had led him there in the first place by building a circuit to install on the main cable coming into the garage to ensure that it could only draw a current that would not be noticed from the central monitoring equipment. This is variable according to what else is going on within the system and has kept them from being discovered by any of the people who took on Andy's job after he *died in a trackside accident* about a month after he'd first met Jack. His story gives me hope for Jim, that he might one day be able to join us, Jack is strangely silent on this subject but I don't push it. We keep chatting generally whilst Andy gets on with his maintenance on Jack's car

By the time he's finished thirty individual cells have been isolated. He briefly disconnects his own vehicle from the charger to ensure that his work is sound, which it is and then switches the charging back. He could charge both vehicles at once but it would be much slower and he thinks it best to get us on our way as soon as possible. Andy decides to make the most of his longer than expected stop-over to go to the transport depot to have a rummage through the scrap for anything that might come in handy. It's late afternoon when he heads off eastwards on foot following the line of the railway but staying under the cover of the woods. He leaves us with instructions to put the other car on charge before we leave or he won't be very happy, the car that we're going to take will be fully charged by midnight giving us a few hours to rest up before the last leg of our journey. We lay and doze while the car continues to charge.

Chapter 16

Friday 30th June 53

None of us really thought we'd sleep given how little we'd actually been doing during the course of the day, therefore it is with a certain amount of surprise that I open my eyes to discover Suzie shaking me awake. But I guess this sort of thing is to be expected when there's no fixed schedule to follow. Jack already has the garage door open and is sitting behind the wheel, a bright glow of moonlight is filtering in from the now full moon, a blue moon. I think the phrase *once in a blue moon* will forever be associated for me with this significant phase in my life. Suzie gets into the front seat next to Jack and after I've rolled my mat and pillow and stored them away - we didn't get into sleeping bags, I crawl somewhat groggily into the back seat. As soon as I'm in, Jack eases the car out of the garage and the door begins to close, we're on our way once more. The seat in this car is nowhere near as comfortable as the other one, I'm not sure whether this is by design or whether it's just more worn out, but it sags quite a lot and it takes me a while to find an almost bearable position.

As before we are running without lights but this time it's not for the sake of saving the batteries, there really is plenty of light from the night sky so there isn't the need. The display is saying that we have a range of seven hundred kilometres, this will reduce when we start to climb to any degree but if needs be we can reduce our speed to compensate, we will have no real problems getting to our destination without having to resort to walking. We reach the point where we turned round yesterday after less than half an hour on the road. This time we are not travelling at a constant speed, the road is in a much worse state than those which we have used previously and is getting gradually worse as we go. Even at the slowest points we are able to better yesterday's constant speed and there are brief sections where the road is virtually undamaged. At one point there is even some intact roadside equipment that used to allow the vehicles to use their fully automatic capability, as we've been on the road for a couple of hours by now, Jack stops the car in order to show us the posts.

They're less than half a metre tall, with three small lenses at the top and still have traces of some markings on them, but they're not very interesting. He explains that they were mainly used to relay information about vehicles that weren't equipped with the navigation system to those that were, it was a very new system when the war started so only really new or slightly older, really expensive cars were able to use it. There were plans to make the system compulsory, which angered quite a lot of people, of course, they saw it as an erosion of their free will. Of course that's precisely what it was, but it's only since the war that Europarl has been able to control its subjects so comprehensively. There are plenty of us outside the system and there's not really much they can do about us, even if they find our group and kill us off or reintegrate us into the system there are other groups like ours around. Although any number of groups like ours are never going to beat the system, it's just not possible, the only way is to change the system from the inside, evolution and not revolution is the only way to win.

We get back into the car and continue our journey, we are now heading due south again and the ground is still flat but we can now see hills and mountains rising up ahead of us. The road is climbing steadily now, Jack has the display configured to show our altitude as well as our speed and battery range, we are now over two hundred metres above sea level. The nature of the trees alongside the road is changing too, there are a lot more evergreens here. This means that the canopy is generally higher as the vast majority of the trees are around the same age and these conifers are quicker growing. There is also less light filtering through to the road so Jack switches on the car's lights for the first time. He briefly demonstrates their impressive full power which really penetrates the gloom but then switches to the far dimmer *side lights* as the power drain is far too great for the distance we've got to cover. Of course the moment he switches them off it is as though we've gone completely blind and it takes several minutes for us all to recover our night vision.

As we continue our journey the mountains ahead of us slowly get more prominent, our own altitude increases as well. We've been on the road for a little under four hours when Jack announces that we are now over half way, we stop again to stretch our legs before continuing. The range indicator when we set off again is indicating that we can travel nearly four hundred kilometres but Jack says that we now have only a little more than three hundred still to go. The mountains are now really starting to loom large ahead of us and as the sky starts to get lighter we can see the bright white snow on the peaks. Despite the fact that we are travelling at a reasonable speed the scenery is so similar, the constant presence of trees either side of us and the view of mountains ahead whenever the trees allow us to see them trick us into thinking that we're getting nowhere. Eventually the direction of the road eases around to the east and we really start to climb, it's much cooler here. Suzie and I wrap our blankets around ourselves as we're both still dressed in the light summer clothes in which we fled from the hospital and we really can't use the car's heater as that uses as much energy as the motor itself.

After nearly seven hours on the road, Jack stops the car without warning or preamble. We're still surrounded by forest and clearly haven't arrived at our destination, although we can't have that much further still to go. We've had the car's lights switched off now for over an hour and the sun has been glaring through the trees straight into our faces for almost as long. Jack is very enigmatic about why we've stopped, saying simply that there is something fabulous to see and for the sake of a little more than half an hour's walk it's worthwhile. There is a narrow track to follow but it is obvious that it has been followed fairly frequently, it is quite straight and heads downhill all the time. Just as we seem about to break out of the wooded area Jack stops again and tells us to close our eyes, we both do so and allow him to lead us out between the trees. He manhandles us into facing in a particular direction and then gives the instruction to open our eyes.

We are standing on the beach of a vast lake, there is a hint of mist floating above the water but it is clear that this will very soon be gone. There is barely a cloud in the sky and the whole lake is surrounded by soaring snow-capped mountains. It is stunningly beautiful and Suzie clearly has exactly the same thought as me, we both strip to our underwear and run down into the cold water. It is very cold but not having washed at all for several days, being able to splash around in pure clear water is glorious quite apart from the setting. Jack is a little more restrained and sits on the edge with his feet in the water and gently massages his ankle in the coolness. We spend no more than a few minutes in the water since it is so cold but we feel refreshed and alive when we come out and shake ourselves off. Our teeth are chattering and we're both shivering but there is now plenty of warmth coming from the sun, the mist has completely disappeared and the pebbles on the beach are also warm underfoot. We lie down to dry off for a while before putting our clothes back on and just breathe the fresh mountain air.

While we're lying in the sunshine with water vapour gradually rising from our wet clothes, Jack explains that the water level in the lake is very slightly lower than it used to be due to the loss of a dam during the war. This change is not dramatic as the lake itself, Lake Geneva, is totally natural, the dam had been built no more than a kilometre from where we are standing with a primary purpose of electricity generation. We crossed the river which is the lake's outlet some twenty kilometres ago by means of a ford which was mainly the remains of a bridge on the motorway that we have been following, this had been painstakingly rearranged by Jack's group to make it possible to get their vehicles across. It was certainly the most significant river crossing that we made on the journey from Reims but still not really any trouble, this in itself is testament to just how much they've managed to achieve over the years. As we get up from the beach to walk back to the car and begin the final leg of our journey I'm full of renewed vigour at the thought of finding out and indeed taking up my place in all of this.

The last part of the journey is where we really begin to climb, the old motorway which we had been following up until now has mainly disappeared due to frequent raised sections having collapsed. This means we are now forced to follow smaller, older roads that stick more closely to the terrain, meaning that there are lots of twists and turns as well as ups and downs. The plants on either side of the road are much smaller now and we can now see the mountains ahead of us all of the time. Despite the fact that these roads were much narrower originally than the motorways, the lack of roadside vegetation means that they have not been encroached upon and the actual width of the surface on which we are able to drive is not noticeably narrower. There are some scary sections where what is left of the road is clinging to the side of the mountain with a huge drop to one side and nothing to stop us going over should we stray too close to the edge. As we get closer to our destination, the road is like this more frequently, progress is really slow for the final few kilometres but after a series of hairpin bends we finally make it to the Mont Blanc tunnel mid-morning.

The original entrance to the tunnel has been destroyed, deliberately by Jack's group, it looks as though there is no tunnel at all until an entrance similar to those of the charging garages begins to open upon our approach. We drive straight through as soon as the opening is large enough and the door begins to close again the moment we're inside. We are in a large maintenance area, there are various other cars dotted around, some of which are jacked up and undergoing maintenance, others are clearly plugged in and charging and a few are simply parked. Jack parks our car in one of the bays, as we get out someone is already plugging in its charging lead, Jack cheerily thanks him and ushers me and Suzie towards a small door at the back of the garage area. We've walked into a small waiting area; there are two three-seater sofas either side of a low-topped table containing a jug of water and several glasses. Jack says to help ourselves to a drink and wait here while he goes to find someone to get us settled in, he then disappears through another door.

I pour a glass of water for each of us and we each sip nervously, we've come a long way and had quite a few adventures on our way but now we're at the culmination of our journey it seems somewhat of an anticlimax. Jack has given us no indication at all as to who we're going to meet, we don't even know if it's a man or a woman. Even though the room we're in is in a tunnel through a tall mountain it just feels like a boring old waiting room. The air is clear and clean, there isn't even any hint of the smells of vehicle maintenance that were lingering in the garage. However the single thing that makes it seem so ordinary is the *window*, it's obviously just a viewing screen but it's like nothing I've ever seen. There are ordinary lights set into the ceiling but they aren't turned on, all of the light in the room is coming from the screen. It's so realistic it's hard to believe that it isn't real, but the really amazing thing for me is that it's a view that I almost recognise from Jack's description of the pictures in his book. This is London; I can't believe it's taken me so long to notice!

We're both staring transfixed at the screen, we're looking down onto the river Thames, there are occasional boats passing and there is a subdued sound of civilisation. Whilst it's a distinctive enough view for me to recognise, it's a really odd picture to be showing when presumably they could have chosen any view that took their fancy. We're on the south bank of the Thames to the west of Westminster Bridge, we can't see anything closer than the middle of the river because although we're fairly high up, on the other side of the river there's a short row of trees and to the right of those is the end of the Houses of Parliament, not the interesting end with the clock tower but the other end! I'm just contemplating this when the door opens again and in walks a woman, she looks a little older than Jack and I suspect she is but if she's one of the two people I think she might be she, like Jack, looks a lot younger than her years. We both stand up and face her.

"Hi, I'm Lucy, I knew Jack would be able to get you here, he was always very resourceful. I see you've noticed the *window*, you're wondering why the view is so boring aren't you?"

"Yes, well no! It's not boring, it's fantastic, so realistic but yes, I'm wondering why the view is not a little bit over to the right…"

"Well that is so that you can see the real trick of the window, walk over and have a look round to the right."

Both Suzie and I do as she says and it's amazing, the closer we get to the window, the more we can see, this screen is just like a real window. Standing right by it I can easily see the clock tower that Jack described. If I move right over to the left of the screen with my head against the cold glass, it's actually cold like a window and not warm like a viewing screen, looking to the right I can see the bridge with traffic flowing. With my ear against it I can even hear the rumble of the buses and then a real treat, the clock begins to chime the hour, and after the Cambridge Chimes the distinctive cracked bell discordantly strikes eleven. It's like nothing I've ever seen and it renders me totally speechless.

"All of the sleeping quarters that are in the tunnel have a screen like this," explains Lucy, "you can choose from a selection of views but we don't have an endless supply, it depends on what video footage we have gathered from before the war. They're mainly tourist spots, but those were tourist spots for a reason and tend to be the most interesting sights. When we get you settled in you can have a little play."

"Can't wait!" says Suzie.

"Anyway, you've had quite an eventful few days so we're not going to burden you with anything straight away. You're both a little bit ripe, I've already sent Jack off to get freshened up, I'll show you to a shower and then we'll all go and have some lunch. After that I'll find someone to give you the grand tour, by then your quarters should be ready for you and tomorrow we can begin in earnest."

"That sounds great!" I reply, "I'm desperate for a shower and a change of clothes."

We're led through the door at the back of the waiting area and find ourselves in some kind of lobby, there is a row of several doors in front of us across the width of the tunnel. To the right there are a large pair of double doors but the rest are marked with traditional male or female symbols for public toilets. Lucy points to two of them and Suzie and I each enter one of the rooms. Inside it is a perfectly ordinary bathroom, on a chair there is a fresh set of clothes and a large towel, there is also a sack clearly labelled *Dirty Clothes*. I don't bother locking the door but immediately strip off and put my smelly clothes into the bag. I open the glass shower door and step inside, there is just a single button to press on the wall alongside a shower gel dispenser. After an initial icy blast the water settles to a temperature that is just slightly cooler than perfect. The shower seems to run for about a minute for each press of the button and nice though it is to keep pressing it, I'm aware that people are waiting for me so I wash quickly and after less than ten minutes I'm sweet-smelling and dressed.

When I step out of the bathroom, Suzie is not yet out but Lucy is standing with a man who looks vaguely familiar, it takes me several seconds to realise it's Jack without his beard and having had a much needed haircut. It makes him look even younger for his age than he did before, looking down I see that his foot is in some kind of special boot, presumably to hold his ankle in place and aid recovery. When Suzie joins us after another ten minutes or so, we all go through the double doors into a large hall encompassing the full width of the tunnel and about three times as long as its width. Like the garage area the ceiling follows the curve of the tunnel's roof but unlike that room there are two huge *skylights*, each of which is about five metres square, they are very impressive indeed. Lucy explains that they are actually showing a live view of the sky above the mountain although not directly above us, the picture in each is different and we can see the white clouds drifting from one to the other. Just like in the other room there are lights on the ceiling but they're not on, the two screens are providing ample light, the only thing that breaks the illusion of reality is the fact that where the sun is visible in the corner of one of the screens we can't feel its heat as we surely would if we were actually under glass. The whole room is empty save for a single table with four chairs, two along each side in one corner, at first I think this is where we're going to be sitting to eat but apparently not. Lucy says that this is one of three large meeting rooms that they have in the complex, one at each end of the tunnel and one near the centre, the other two are slightly narrower to allow their train to pass but they all have the same image shown on the ceiling windows.

At the far end of the hall there are five sets of double doors, we go through the middle pair into an entrance area, all the doors lead here. Over to the right there is a tiny little train, the track is only about half a metre in gauge and the seats are back to back along the length of the carriages facing to each side. We all take a seat onboard and it sets off further into the tunnel, in some places we are in open areas like where we boarded and in others the train passes through a tunnel within the tunnel. The train doesn't feel like it's moving at all as the track is so smooth and well laid but it is deceptively quick and actually makes me feel a bit travel sick. After less than fifteen minutes we glide silently to a halt in another station similar to that at which we boarded, we are now right at the other end of the tunnel. There is a similar set of double doors which presumably lead into one of the meeting rooms, but we don't go through these, instead we double back on ourselves and walk along a corridor heading back into the mountain. We don't go far before we go through a door into one of their canteens.

It's still fairly early for lunch but the delicious smell that hits my nostrils as Lucy opens the door has my mouth watering. There are a few people collecting food from a self-service counter, there are others seated at various tables but it is by no means busy at the moment. Some of the people are eating things that I would consider to be breakfast but there is quite a selection of food on offer. We can hear the occasional crash and bang from the kitchen but the atmosphere is generally calm and relaxed, the people whose eyes I catch smile at me and I smile back but nobody seems to be bothered by the presence of strangers here. There is a bank of six viewing screen *windows* along one side of the room, the view is that of a big city square I've no idea where, but I don't think it's London. I take a bowl of onion soup and a nice chunk of buttered bread, Jack satisfies a craving he's had for a while and indulges in a bacon sandwich. We all sit down at a vacant table, while we eat and then get a main course and dessert the room gradually fills and when we finally get up to go our table is taken straight away.

When we leave the canteen we head along a corridor that runs alongside the small railway and once we've passed the meeting room at this end of the tunnel we are in another area similar to the vehicle maintenance area at the other end. There are no vehicles here though, except when the train happens to be passing through, the main difference is the fact that the end of the tunnel is open here. We are looking out onto a winding road that leads down the hill, there are buildings either side, but it's nothing like one of the settlements that I've been used to. The buildings aren't all the same; they differ not only in colour but also in style and the means in which they've been built. Some are stone, others are brick, many are made out of wood, on the roofs there are tiles of several different colours as well as shingles and one of the buildings has a roof that appears to be made out of grass. Never before have I seen such variety of architecture, even in pictures of Luxburg, but it all fits together well and is a lot more pleasing on the eye that the regimented similarity back home.

The Village as Jack and Lucy call it now houses the majority of their population, in reality it is far larger than anything that would ever be classed as a village, but it needs to be. As of this year, their population stands at more than ten thousand, just under half of whom are children, even allowing for that this *village* has five times the population of a standard settlement. It's amazing! During the course of the afternoon Suzie and I are left with Stephen and Julie as Jack and Lucy have various things to sort out. Stephen is twenty and Julie is nineteen and they were both born in this community, they live together but they are not married. They have chosen to be together, they have not been assigned to each other, they don't have any children as they consider themselves to be too young at the moment, they want to live a little first. They begin the tour by showing us their own little cottage, it is one of the smallest wooden houses and is in total contrast to the houses that we're used to. Ours are comparatively spacious but soulless, this has only a single room downstairs that doubles as a sitting room and kitchen but it is filled with the character of our two young hosts with ornaments and trinkets everywhere. Upstairs there is a single bedroom under the eaves with a stained glass dormer window shining a colourful pattern across the bedspread. We duck through a low door into a small bathroom where Stephen shows off his efforts at tiling with justified pride.

They show us around the whole of the village, showing us in shops and other public places as well as visiting some of their friends. We visit a school, one of several and captivate a class with the story of our journey. Everywhere we go all the people we meet are so friendly, so much so that in the space of a few hours we both feel that we've come home. We finish our tour with the tunnel itself, this, while not as homely as the village and much more like the kind of environment we've been used to in the past, is every bit as interesting. There are huge labs where technical development is going on, a hospital, as well as the bulk of all the manufacturing. The only major industry that is not in the tunnel is the farming for obviously reasons, but even so a fair amount of the packaging and preserving and cooking goes on in here. We finish our tour with only Julie as Stephen has to begin a night shift in one of the electronics labs, we are starting to feel tired by the time she takes us to Lucy's office and bids us farewell.

Lucy is also looking tired when she looks up from a desk full of papers. She takes us to the canteen again, a different one from the one that we used earlier and we all enjoy a rather nice meal of fish and chips, this apparently was once a very popular British meal and was traditional for a Friday. After this she shows us to our quarters herself, we are housed in sleeping quarters in the tunnel along with the majority of the people who are single. Most, but not all of the couples rent houses in the village and most people live in the tunnel quarters until they pair off but there are no rules governing this at all. Suzie and I are given adjacent rooms on the first floor, these are slightly smaller than the ground floor apartments due to the curvature of the roof but they both have the promised *windows*. There are a selection of spare clothes and toiletries laid out for each of us, the apartments each consist of one large room with a bed and sofa as well as a small desk and chair with a separate bathroom, not large but perfectly adequate. We say good night to Lucy arranging to meet in the canteen in the morning and then Suzie and I have a long relieved hug, sharing our gladness at having come here before turning in for the night.

Chapter 17

Saturday 1ˢᵗ July 53

The sun streaming in through the window wakes me from a pleasant sleep, I've been dreaming but before I can remember any details the lingering memory fades to nothing. It takes me a while to realise where I am and when I do I gaze up at the window that isn't a window, all I can see from the bed is a pure blue sky. Slowly I get up and wander over to the window, I'm at or near the top of a very tall building overlooking a vast city, it's not London. Along the bottom of the window frame I find the control for the display, it consists of a miniature touch screen just like that on Jack's portable device. It is displaying a still picture of the view that is currently showing as well as a description which says "View from Eiffel Tower", there are also four buttons with arrows pointing up, down, left and right, touching these moves the position of the window within the display. This allows me to look right up at the sky or almost vertically downwards which makes me feel a little sick, more interestingly I can move the view round through a full circle effectively allowing me to put the window on any side of the building. The building appears to be a metal structure with little or no accommodation, simply built for the sake of the view I suppose. I play with this for a little while before touching the button marked *Next*.

The view fades to total darkness and then fades back to a different view, this one is captioned as *View from Elizabeth Tower*, it would seem that these scenes are very imaginatively named. This one I recognise as being London, I appear to be in the clock tower that I viewed from ground level on the other side of the river, yesterday morning. I don't get a chance to do any more playing as there's a knock at the door. I walk over and open the door, the only lock on this is a mechanical one and the key is sitting in the lock on the inside of the door. I hadn't locked it last night, an easy mistake to make having been used to automatic locks and restrictions on access. Suzie steps into the room full of enthusiasm.

"It's great here isn't it? Did you sleep OK? My bed was so comfortable, I can't remember the last time I had such a good night!"

"Yes, it's great, but I wish I knew what they want me for. What could I possibly do for them that the thousands of people that are already here can't?"

"I don't know, but I'm sure they'll tell you when they're ready. It's not as if we've been used to being told anything in the past, the orders from Luxburg are always a surprise come the summer solstice."

"I suppose so, well yes, but even so I thought they'd be desperate to fill me in having dragged us half way across the country!"

"Just be patient. Have you had a play with the window yet?"

"Yes, I was just looking at it when you knocked. I've only looked at two different views so far, I only woke up a couple of minutes ago."

We both go over to the window and start to flick through the scenes, most of them seem to be views from tall towers but there are others as well including great parks. One called *View from Arc De Triomphe* is obviously in the same city as the first scene that I encountered as I can see the other tower from here, the thing that I find incredible is how busy it is. There is a constant mass of cars very similar to the ones that we've travelled in moving around the base of the tower, the sheer number of people that used to live here is so hard to comprehend. Some of the views are more restricted as to moving the viewing position, presumably depending upon the scope of the original recording. I find a few which won't move at all, one of these is of a street lined with shops, so many shops, the pavements full of people clutching bags with long sticks of freshly-baked bread, so much has totally vanished. I wonder if we'll ever get back to a population anything like what we once had or whether we're doomed to disappear, the end of human civilisation.

We continue flicking through the views on the window until we wrap around back to the beginning. One of the most surprising images was that of the square in Luxburg overlooking the main Europarl building, there is no means of moving the view which makes me wonder if this is actually a live camera. Suzie agrees with me, she thinks that the shopping street is also a live view of Luxburg. We switch back to them one after the other and the sky does indeed look remarkably similar in each, could it possibly be true? I don't see how it can, but we decide to ask Lucy or Jack when we meet them for breakfast. It's nearly time to go down so Suzie goes back to her room to get washed and dressed while I do the same. It's seems almost like a luxury to be able to put on a different set of clothes, living as we have for what seems like ages but is actually less than a week, in the same dirty smelly clothes. The real novelty though, is not their cleanliness but the fact that they are different, even the socks that I pull out of my top drawer are navy blue rather than the black ones that I wore yesterday. It takes me a little while to find a pair of trousers that look good with the pale green shirt that I've chosen, so long in fact that Suzie is ready and bursts in while I'm only half dressed.

We manage to find the canteen without much trouble, arriving just before the agreed time of nine o'clock. Lucy and Jack are both already seated at a table together when we walk in but neither of them have any food as yet, they both smile broadly and get up. All of us serve ourselves from the buffet and once we're sat at a table and tucking in, Suzie asks Lucy about the views on the window.

"That's very perceptive," she replies, "you're absolutely right both of those views are from cameras planted by our operatives in Luxburg. They're actually showing live pictures of what's going on in Luxburg right now! Well not quite live, if the transmissions were powerful enough for us to receive here they would be spotted by Europarl very quickly. The actual signal from those cameras is encrypted and transmitted continuously on Luxburg's own wireless network, the same network that connects all their computers. We've then got a small receiving station right on the edge of the transmission area that overlays our transmission onto the railway's electrical supply. This is then picked up in our charging garage at Reims and beamed to us here via a powerful and very directional transmitter, it's all very clever but the various transitions mean there's a delay of about twenty seconds. It was worked out by Andy our electronics whizz, there's been no hint that it's been discovered either."

"We met him on the way here; he seems to be a useful chap."

"Useful is putting it mildly, in many ways we're more technologically advanced than Europarl themselves and that's nearly all thanks to him. Of course it's a lot harder for us to get hold of some of the components that we need, there's a certain amount of make do and mend. It's too risky to take too much that hasn't already been thrown away, even an organisation as large as Europarl will spot a high level of loss. Although we have ways of influencing what actually gets thrown away if we especially need something."

"I'm really looking forward to getting started with whatever it is you've got planned for me!"

"All in good time Ed, you've only just got here. I think it would be a good idea for you two to spend at least today wandering around the village. Meeting people, get the feel of the place and we can start with the serious stuff tomorrow or Monday."

"If you think that's best…"

"Oh yes, it's definitely best. Once you've finished eating you should head over to the village hall, there'll be lots going on there."

We finish off our breakfast and then leave Jack and Lucy to it. We are only a short walk from the end of the tunnel, but as we come out of the canteen the train arrives so we hop on. The train itself is very interesting, it runs without a driver from one end of the track to the other stopping briefly at each designated station. It monitors people getting on and off and never seems to leave while people are still boarding. Their electricity supply is ample for their needs coming from three separate sources, they have a huge bank of solar panels on the southern facing slope of Mont Blanc itself, wind turbines near the top and hydro-generation on three separate rivers. The train quickly delivers us to the main entrance hallway on the Italian end of the tunnel, we get off and head out into the morning sunshine. It's pleasantly warm but not hot, we walk down the hill past the houses taking in their variety once again. Every now and again we pass people on the path and without exception they greet us with a smile and a friendly "good morning". I realise that I'm already thinking of this as my home, for the first time in my life I feel like I belong. Of course I never had a chance to settle into Sevenoaks but before that I'd lived my whole life in Chelmsford and yet it never felt like home. The only thing that is missing here is family but the people are so friendly that they feel like an extended family and I really feel that I can bring up my own family here one day.

The further we get from the tunnel mouth the steeper the path gets, the houses further down the slope are more spread out. Some of them have nicely tended gardens with a glorious display of flowers, others have grassed areas surrounding them with folding chairs and parasols set out. We get to Stephen and Julie's house just before the curve of the path where it turns through almost a hundred and eighty degrees and continues down the hill. She's in the garden tending to her plants; we greet her and say that we're heading to the village hall. She says that she and Stephen will probably see us there when he's out of bed, as he didn't get in from work until just after six o'clock this morning she thinks that'll probably be about eleven as he's not working this evening. We carry on round the bend and down the hill and we get to the next turning point which is only about two hundred metres away from the main tunnel entrance but quite a lot lower down the hillside. Here is the *Village Hall* which is in fact another tunnel, although compared with the main tunnel which is over eleven kilometres long this at a mere two hundred metres or so is tiny. This tunnel however has been set up as a single space so it seems huge, indeed it is larger than the large meeting rooms in the main tunnel.

We step through the main doors into the hum of excited chatter. There are various groups of people of all ages dotted around the vast area doing various different things. By the entrance is a small desk with a young man seated behind it, he has a list of all the activities available.

"Hi guys!" he greets us. "You're new here aren't you? I'm Jimmy, now let's see if we can find something you fancy. We've got all sorts different things that you can try, various life skills like cooking or gardening. Or there's keep fit, we have loads of gym equipment and instructors. Ah I know, you're just in time for the film…"

"The film?"

"Yes you know, the cinema?"

"Cinema?"

"Oh, you really are completely new aren't you! Trust me, you'll love it, right to the back of the hall and through the double doors."

With that, he's finished and is welcoming another group slightly younger than us. We walk down the centre of the tunnel and my initial impression of the hall appears to be wrong, the whole back wall that I had taken as being glass, just like that through which we entered is in fact a giant example of their fake windows. As we reach the doors I can see that it is made up of quite a few individual panels but the matching of the pictures between them is flawless. We step through the doors into a totally different environment. It's almost completely dark, but once our eyes have adjusted to the relative gloom we can see that there are about ten long rows of staged seating facing some tall red curtains with an aisle down the centre and another on either side. About half the seats are occupied, but before we get a chance to choose a place the lights all dim abruptly to almost nothing and the curtains begin to open. Hurriedly we shuffle over to the closest seats and sit.

There is a fanfare of trumpets and an image appears, projected on the screen that had previously been hidden by the curtains which are now fully open, I can read the words but they have no meaning

20th CENTURY FOX

Then there is a sudden crescendo of a full orchestra and some blue text appears

A long time ago in a galaxy far, far away. . . .

From that moment on I am totally hooked, this is incredible, a story of good against evil with the goodies finally winning by the skin of their teeth. Technically the picture is not even as good as the viewing screens that I've been used to, let alone the fake windows but it is still nothing short of spectacular. When we finally emerge, blinking, from the cinema we're dazzled by the daylight. I can see that Suzie has felt the same awe that I have, this is entertainment on a scale that just doesn't exist anymore. The film that we have watched is over a hundred years old but the story is the same as what faces us right here and right now. I'm starting to wonder whether *making a difference* is something that only happens in stories. Even though I'm still unaware of how I fit into place, I like being here; I can live quite happily here.

They're showing another film in a little while, but as much as we enjoyed ourselves, to go straight back in for a second helping would devalue the experience. We wander back through the large area looking at the groups of people doing what they've chosen; suddenly we hear our names being called from behind. Turning around to look, Julie is skipping through the crowd of people leaving the cinema, dragging an embarrassed and tired looking Stephen behind her. Catching us up she greets us breathlessly and suggests that we go together to get something to eat which seems like a good idea to me. Instead of heading back up the hill, Julie leads us in the opposite direction and a couple of minutes later we are all sitting around an outside table at a small café. In the shade of a brightly coloured parasol we glance at the menu, it's not very extensive consisting only of sandwiches with various fillings available but after finding out what sort of things Suzie and I like, Julie orders our lunch enthusiastically and with a knowing smile.

When our food arrives it is rather more special than the menu would have you believe, the bread is freshly baked and absolutely perfect. It's very difficult to avoid making noises of appreciation whilst eating. As we finish off our lunch Julie suggests that this afternoon she and Suzie go off together and do *girl things*, leaving Stephen and me to do whatever we fancy. I agree that it's a good idea and Stephen says there's a great stream in which we can go and fish, he has a spare rod for me so that's settled. We leave the café and head back up the hill, the girls go back into the village hall but Stephen and I carry on up to their house. I wait outside and admire Julie's handiwork in the garden whilst he goes in to collect the equipment. He takes a little longer than I expect but presently he comes out again struggling with two rods, two folding chairs one of which is pink and decorated with flowers, presumably I'm borrowing Julie's chair, he also has a rather large rucksack on his back. Abruptly I'm handed both of the chairs and we head off down the hill once again.

A little way past the café we turn off the main pathway and make our way down a steep winding track between the trees, it gets steeper as we make our way down and just as I'm contemplating holding onto the trees for support we break out onto the bank of what could be described as a large stream or a very small river. Despite the mountainous terrain it is fairly calm and slow flowing at this point, there is a faster flowing stretch about half a kilometre upstream which we can hear but not see, this is where some of their hydropower equipment is situated. I unfold the chairs and Stephen takes off his rucksack which looks incredibly heavy and sets it down along with the rods, he takes a seat and I follow suit, then he shows me how to set up the rod. He shows me how to cast the line and after a few practice throws I begin to get the hang of it, at that point we bait our hooks with maggots that he has in a small tin in his pocket and cast them out for real. I'm beginning to wonder about the rucksack which has been untouched since we arrived. He opens the top of the pack and passes me a y-shaped piece of metal, taking another for himself he pushes it into the ground and rests his rod on it, I do the same.

Then the real reason for the large rucksack and also its apparent weight becomes clear, he removes two bottles and passes me one with a smile. They're beer, nice and cold too, I unscrew mine and the pale liquid fizzes out of the top slightly. I've never tasted beer before, in fact the only alcoholic drink I've ever had has been the fizzy wine for the toast at the Human Rights celebrations every year. This is much less sweet but is pleasant enough and the second bottle goes down even better. After the second bottle I feel a little peculiar, my senses are slightly dulled and when I see the line on my fishing rod being tugged it takes me a little while to realise. After half a minute or so I manage to reel in the line and surprisingly the fish is still attached. Stephen shows me how to remove the hook without harming the fish, it's too small to warrant keeping so we throw it back into the water. This afternoon is the most relaxing time I've had for a while, possibly the most relaxing time ever. When we pack up our things to head back up the hill a few hours later we have quite a few fish to show for our effort. The best thing though, is that I feel Stephen and I have got to know each other, that I've made a friend.

Whilst Stephen drank most of the beer, it seems to have affected me rather more and it's much more of an effort to get back up the track than it was coming down. When we get back to Stephen and Julie's house the girls are already there and have a meal ready for us, all we have to do is prepare the fish and cook it over the barbecue that is already lit in the corner of the garden. Stephen does this with ease and before long we're enjoying a fantastic homemade dinner with another beer to wash it down. When Suzie and I finally head back up to the main tunnel it's not especially late but I can definitely hear my bed calling me. When we get inside the train is not there and as our quarters are only a short distance into the tunnel we carry on walking, we are just climbing the staircase when we hear it pass. A couple of minutes later we arrive at our adjacent doors, we say 'goodnight' but then as Suzie is just about to go inside I have a sudden urge to kiss her. She kisses me back and smiles, then she tells me not to do anything I'll regret in the morning and with a wink she's gone. I go into my room and lie down on the bed without bothering to undress and within seconds I'm fast asleep.

Chapter 18

Sunday 2nd July 53

It's quite early when I wake up, I have a bit of a headache and I'm desperate for a drink. I jump out of bed and that's when the true extent of my headache reveals itself, I drag myself slowly into the bathroom and put my mouth under the running water and slurp greedily. It seems like I'm drinking for ages but it can't actually be any more than a minute, I turn off the tap and look at myself in the mirror behind the sink. I'm not looking my best, my eyes are slightly bloodshot but since my drink I feel a bit better although I still have quite an unpleasant pounding in my head. What I really need is some paracetamol, I open the cabinet without much hope but there inside is a likely looking bottle. I read the label, it says *Aspirin* which I've never heard of but the other text would imply that it will do the same job as what I have been used to. I take a couple and wash them down with another blast from the tap and decide to take a shower whilst I wait for them to take effect.

Fifteen minutes later I'm feeling a lot better; I get out of the shower and dry myself off before getting dressed. It's still early but I'm so excited about finding out the reason why I'm here that I don't let the early hour worry me, so I go next door to wake up Suzie. The instant I raise my hand to tap on her door it bursts open and there she is fully dressed.

"I thought you'd be up early today, come on, let's go and get some breakfast!"

"How do you do that?"

"Do what?"

"Know exactly what I'm going to do, even when I don't really know myself?"

"I can read you like a book, come on!"

We make our way down to the canteen. Even with the time just before seven, there are a few people eating here including Lucy much to my surprise. She smiles as we enter and when we've filled our plates we sit down at the same table.

"I thought you'd be here early this morning!" says Lucy. "Once we've finished eating we'll go to my office, until then not a word about it. Julie's expecting you down at her place Suzie."

"I can't come with Ed then?"

"Not this time, this is just for Ed at the moment, it's going to be a lot for him to take in so it's going to be best with as few distractions as possible."

Suzie leaves it at that with a slight frown but doesn't push the point, I'm now feeling a little apprehensive about the whole thing. It's a miracle that I manage to finish my breakfast. The three of us leave the canteen together but then Suzie heads off on her own to find Julie while Lucy and I go in the opposite direction to her office. It's not yet eight o'clock when we sit down, Lucy doesn't seem eager to get started but just as I'm about to break the awkward silence there is a knock at the door and Jack comes in. It seems like ages since I last saw him although it's actually only about a day, I suppose I'd become so used to him being around all the time that it feels longer. Jack sits down next to me and Lucy touches a panel on her desk, a picture appears on the wall to my left, it gives me a really strange feeling because of the mixture of familiarity and unfamiliarity. Lucy addresses me while I'm still mildly shocked.

"Do you recognise that picture?"

"Parts of it, there's me in the middle but I'm with the president of Europarl and his wife and we're standing on the steps of the main Europarl building. It can't be a real picture because I've never been there and I've never met them."

Lucy and Jack are now grinning broadly, she carries on.

"Ed, that is a real photograph but the person in the middle is not you, he's the president's son and the heir to the presidency. It's uncanny but he is the spitting image of you, that is why you're so valuable to our cause. If we can make a switch, get you into Luxburg as the heir then you can facilitate change, you can bring about reform when you become the president!"

My brain is in overdrive, I'm aware that my mouth is hanging open but I can't say anything. So I look a bit like the president's son, well

I look exactly like the president's son, so like him that I'm even fooled myself, but there's no way I can just be put in his place. Any person is far more than what they happen to look like, I don't have his experiences, I don't know any of the people he knows, I won't speak the same way as he does. Then there's my hatred of the president and all he stands for, this is never going to work!

"Ed, I can see by the look on your face that you don't believe you can do this, but you won't be on your own. We have plenty of information and we have just about enough time, you're roughly the same age as Benoit Gilles but he was born on the summer solstice which means we only have until next summer before he or rather you will be assigned a junior post in Europarl. We need to get you in before then so that you work through the system in the usual way and when you replace President Michael Gilles you'll be ready for the job. We also have other people in Europarl, quite a few in fact, they'll be there to help you all the time. Most importantly, ever since we became aware of your presence and this opportunity we've concentrated on getting some of our people to become friends with Benoit. They will help significantly when we make the switch. It's not going to be easy for you, but you can do it."

"What about my voice? I'm sure I don't speak the way he does."

"You're right, but we have recordings, it will be no different than what actors used to do to get into character for a play or a film, you'll be learning a part."

"Maybe. Surely his family will spot me as an imposter, what about medical records, things like that, finger prints even?"

"That's the biggest risk but even that is small as you look so alike, anything that you do differently will be attributed to a change of attitude, they really won't be expecting a swap. The medical records will be switched as well, Benoit hasn't had any significant operations or anything like that so there's no risk of you having your appendix removed twice or anything like that! He happens to have the same blood group as you so that's not a problem, there are no DNA records although if you were ever to get tested there's a possibility of discovery as obviously Michael and Anais Gilles are not your parents but there's no reason to suppose that this is going to happen."

"How are you proposing to get me in?"

"We have a plan in place, but because of the nature of the plan it will have the best chance of success if you don't know how it's going to be achieved."

"What about Suzie, will she be able to come too?"

"Not straight away, no. We should be able to get her in at next year's Human Rights Celebrations. We're anticipating doing the switch sometime in January or February so it will only be a matter of a few months."

"Okay, there's no reason not to do this. When do we start?"

"Right now. Jack will take you to your office where you'll have access to all the information that is available but from now on everyone will refer to you as Benoit, you have to live the part."

"It's going to be hard work getting used to a different name."

Jack and I get up and he leads me along the corridor to my office which is not far away from Lucy's, on the door is a plaque that reads *Benoit Eduard Gilles*. Jack opens the door and stands aside to let me walk in. The office is slightly smaller than Lucy's, there is a single window behind the desk that shows the now familiar view of the square outside the Europarl building. There is a large viewing screen on the desk and I sit down in front of it. Jack asks if I'd like him to stay for a while or whether I'd rather be left. Sensing my indecision he makes the choice for me and gets up to leave, saying that he'll come back at lunchtime to see how I'm getting on. Left to my own devices I touch the screen and it fades into life, the display is showing a picture of Benoit. It's uncanny, I really could be looking at a picture of myself, maybe this crazy plan really can be made to work. I start to read through his biography, it covers all sorts of details including such things as favourite foods, some of these are things that I've never even heard of let alone tasted. The thought occurs to me that I'm going to need to taste all of these things or at the very least learn to recognise them, it could be a real problem if I'm offered something that's *my favourite* and I don't even realise. There is a huge amount of information available to me, I know Lucy said that we have enough time but I'm really not so sure.

I jump out of my skin when Jack knocks at the door and comes in, I hadn't noticed the passing of the morning. Jack asks if I'm hungry and I realise that I am very hungry indeed, I've also not drunk anything since breakfast. I'm just about to get up to go with Jack to the canteen when it occurs to me that it might be a good idea to note down some of Benoit's favourites, I ask Jack if he thinks the canteen is up to it. As usual, they're one step ahead of me, as part of my training the canteen has been instructed to do this anyway, in fact from now on I don't have a choice with regard to what appears on my plate. Even Europarl's regime didn't extend to dictating everything I eat, I can see that the next few months are not going to be easy at all. We get to the canteen and with a sense of resignation I approach the serving window, the head cook hands me a tray with a smile. There is a little card beside the plate which says *Judd mat*

Gaardebounen but underneath is written a little explanation which says that it is *smoked collar of pork with broad beans (a traditional dish from Luxburg)*. I don't know what language the name of the dish is, but I do know that before the war many of the different countries that now make up the U.S.E. had their own languages so this could well be Luxburgish if there ever was such a thing.

Jack and I sit down together at a table, he also has pork but his is roast and served with roast potatoes, other vegetables and gravy. Nevertheless I pick up a fork and tuck in, it's actually very nice indeed, maybe this is going to be easier than I'd expected. Jack asks me how I've got on this morning and I tell him about my morning of reading. He seems quite enthusiastic about the way I've settled into the task at hand. We return to the hatch once again to get a dessert, I have a small individual tart which is called *Quetschentaart* but is just a fairly ordinary plum tart which is harmless enough. When we finish eating Jack comes back with me to my office and points me in the direction of some recordings of Benoit talking. The tone of his voice is the same as mine but his accent is different, not remarkably so but I will sound really strange to the people who know him unless I work on that. The display on my desk shows the sound waves of his speech on screen, when I say the same thing it overlays the display of my own speech and shows a percentage match. If I speak in my normal manner this is consistently in the sixties, with a supreme effort on one phrase I am able to reach ninety-five percent which Jack says will be fine if I can make all the things I say hit that level.

I spend the rest of the afternoon after Jack has left practising and it starts to become significantly easier as the day wears on. I've just about finished for the day when there's a knock at the door, it opens straight away and Suzie pops her head round, I tell her to come in and she remarks that I'm already starting to sound different. We go to the canteen again and get our dinner, mine is specially arranged as expected and compared with what I've been eating since I became Benoit is fairly ordinary, steak and chips. The main difference being that it is very rare indeed whereas I would normally have it well done, once I overcome my initial misgivings I realise that it is actually much nicer that way. While we're eating Suzie mentions that there's another film showing in the cinema this evening so after we've finished our meal we head out to the village again. This evening's film after starting in exactly the same way as yesterday's with a fanfare of trumpets and those same words *20th CENTURY FOX*, is totally different from then on. This one is called *Home Alone* and after a slightly slow start, the final half hour or so has me and many others in the cinema laughing out loud.

It's starting to get dark as we head back up the hill to the main tunnel entrance; we walk hand in hand laughing about the film. There are some benches just outside the tunnel and rather than go straight inside we decide to sit down on one of these the watch the sun set in a gap between the mountains. It's a perfect end to the evening until I start to think about going to Luxburg. A few months seems like a long time after the whirlwind few weeks that we've just had but I know that it's going to go very quickly, then I'm going to be on my own. Maybe not actually on my own, as we have people in Luxburg but Suzie won't be there at the beginning, when I'll be struggling to play the part of the president's son and heir. I know things will get easier as time goes on but it seems to me that this plan is going to take a long time to come to fruition. It's going to be several years before I'm involved in anything of any importance at all, but it's going to be many years before I have any actual power, before I can actually start to do anything. I notice Suzie looking at me quizzically and I force a smile to replace my contemplative frown, but as usual she's already read my mind.

"You'll be fine!" she says. "There are plenty of people who'll be there to help you, I can tell how hard you're working, you've already started to change the way you speak and it's only day one! You really should have a little bit more confidence in your own abilities, look how far you've come in the last couple of weeks. Remember that if it weren't for you, I'd still be stuck in Sevenoaks."

"That's not true, you're so much more suited to this than I am. You'd have found these guys all by yourself, if they'd not been looking for me, if it weren't for Jack I'd never have been here at all."

"However you came to be here, you're important to the cause."

"What if the cause is wrong?"

"How do you mean wrong? That implies that Luxburg's regime is right!"

"Not at all, maybe it's not possible to rule the country well. What if the current system really is the best, the best of a bad lot? There hasn't been a war for fifty-three years!"

"Only because there's nobody left to fight one. Anyway, I don't think we should talk about this anymore, I want to enjoy myself while you're still here. We should make the most of the freedom we have here, I know I've got a bit more freedom than you but even so you've still got more freedom than you've ever had before."

"You're right, come on, let's go inside. It's starting to get a bit cold."

We get up from the bench and go into the main entrance hallway, the train is sitting there and we hop onto it. The moment we're seated it sets off smoothly into the tunnel, a very short ride later it glides to a halt by the now familiar canteen. We decide to go in and see what kind of food is available for a quick snack before bed. There are a few people sitting around in small groups but nobody I recognise, we approach the counter and are surprised to see that a full menu is available. We decide to share a plate of chips, Suzie does the ordering just in case my request is rejected on the grounds that Benoit wouldn't be eating chips at this time of the evening, but the cook on duty doesn't bat an eyelid anyway. We go and sit in a quiet corner, grabbing a pot of tomato ketchup and a couple of drinks on the way over, the chips are fabulous. After we've finished them off we sit quietly for a while before heading up to our quarters. We kiss again in the corridor before turning in and this time it seems much more natural and lasts a lot longer than last night but again I'm not allowed to follow her in. Sleep comes to me easily however, after such an intensive day.

Chapter 19

Friday 5th January 54

I wake up early, the window is showing a live view of the mountain outside, it's still dark but the sky is clear and I can see the deep snow glistening in the starlight. I have now been here over six months and it feels like home, this is a bad thing because it means the wrench when I leave is going to be so much worse. But what I'm really dreading is leaving Suzie behind, ever since we were thrown together we've been close but we've grown closer still until now I feel like I'm going to be leaving part of me behind. In a way of course I've already done that, I speak with a Luxburg accent. Not only that I speak with Benoit Eduard Gille's Luxburg accent, I'm no longer Ed Bush, if someone called my old name I probably wouldn't even turn around. I'm fully in character and I'm ready, however the fact remains that I don't want to say goodbye to Suzie but in less than two hours that is exactly what I'm going to have to do. It's going to be the hardest thing I've ever done but then tomorrow I begin another phase of my life and will be doing something even harder. I'll be entering Luxburg and becoming Benoit for real and I still don't know how the switch is going to be done.

I get up and head for the shower, my face is itchy because of my stubble but I can't shave because Benoit has decided to try and grow a beard and a sudden loss of facial hair would be a bit of a giveaway. As soon as I'm in place though, it's going! I'm not especially happy with my hairstyle either, I suppose simply because it is a *style*. Until I came here when my hair got too long I got dad or Jim to go over it with the clippers once every month or so and I did the same for them but in Luxburg things are different. Since I've been in character we've been monitoring Benoit for changes to ensure that the swap will be as unobtrusive as possible to those around him and he's at the hairdresser's every other week. This means that last week my hair was cut to match his so that I'll be ready to step in. Once I'm dressed, despite the fact that it's only just after six I go next door to see Suzie. For the first time ever she's not already awake, it takes her a couple of minutes to open the door but she's still pleased to see me and I get a quick kiss. I sit on her bed and we have a conversation through the door while she gets ready in the bathroom. Then we head down to the canteen to have our last breakfast together for several months at least.

As we approach the counter the cook on duty greets me, saying "Morning Benoit, big day today then!"

I smile as he hands me my usual breakfast tray and go to find an empty table, Suzie joins me with her fried eggs and bacon as I bite into a croissant. She's done this deliberately judging by the grin on her face but I let her off because I think she's probably going to have a worse wait until we're together again than I am, at least I'll be getting on with what I came here for. We finish eating just after seven o'clock and we head to Lucy's office together. Lucy and Jack are already there as well as Andy who will be accompanying me to Luxburg, I've only seen him a few times since I've been here as he spends most of his time locked away in a lab when he's not out and about. There are two spare seats for me and Suzie which we take without being told and Lucy addresses me.

"So Benoit, this is it, the moment of truth. I know you can make this work as you've really worked so hard over the last five months. Are you all set?"

"Yes, I'm as prepared as I can be. All I need to know now is the plan."

"You already know as much of the plan as you need to, you'll be travelling down to Reims today with Andy. You'll be staying overnight in the charging garage there and tomorrow you'll be heading on to Luxburg. Everything is set to make the switch early tomorrow evening, all you need to do is go along for the ride."

"I suppose so, I just wish I knew."

"Believe me, it's best that you don't" says Andy with a wink, "anyway it's time to get going. I assume you're going to come with us to the garage Suzie?"

"Just try and stop me!" she replies.

I guess I'll just have to drop it, but I have a definite feeling of being in the dark about something that everyone else knows in intricate detail. Jack and Lucy wish me a final good luck and the three of us leave Lucy's office and head to the internal train. We have to wait for it to head to the Italian end of the tunnel before it collects us on its return to the French end. Less than fifteen minutes later we're back at the other end of the tunnel, unbelievably I've not been here since arriving last summer. As we walk through the hall which so impressed me first time around I can't help looking up at the skylights, it's fair to say that they were much better the first time around when there was a blue sky with gently drifting clouds. Today it's just shades of grey, we don't linger but pass straight through the doors at the far end, then through the waiting area where I first saw one of the windows. Here there are thick insulated all in one suits and protective helmets for me and Andy to wear on our journey, it's going to be a very different experience from the inward journey.

Before I put these on I turn to face Suzie, she's smiling at me but there are tears streaming down her face. That's all it takes to make me cry too, it feels a little embarrassing until I look around and see that Andy has left us to it. I put my arms around her, hold her close and let the tears flow. Time stands still while we slowly gain control of our breathing, then it happens Suzie whispers it but I hear it clearly.

"I love you…"

"I love you too, I'm going to miss you so much. Roll on June…"

"Yes, I be with you before you know it. Now you'd better go, be safe."

With that we kiss one last time then I put on my insulated suit and pick up my helmet which has a pair of gloves tucked inside. I open the door to the garage and it's like stepping into the fridge or even a freezer but I only feel it on my face and hands, the jacket is remarkably good at keeping my body warm. In spite of the cold Suzie follows me through, by the main entrance door Andy is sitting on a strange vehicle, one of his hands is resting on the handlebars which are connected to a curved skid. There is a saddle in the centre with room for a single passenger behind the driver, behind that is a large boxy structure presumably containing the batteries and this whole section sits upon a single track driven by a series of several wheels inside. I put on my gloves and helmet, blowing Suzie a kiss as I lower the tinted visor and awkwardly clamber into my seat behind Andy.

"Don't worry," says Andy through a communication device that is evidently built into our helmets, "we're not travelling like this all the way, only while we're in the thick snow. There's a normal car waiting for us about a third of the way to Reims."

"I'm relieved to hear that, this doesn't seem all that comfortable."

"You wait until we're moving!"

With that he flicks a switch on the frame in front of him, twists the right hand grip towards himself and with a whine of an electric motor and a scrape of the metal skid across the concrete floor we head out through the garage door. I glance behind and wave to Suzie as we go, once outside we're on thick packed snow and ice and the movement is much quieter, just a slight rattle from the track and the hum of the motor but Andy's right, it's really bumpy. I'm glad that he's driving and not me as I can barely make out the track, luckily it's not snowing at the moment but there's a definite threat in the clouds. There is no readout of speed that I can see but it feels as though we're going quite fast, too fast in fact. After narrowly missing a tree at the edge of the track there's a perceptible drop in speed, we make our way gradually down the mountain. I find that I'm more comfortable with my eyes closed as this way I don't see the huge drops on alternating sides of the road but after a while of travelling like this I find myself on the edge of sleeping so I force my eyes open once again. Looking behind I can barely see anything, the top of the mountain is veiled in low cloud but it seems to be slightly brighter ahead of us. Instead of dwelling on the mountain road's dangerous nature I focus my eyes on the back of Andy's head and my brain on being Benoit.

As the journey progresses the track that we are following gradually starts to get easier and we are able to increase our speed little by little. After we've been travelling for about an hour there is noticeably less snow and more trees around us. I'm starting to get a little bit stiff so I ask Andy if we can take a break, he eases the speed down and we come to a halt. I struggle to get my leg across the saddle and I have pins and needles in my right foot, Andy jumps off seemingly without any trouble at all. I decide to take off my gloves to flex my fingers but change my mind after removing only one, it's still very cold. We both walk around a little bit swinging our arms and then get back on, Andy says that we only have just over a hundred kilometres to go before we reach the car. As we pull down our visors to set off again a few flakes of snow begin to flutter down around us, unfortunately this soon turns into a fairly steady fall. This restricts visibility quite badly meaning we're not even travelling at half the speed that we were until we stopped. We also have to keep clearing the snow that builds up on our visors.

Fortunately after little more than half an hour the snow stops and we're able to pick up speed once again. Although the weather is not that great for travelling from a comfort point of view, the fact that there is snow on the ground evening out the potholed track, we're on a vehicle designed with this kind of weather in mind and we're going downhill combine to mean that we are actually making far faster progress than when I made this journey the other way. All of a sudden Andy's voice bursts into my thoughts, he says we're probably close enough to the car now to be able to get a reading from it on his mobile device so we come to a halt once again so that he can retrieve it from the inside pocket of his suit. He has to take off one of his gloves to work the screen with a finger tip, when he gets the right mode activated there is an arrow pointing almost straight ahead and beside that it says the distance, just over three and a half kilometres. There's nowhere near as much snow now, looking into the woodland at the sides of the track it is possible to see small patches of dark brown earthy ground breaking the continuous white blanket. He hands me the device and puts his glove back on before setting off again with me watching the numbers on the screen count downwards.

When it gets down to five hundred metres I tell Andy and he slows right down, we don't know exactly where the car is going to be and it could be a little way from the track itself. When we're fifty metres away we slow down to a walking pace just in case and I can see that the direction of the arrow is pointing away to the right of the track, the distance goes down to twelve metres and then starts to increase again so we stop. Peering into the woods in the direction of the arrow I can't see anything that looks like a car, we get off and start to walk carefully through the snow. Having walked past several trees we're in a relatively small clearing and there in the middle is a white mound, the whole car is covered in about ten centimetres of snow, the snow has drifted around the car as well so apart from the mound it is completely hidden from view. It's been here long enough for the snow to freeze onto it, brushing it with our hands only clears the recent fall and still leaves a covering of hard ice.

This leaves us with a bit of a problem, I wonder whether we should carry on as we were on the tracked vehicle but Andy says the snow is only thick enough for another twenty or thirty kilometres so that's a non starter. We have to clear the ice off the car but we can't even open the doors as they're frozen shut. We don't have anything to hand that will scrape the ice away without damaging the car itself although there is an ice-scraper inside the car. There's only one thing for it, we need to light a fire near the car and warm it up a bit, we both head off into the woods to collect some wood. After about twenty minutes we have a good pile of small branches and twigs, there are plenty of dead pieces around and I even manage to find a large and sprawling hawthorn tree which I remember is good from Jack's instructions all those months ago, Andy has also found a reasonable amount of silver birch bark. We decide to build a fire on each side of the car near the front, primarily to get the doors open but we're also hoping that it will melt some of the ice from the windscreen. Andy lights the fire on the driver's side and makes it look so easy that I'm inspired to take his flint to light the other one. With a bit of effort I get it going but it wasn't as easy as it had looked.

After only a few minutes there's a good amount of heat coming from both the fires and the car is beginning to drip, we're able to get the doors open shortly afterwards. Andy leans into the car with difficulty as with hindsight we've lit the fires a little too close and pulls out a small plastic ice-scraper. He then gets to work, the ice just falls away from the side windows and the edges of the windscreen are not much harder but he has to push quite hard towards the centre, there's no hope of clearing the rear window but we're not going to need to see where we've been. I kick out what's left of the fires while Andy brings the tracked vehicle into the clearing, I pick up our helmets and hang them on the handlebars before both of us climb into the car. Andy slips his mobile device into the cradle behind the steering wheel and it fades into life revealing a healthy range of over five hundred kilometres. It's a tricky job to ease the car out of the clearing as the tyres don't bite the snow particularly well but once we've made it to the track progress is much better, it feels a lot slower than we have been travelling up to now but in reality it's just the fact that it's a much more refined method of transport, we are only going very slightly slower and when we clear the snowy region we'll be able to move dramatically faster.

Andy's prediction of twenty to thirty kilometres more snow proves to be a little optimistic but three quarters of an hour and nearly forty kilometres after leaving the clearing we can finally see the gravel surface of the track in front of us. There is still the odd drift of snow here and there but nothing of any significance, so gradually Andy increases our speed. We're now off the wiggly roads and on the old motorway which is much straighter so there isn't too much risk of skidding off although we do have the occasional scary moment where the track curves relatively tightly. The tyres fitted to the car are actually quite good for the conditions, despite having been remoulded many times on old ones discarded from the vehicles running in Luxburg, the set on this car have got deep treads to improve the grip and metal studs as well. Andy has brought a bag containing some provisions, we eat and drink as we travel along without bothering to stop. Even though I have been taught how to drive a car as this is a skill that Benoit has, we don't share the driving, I have not driven in these icy conditions and if I were to start now it would either make it too slow or too dangerous.

Late in the afternoon we arrive at the charging garage by the railway line just outside Reims, the cloud has broken up slightly for the first time all day and we're able to see a few rays from the setting sun. It's cold here but nowhere near as cold as it is back at base where the daytime high temperature has not been above freezing for weeks, here there is no ice at all at the moment even in the shade of the forest. As soon as we have the car inside the garage Andy plugs it in to charge up ready for the last leg of our journey tomorrow. It's less than two hundred kilometres from here to Luxburg and the track that will take us there is very good, we'll be leaving first thing in the morning and we should be there by midday. We'll be heading to an old warehouse building on the edge of the city which is basically a base for our agents in Luxburg, it will be there that we make the final preparations for the swap. I must admit that now we're so close to doing this I'm starting to feel very uneasy about the whole thing, but everything has gone to plan so far so I suppose I really shouldn't be worrying. I take my mind off things by heading off into the woods to collect firewood to cook our dinner while Andy is tinkering with the car.

After we've finished eating we continue to sit by the fire, putting the occasional piece of wood in and absent-mindedly prodding it, there's something about this kind of activity that seems very natural. However as I gaze into the flames my mind plays tricks with me and I see Suzie's face there which makes me miss her even though it's barely twelve hours since last I saw her. The only way I'm going to cope is by not thinking about her, otherwise I'm going to be counting the days until the Human Rights celebrations. I chuck another log into the fire with rather more force than I intended and a shower of sparks flies around prompting Andy to ask if I'm alright. Rather foolishly I tell him of my internal conflict but instead of telling me to get a grip he then proceeds to tell me about the family that he left behind when he ran away to Mont Blanc. It hadn't occurred to me before when Jack had told the story of how he and Andy had first met but of course he would have been married when he left. I suppose it was much harder for him too, he left a wife and three young children to join the cause and he's not been able to see them since, as far as they're concerned he's dead. That's good enough for me, I resolve to do the best job that I can for the good of the country and for humanity itself.

We sit and chat by the fire until it dies away to embers and we turn in for the night, in the time we've been here it's become colder, we've not noticed as we've been close to the fire and wearing thick clothing but when we stand up there is a frosty crispness under foot. We root out a couple of foam mats to sleep on and a pillow each, I decide not to bother with a sleeping bag electing instead just to rely on my insulated overalls to keep me warm but Andy takes his off and slides into a bag. There is no heating as such in the garage but once the door is shut the heat that comes from the charger as well as the batteries themselves in the car as they take their charge and the radiator on the back of the freezer is trapped inside so it is soon significantly warmer than outside. Half an hour later I've decided that I'm actually a little on the warm side so I take off my insulated suit and get a sleeping bag after all. Sleep still evades me even though I am quite tired after a day of travelling and well fed, I can't help but dwell on what's going to happen tomorrow. I can hear Andy snoring gently long before I manage to drift into slumber.

Chapter 20

Saturday 6th January 54

After having had trouble settling I surprise myself by sleeping very well, it looks like Andy has been up for some time when I wake. I'm even more surprised when he tells me that it's nearly eight o'clock, I scrabble out of my sleeping bag and get my suit back on before I get too cold. Breakfast is rather less than impressive being just some cold toast that Andy brought from home, still it's better than nothing and I'm not terribly hungry anyway. I'm not exactly eager to get going but I know it's got to be done and once I'm in Luxburg I'll be doing something rather than simply waiting. We get into the car, Andy sets the door opening remotely and we ease onto the frosty track, once the door has finished closing we can hear the crunch of the ice under the wheels. We follow a different track away from the garage which takes us alongside the railway line, so close that we actually see a train go past on the other side of the trees. Before long the track heads away from the railway to the south and we come out of the wooded area onto what was clearly once a motorway, it is in a significantly better state of repair than the road from here to Mont Blanc but not quite as good as the road we followed away from the Channel Tunnel.

Despite our destination this morning's journey is the easiest that I've ever made, we simply drive the two hundred kilometres or so along the road and two hours later we're approaching the outskirts of the biggest city that I have ever seen. The only city that I have ever seen. The tops of the buildings are visible on the skyline from over ten kilometres away but the closer we get the more prominent and impressive they become. Of course I've seen pictures of the Europarl building in Luxburg and then I've seen the views on the windows at Mont Blanc but nothing has prepared me for the scale of the place, it's huge. Then just as we seem to be arriving the road curves away to the south, Andy is ready and winks, saying that we're obviously not going to drive straight into the city in broad daylight. After a couple of hundred metres we turn off the road onto a track and after a short distance over a deeply rutted surface we arrive at the now familiar sight of a charging garage. The camouflaged door opens upon our approach and we drive straight in, before Andy has stopped the car it's shutting again. It's quite dark inside once the door has closed fully, there's just a small dim lamp glowing ahead of us. As my eyes adjust to the gloom I realise that there is a string of lights stretching away into the distance.

Andy explains that despite looking like a charging garage there is actually no charging facility here, the only electricity runs a string of lights running the length of the tunnel that will take us underground into the basement of the building that is their Luxburg hideout. Opening the door of the car switches on a bright light in the ceiling of the car which has the effect of rendering the dim tunnel lights virtually invisible, we get out and shut the doors and the light in the car fades away after a brief delay. We give ourselves a minute or so to regain our night vision and then start to follow the lights along the tunnel. It feels damp and the lights really don't allow us to see anything more than the direction in which to travel. Andy explains that they are actually light emitting diodes, this particular set was in fact bought in a shop in Luxburg and was intended for decorating what he calls Winterval Trees. I look at him blankly and despite the darkness he detects my puzzlement and goes on to explain further.

Before the war there were various mid-winter festivals belonging to various different cultures which were officially merged together into a single entity called Winterval and part of the traditional celebration involved cutting down a tree and decorating it in the main living room for the duration. These lights were ideal for lighting the tunnel in a way that would not be detected although he did have to lengthen the wire more than a little. Because of the continuous nature of the habitation of Luxburg, all the old festivals have survived to this day, several of them each year, it makes me feel a little hard done by with regard to the single Human Rights celebration per year that I've had all my life. In the time before the war this festival was only really celebrated in the more northerly states where the longest day is most significant. In fact the Human Rights celebration has very little impact in Luxburg itself which I find absolutely staggering. With this revelation I can see a glow at the end of the tunnel, we're almost there.

The light gradually gets less dim until suddenly we turn a corner and we're standing at the end of the tunnel behind what looks like some rough wooden panelling, the light is coming from cracks between the panels. There is a small illuminated button right at the top of the tunnel which turns yellow when Andy presses it, he warns me in a whisper that we might have to wait a little while before we can go in. The moment he says this the light in the button changes to green and the wooden panel slides surprisingly smoothly to the side. We step forward into a room that is about twenty metres square, there are no windows but it is brightly lit with strip lighting which after the darkness of the tunnel makes me feel a bit peculiar due to the flicker. There are a few crates dotted around the room and a desk in a far corner next to what looks like it is probably a lift, apart from that the room is empty. The man sitting at the desk turns on his chair to face us as we walk across to him our footsteps echoing slightly.

"Alright John?" says Andy offering his hand, "Is everything ready?"

"Yes, we're all set. Just a matter of waiting until Benoit sets off, which if he sticks to his usual routine should be between about five thirty and sixish. Come on, I'll take you upstairs"

John gets up and presses the button by the lift doors, we hear a distant clanking and after about a minute the doors slide open with the ding of a bell. We all step inside even though we only just fit, there's a sign below the button panel by the door which says *Weight Limit 500kg or 4 Persons Max,* it's no larger than a shower cubicle. There is no way we'd fit a fourth person in with us even if we were really friendly, according to the display we are currently on floor B which is lowest indicated level, the button above this is G and then they go all the way up to 9. However John presses B, and proceeds to explain that we are actually quite a long way below the bottom level of the building but the control panel has a special system for accessing the secret floor. The lift gives a sickening lurch, then slowly and noisily ascends, how far I cannot tell but it takes very nearly a whole minute, John apologises explaining that the lift is original to the building and is now at least a hundred and fifty years old, also there are no stairs to act as an alternative as these stop when they reach the actual basement. Once the doors drag themselves open we alight into a relatively normal looking open plan office.

I sense that there are quite a lot of people looking at me and trying not to make it obvious. John recognises this as well and announces my arrival as the replacement Benoit Gilles to the room at large giving everyone a chance to give me a good look up and down, there is a general murmur in the room of people acknowledging that I look just like him and that they'd never tell the difference all of which is quite encouraging. Once everybody has gone back to their work John leads me and Andy over to a desk where a girl is sitting monitoring a bank of three viewing screens. She's not much older than me, she gets up at our approach and smiles a smile that lights up her whole face and introduces herself as Sarah, she then tells John that she's just completed assembling the footage. John explains that he's asked her to put together all the footage they have of Benoit's movements around the city over the past week pulled from the CCTV cameras that are spread around the city. John wheels a second chair over to the desk and I sit down next to Sarah to watch what she's assembled.

There isn't a great deal and it takes us less than half an hour to watch it through, it does however give me more of an insight into his life than some of what I've been looking at up until now. In most of the videos I've been watching he's aware he's being recorded whereas in the CCTV footage he doesn't seem to be aware of the camera. He seems to spend a large amount of his time going in and out of bars and clubs which could be a little bit of a struggle if I'm going to have to continue this behaviour exactly as before. I notice that he had yet another haircut at some point yesterday and remark upon it, to my eyes it looks ridiculous but I'm going to have to put up with it until it grows a bit, at least this will be the last time. It's slightly annoying that he's still continuing his attempts with facial hair, that's another change I'll be making as soon as I'm in his place. After we've finished with the video one of the girls cuts my hair to match which doesn't take long, I ask about dressing in the same clothes but I'm told that the nature of the swap will be such that I'll be able to change into the actual clothes he's wearing at the time.

Now we seem to be back to waiting again, I must admit that I am starting to feel a little on edge. I would probably be running my fingers through my hair if I could, but now it's so short it might as well not be there apart from a slightly longer strip along the top of my head. It actually wouldn't be too bad if it weren't for the lettering shaved into each side that reads "Euro" on the left and "Parl" on the right with a zigzag hyphen across the back of my head, subtle Benoit is not! Absent-mindedly I start to bite one of my fingernails and suddenly John grabs my hand and tells me not to do that as Benoit doesn't bite his nails. With a sinking feeling of embarrassment I look at my hands, all my nails are quite badly bitten, John gives me a reproachful look and I can tell this is a potential problem. I've never been a nail-biter before but the last few months have been fairly intense it's something I've just started doing over that period without really noticing. Evidently nobody else has noticed either, I'm rather surprised that Suzie never mentioned it but I feel a little silly now as this wouldn't be a problem now if I'd stopped even just a few weeks ago.

"Well there's not really anything we can do about it now" says John, "it probably won't be noticed. Just try and stop going forward because any obviously changed behaviour could draw attention to the swap."

"Yes, actually while we're talking about *the swap*, what's going to happen to Benoit?"

"You don't need to know, in fact we won't really know until we find out how he takes it himself but whatever happens he'll be well looked after."

I'll try not to worry any more about this as if I do it could impact on my ability to play my part, the words *looked after* have unpleasant connotations as I think back to how Europarl looked after my mum. Although of course that is exactly the sort of thing that I'm here to stop, ultimately so there's no reason to think that we'll be using those methods ourselves. Luckily for my sanity at this moment there is a distraction for me, Sarah announces that news has just come in from one of the maids in the presidential residence that they are just about to take lunch. It strikes me that it's slightly early for that but then I realise that it is actually after midday so not as early as I'd thought. As soon as they know what Benoit has been eating they'll be bringing me the same food, this is important apparently in case I'm sick. I'm just about to ask why there is any reason to think that I'm going to be sick as I feel fine at the moment apart from slight apprehension but I decide that I probably don't really want to know the answer to that question. Then Sarah asks me how I fancy steak and chips, which is a bit of luck because given a free choice that sounds very good to me.

We all sit round a huge wooden table that is in a room on one of the upper floors in the building, this is nominally *the board room* but is more often used as a place to dine. The food is good but the conversation is a little strained as I would really like to know how the swap is going to happen but that's the one thing that nobody else is going to talk about. Pudding is some kind of custard tart that I really don't fancy but since according to our spy within the presidential staff, Benoit has eaten a large portion of the very same, I have no choice in the matter. It tastes better than it looks but even so there's far more of it than I really want right now. I've nearly finished forcing it down when there's a knock on the door and someone else who was in the room downstairs but to whom I've not been introduced bursts in saying that it's time to go, that he's a lot earlier than usual and we need to get ready right now.

John gets up and tells me to come with him, Andy and Sarah remain seated at the table but Sarah silently mouths "good luck" to me with a smile. We take the lift down to the ground floor and go out through a side door which leads out into an alleyway between two buildings. There are a pair of wooden gates at each end and there is a stretcher leaning against the wall, there is a distant sound of a siren that seems to be getting nearer. Something about the noise is unsettling, that and the stretcher, I know they're something to do with the process of the swap and I'm now feeling really uneasy. The siren gets louder until suddenly with a rattle of the gates a vehicle zooms past the end of the alley, I can see blue lights flashing on its roof above the gate. About a minute after the vehicle has passed the siren stops and all I can hear is the ordinary background noise of daily life in a city. John is starting to fidget and I wonder whether something has gone wrong, he jumps out of his skin when his mobile starts to play an annoying tune very loudly in his pocket, I then hear half a conversation that doesn't sound good at all.

"This is John... Oh no... Are you sure it's that obvious?.. Well, I suppose we'll have to then, but I really don't like it... You don't think there's another way?.. Alright... See you in a few minutes."

"Is there a problem?" I ask.

"Yes and no, we can still do the swap but there's a complication that we didn't expect. Benoit was on his way out just as we planned for, we have fitted a device to his car that allows us to lock up the steering and cause an accident. It was all planned meticulously, the ambulance that's just gone past is being driven by two of our people, the plan was for them to stop off here on the way to the hospital and we'd swap you round. That is still the plan, the problem is that Benoit has actually crashed his car without our assistance and it's worse than what we had planned…"

At that point I hear a siren start up again and I know it's not going to be long now and John has yet to come to the point.

"We were expecting only minor injuries but he has a broken leg as well, the problem is that there were witnesses to the crash who have seen his leg badly broken, people who could be a massive problem if you turn up at the hospital without a broken leg."

I have no more time to think what this means, the siren is almost upon us, it stops suddenly as the gates open and then the ambulance arrives in the alley. The back door opens quickly and two men carry a stretcher out with *me* on it, he's obviously been drugged as he is sleeping peacefully and he is wearing nothing except for his underpants. It is clear that his left leg is badly broken near his ankle even though it has been put in a splint, despite all this I can't help but wonder at how much like me he is in the flesh. One of the men from the ambulance hands me a pile of clothes telling me to get them on. I quickly discard my own clothes and get the others on, it's cold in the alley and I don't want to be undressed for too long. While I'm changing they take Benoit inside, the left trouser leg has been cut up above the knee which focuses my mind all too clearly on what is about to happen. Then the two ambulance men are back.

"Okay, we're going to have to do this now," says one of the ambulance men, "there's no easy way to do it unfortunately but we'll give you a local anaesthetic so it won't hurt."

There's nothing to say really, I take up my position on the spare stretcher. His partner takes out a syringe with a large and vicious looking needle and rolling the tattered remains of my trouser leg up above my knee he injects the drug into my leg. I feel the initial prick but then my leg quickly becomes numb. We've not got much time now before the ambulance needs to be at the hospital. They don't need to worry about getting the break exactly right as it is only the two ambulance men who've seen it in any detail but it still needs to be consistent with the way in which it happened. This means that I need to roll over onto my front which is not easy with a leg that has no feeling whatsoever but with some help I manage. I close my eyes and wait for the inevitable, I feel the weight of someone sitting on the top of my leg but I can't feel anything any further down. Then I hear it, a surprisingly loud crack that almost seems to echo off the walls of the alleyway as both my fibula and tibia break. Quickly they roll me back onto my back and get the stretcher secured in the back of the ambulance; one of the ambulance men stays in the back with me and the other takes up his position in the driving seat.

Although I can't see anything outside as we set off, I can tell that we're going forwards to exit the alleyway at the other end. The siren comes to life as we clear the gates and I can see reflections of the blue flashing lights through the dark tinted windows. In spite of the anaesthetic I'm beginning to feel the occasional twinge of pain in my leg which makes me wonder just how painful it must have been for Benoit himself. It only takes a couple of minutes for us to arrive at the hospital entrance, in that time my leg has been splinted in the same way as Benoit's was. As soon as the ambulance stops, the stretcher on which I'm lying is removed and attached to a trolley of some description, the thing that I'm really not expecting is the flashing of cameras as I'm wheeled in through the big automatic doors of the hospital. The baptism of fire doesn't stop once inside though, there is Anais Gilles, my *mother* alternating between concern for my welfare and anger at my reckless driving. She walks alongside keeping pace with the trolley as I'm taken to have my leg examined.

I'm taken into a room where a doctor runs a scanner over my leg which displays an image of the two broken bones on a monitor beside the bed, he says that I've been lucky. Both breaks are clean with no splintered ends and they won't have to operate, the ambulance team have managed to get the bones into to correct position so all they'll need to do is put it in a plaster cast. I get my first proper sight of my leg now and it is quite badly bruised, but within a few minutes I have a neat cast enclosing my heel and stopping just short of my knee. At first I find the experience very stressful as I am convinced that I'm going to be found out as an imposter at any moment, but my *mother* is present the whole time and if she doesn't spot the swap then I guess I must be relatively safe. She's calmed down a lot since my arrival and she's been looking at me most of the time I've been here, I've yet to meet my *father* of course but my research over the last few months has led me to suppose that he's unlikely to present problems.

There is no reason for me to remain in the hospital any longer so as soon as an orderly has brought us a wheelchair we're heading out of the main doors again. There is a large and shiny presidential limousine standing in the *Ambulances Only* area. As we approach the car, the chauffeur sees us and gets out to open the rear door, he helps me out of the wheelchair and into the comfortable leather seat. This is a far cry from the ancient things that I've ridden in up to now, once mum is seated next to me and the door is closed I can hear no external noises at all and as the car pulls away there is silence. I can't even hear the noise of the wheels on the road, let alone the sound of the motor. The road we are travelling on is properly maintained so perhaps it is not fair to compare it with the tracks on which I travelled half way across the country but if I close my eyes it really is impossible to tell that we are moving. The real difference for me though is not within the car itself, it's the number of people around. On every pavement there are people walking, there are other cars on the roads, not many but far more on every street than I have ever seen before. I am making a conscious effort not to stare in wonderment at everything around me but it's hard to keep it up. Then all of a sudden we turn into a long avenue and we're approaching the presidential residence, we're back home. Now I have to prove myself as an actor.

Epilogue

Tuesday 6th June 75

It's hard work running a country, most people would assume this to be the case if they stopped to think about it but how many people actually think about running a country? I mean really running a country, not simply thinking of a few policies whilst talking to one's friends. I know I didn't, I never thought about it at all, I never imagined it even to be possible that one day I'd be here in charge of a country larger than ten million square kilometres but nevertheless here I am. I wasn't born to be the president, or maybe I was, but I was put here for a purpose, to bring change. It was such a long time ago that I can't really remember what I was supposed to be changing but I have advisors and I have my wife. It was never going to happen overnight, everyone knew that, even me, but I don't think I realised just how long we would have to wait.

The Europarl system is not fair, on so many levels, I'm the president simply because my father was the president until he died. I should feel slightly guilty about it, especially as I know that the person whose actual birthright this was is living a very different life from what he expected but I don't. I'm told that he's not unhappy, but then again I'm not sure if I even know what happiness is, most of the people of this country, those who live or die at my say so would claim to be happy. My real mother went to her death happily all those years ago and my father and brother looked on with no sense of anger or impotence. It was only me who thought it was wrong. Now my real father is gone too, the irony is not lost on me that he went to his death at the order of the president. The president who then proceeded to die of a heart attack no more than minutes later, I lost two fathers in one go. If it had been a few weeks earlier I'd still have my real father but in all honesty I was closer to the president, it's a really strange situation in which to find myself and despite the anticipation I wasn't ready.

How important is family? I don't have any children yet but I'm sure I will one day. Right now I can look at the viewing screen on my desk and see my brother, he's actually travelling towards me at almost three hundred kilometres per hour driving a train. He has a wife and three children, none of whom I have ever seen in real life. A few taps on the screen and I can see them too, his wife at home with the two babies and little Ed at school, yes my brother named his son after me. Sooner or later I would like to reveal myself to them but I don't know how to do it, I know who I'd really like to help me with that, Jack. But he died a long time ago, I had more of a connection with him than anyone else except for my wife. The truth is that right now I feel more a part of the old Europarl than I do part of the new regime even though I'm supposedly leading it, this will change though it's early days and it's all I can do at the moment to keep things ticking over.

It's June, and this is a busy time of the year in the U.S.E., we have to sort out the placements for all the people who have come of age in the last year. It's the first time I've done it myself but I've helped my father for several years now. Originally we'd thought it would be best to do away with this altogether but it's not as easy as just stopping, the population have expectations, they have their Human Rights. If we stopped everything suddenly there would be a public outcry, this has to be taken slowly and steadily and as we've waited this long already a little longer won't hurt. This will be the last year that things remain the same as they've always been, next year things will be different although we haven't yet decided how different. People currently have everything provided for them whether they like it or not, the real problem that I have in my mind is that it seems to me that far more people like it than don't. I can't help but feel that things are going to get far, far worse before they get any better at all.

About The Author

Philip Hoyle has always been an avid reader with a particular fondness of post-apocalyptic fiction. Aside from creating bespoke computer software along with its associated technical documentation and having kept a diary since 1986, *Human Rights* is his first foray into writing. Most of his writing has been done whist watching his son at athletics or ice hockey training which has led to cold fingers whilst typing.

He lives in Chelmsford with his wife Clare and two children Victoria and James. He is a fan of classic cars and has owned a Triumph TR7 for nearly twenty years. In what's left of his spare time he helps run a Cub pack and tries to keep fit by running on a fairly regular basis. He is currently working on the remaining two books in the trilogy.

Also from Stanhope Books

Sofiah

Rob Shepherd's WWII film, now turned into a story. Set in 1944, "Sofiah" features two men from opposite sides of the battle for Europe. Soon the two men find they have more in common than they could have bargained for.

When Dreams Converge

Stephen Massie's first novel, charting the adventures of Luke, a keen amateur sailor, and his wife, as they set to sea to live their dream of freedom. During their voyage they are thrust into a world of crime, terrorism and murder. In a web of deceit and intrigue they are pursued by ruthless criminal organisations.

Life With Boris Karloff!

Read the extracts of a fictional diary of one man's experiences of living with bogeymen and his struggle in the end to figure out who are family and who are the real monsters.

Rob Shepherd's unique and humorous look at a ridiculous situation.

www.stanhopebooks.com

facebook.com/stanhopebooks

Twitter @stanhopebooks

www.ingramcontent.com/pod-product-compliance
Lightning Source LLC
Chambersburg PA
CBHW070917180626
46817CB00003B/1104